Celeste Unraveled

by Karen Gansel

Published by Amazon.com and Kobo.com

Library and Archives Canada Cataloguing in Publication

Gansel, Karen

   Celeste Unraveled: a novel by Karen Gansel

ISBN   978-0-9690556-7-9

   1. Title

Book cover art by Karen Gansel

Book cover Design by Ken Gansel

Printed in 2020 by Amazon.com and Kobo.com

Available in eBook format or Print on Demand

Contents

Chapter One

Celeste

Celeste missed her comrades from the UHN, her hospital when they lived in Toronto. She no longer had the energy to drive back there for lunches with them. After a while there wasn't much to talk about anyway. Sure, she had acquaintances here in Niagara on the Lake, but no one really with whom she could share her deeper worries.

On the drive back home from shopping, for the first time in years, Celeste relived the day she learned she'd be one of the victims of the hospital's downsizing. The Director of Nursing had sent out a memo to all her staff advising them to be in the auditorium for a special meeting at ten. Celeste had been shocked and worried. Management normally broke the nurses up into smaller groups for meetings, so they left a strong group for patients on the floors.

Even more surprising, the CEO was leading the meeting. She fidgeted as he droned on about the future goals and objectives of the hospital. Who cared about what the inner circle felt? She noticed other management staff who were clustered near the front of the room had their heads down. The more he talked, the more they shifted in their chairs. Not a good sign. She snapped to attention when he began to outline the restructuring plan and the new organization chart. Nursing would be grouped into larger teams with fewer managers. It didn't sound good for her. She began to perspire then switched to feeling chilled. By the time the CEO finished, she had a stabbing pain in her head. As he wound up the talk, the Director of Nursing, Sharon, asked all her staff to remain in the room when others left.

Once they were alone, the quiet in the room felt like a funeral even with some low sobbing. Packages were distributed while Sharon began her slide show with the new organization charts. The nurses were frantically flipping through the deck of slides on their tables. *Which page? Did she say which page?*

Not able to contain her anxiety, Celeste blurted it out loud. "Which page are you on?"

Sharon turned her attention to them and gave the number. "I'm sorry. I should have waited until you got there."

With the explanation going on and on, all Celeste could take in was she was probably out. Her current two units were being consolidated with two others into a new much larger team. Sharon was explaining it would mean some nurse mangers, which meant her, would be encouraged to apply for the new jobs and others may choose to pursue careers elsewhere. *Where was elsewhere?* They'd be setting up individual meetings with those involved tomorrow morning.

Soon they all stumbled out of the room and headed back to their own cubicles, heads down and eyes straight ahead. Most of the regular nurses where unlikely to be directly affected by the change. However, they would worry about losing a manager they'd learned to trust and about who would replace her. Celeste stared at the chart lying in front of her. Even before her talk tomorrow with Sharon, she could see there was no place for her. The other managers all had been there longer than her.

The next day, the content of the talk was routine. Sharon explained there were several other nurse managers who had years of seniority over Celeste who'd expressed an interest in the new jobs. She could still apply but her chances were limited, and she could be bumped from her position if she won. The pros and cons of unions. If she decided to leave, there was a severance package and career planning opportunities open to her. Angry and disappointed, she said right there, she'd be leaving. Sharon told her she'd remain on the job for the next two weeks while final details were worked out.

How those two weeks had dragged. Celeste was ashamed to confide in her spouse, Adrian. about what was going on. As a senior executive, he was probably part of it anyway. Why hadn't he warned her this could happen? The shock was too much for her. Work had become an agony. When she walked down the hallway, other nurses changed direction and walked the other way. When she went to the cafeteria, people would quickly gobble their lunch and scatter for the door. Even her best friends, who had said they were sorry to hear about her leaving during the first one or two days, later began to avoid her. Her team members looked miserable and did their best to comfort her and to cause her no problems. But by the end of the two weeks, they'd already begun to seek out the three remaining nurse managers to get a step up with them.

When she did eventually tell Adrian what had happened, he said. "I've been waiting for you to tell me. I heard about it after the meeting. You'll apply for one of those jobs, won't you?" He gave her a quizzical look.

He didn't understand about seniority. As an executive, it was merit that counted. Merit and who your friends were. She tried her best to explain.

"It wouldn't matter if I did. At least three nurse managers have seniority and Sharon didn't encourage me to apply. She'd have told me if I had a chance."

Adrian clenched his jaw. "So, you're giving up, are you?" He shook his head.

Celeste's spirits dropped even lower. "I'll take the severance. Something will come up. You'll see."

But a year later, nothing had. She'd settled into long lunches with the neighbourhood women's group and afternoon bridge games.

Later when the downsizing hit him, Adrian had acted. Within a month, he had a new business set up and had feelers out for contracts. But for both, the bright lights of the city had dimmed, and the crazy activity seemed forced. The move had been a refreshing new event for them.

*   *   *

Celeste danced with excitement as she pulled her long denim coat over navy jeans. A glance in the mirror reassured her that the tight blue sweater she'd chosen complimented her shoulder-length hair. Looking good for their Friday night out was important. Adrian had invited Ian and Dennis from the local golf club to join them at Bistro 77, along with their wives, Sabrina, and Marjorie. He wanted to set up a regular dinner group. Something he'd look forward to after a long hard week. She pushed thoughts of another dreary Monday to the back of her mind. Nothing more than watercolours class with aerobics on Tuesday.

Now with her husband back home, she'd have fewer nights of sipping white wine and watching the TV alone while the sun blinked behind the horizon. She turned to admire Adrian as he strode down the staircase dressed in new designer jeans, slinky black T-shirt, and grey micro-fiber jacket.

"It's great to have you home, darling." She caught Adrian admiring his reflection in the mirror and as he patted a few stray hairs into place when he reached the bottom step.

"Do you like these new jeans? I picked them up in Colorado on this last trip."

Celeste frowned. Why did he always have to upstage her when they were going out? Not wanting to spoil the evening, she forced a smile. "You look great as always. I still don't know your golf partners that well. What can you tell me about them?"

He picked up his wallet and car keys from the counter. "You remember Ian. He's the uptight former engineer from Britain. His claim to fame is working at Ellis Don when they built the Sky dome."

"How long have they lived in this town?"

Adrian stood still, concentrating. "Well, they moved to Toronto straight from Manchester in the 80s when he was in his mid-forties. He seems to have retired before sixty-five. So probably five or six years."

She set the security alarm and opened the door to the garage. "Well, aren't you precise." Celeste walked to the car. "Let's go. We don't want to be late. She opened the door and slid onto the grey leather seat. "I remember Sabrina from last time. She's funny. Always has colourful stories to tell and knows everyone in town."

Adrian followed her out. "That's her. I could never see why she married him. I guess, Ian provided her with the luxuries she wanted. He could afford it with being next in line for CEO.

As he dropped into the driver's seat, he continued. "I don't know Dennis as well, but he retired from Scotiabank, managed private investment accounts or something like that."

Celeste nodded. "I know his wife. Marjorie and I belong to the same book club in town. I'm glad they're joining us."

Adrian loved the atmosphere at Bistro 77, a cozy restaurant on Queen Street in town, a favourite with the locals. On a Friday night in late May, it was busy but not yet overwhelmed with tourists. That would come during the summer when the locals would move to the Golf Club or The Vintage Wine Restaurant farther out of town. While waiting for a table, Celeste admired the dark wooden booths and oak floors highlighted by the sand palette of the walls. She and Adrian slid into a circular booth at the back where they could keep an eye on the door. The new cone shaped lights softened the magenta and hunter green wallpaper ending in dark mahogany panels. Relaxing in her seat, she smiled at Adrian and placed her hand over his.

Precisely at seven, Dennis entered wearing a camel wool coat which he removed and handed to the host. He turned to assist Marjorie with her black wool cape over a designer sweater. Adrian's wild wave soon caught their attention and they headed toward the booth in the back. Marjorie's sensible leather oxfords were just visible under her pants as she shifted herself into the booth next to Dennis and smoothed her short brown hair.

Dennis scanned the crowd in the restaurant, obviously looking to see who else was there tonight. "No sign of Ian yet? He's probably still looking for a safe place to park his Jag," Dennis smirked.

"Oh Dennis. Don't be so hard on him." Marjorie gave him a stern look. "You know that car is his pride and joy."

Dennis and Adrian were still chuckling when Ian appeared and joined the group, hanging his leather jacket on a coat tree nearby. Celeste noticed his olive skin and black eyes were sparked by the pale grey cashmere sweater. He knew how to dress to effect.

"Sabrina will join us shortly," Ian sighed. "Her first bathroom visit already." He turned to glance at the table next to them with a suspicious look at the two men seated there. Then took his seat.

Adrian's eyes lit up when Sabrina arrived. She removed her red cashmere coat and joined them in the booth cuddling up against Adrian. When the waiter arrived, they ordered from the list of wine specials, a Baco Noir and a Cabernet Merlot from local vineyards, a Chardonnay from California. Celeste proposed a toast. "To another summer of great food, exceptional wine and good company."

"Cheers." Ian responded by raising his glass. "We couldn't ask for a nicer location to live out our old age."

Sabrina quickly answered his challenge. "Who's old? Speak for yourself."

Celeste could feel the heat rise to her face. "What's so great about retirement? I for one enjoyed the long hours at the Toronto General. In fact, I'd probably still be there if I hadn't clashed with the new CEO."

"Come on now, Celeste," said Adrian. "You know that the reason they forced you out was the usual hospital cost cutting. The Board chose to lay-off staff to save money needed to pay for those high-end executive salaries. Anyway, get over it. That was two years ago."

"That's fine for you to say." Celeste frowned at him. "You've just moved from one job to another. Now you're known as a consultant flitting around the continent to new jobs."

Adrian sat up straighter, his eyes like steel. "The life of a consultant isn't always as easy as you think. And one hotel room is much like the next."

Dennis shook his head. "Lighten up you two. We agreed to a fun Friday night out, not to listen to each other's quarrels. I'd still be with the bank if it weren't for my heart attack, but I got over it."

His wife touched his arm. "I've never been so frightened."

Dennis smiled. "I know I've got a new life now. I'm just waiting to discover it."

"What do you mean? You got the Volunteer of the Year award in December." Marjorie smiled at him. "I keep telling him, we need to leave some jobs for the next generation."

Ian squirmed in his seat. "We need to keep our conversation down." He hunched over the table towards the others. "See those two swarthy men at the next table? I've watched them listening to us closely. You can never be too careful."

Dennis shook with laughter, "Not that again, Ian. Remember when you were certain the bartender at the club was selling membership information over the internet to a gang involved in identity theft?"

Ian glared at him. "Well, he was crooked. Caught with a pocket full of cash from the till. I wasn't totally wrong." The two men stared at each other in silence.

Sabrina broke the tension. "Leaving the brokerage world behind didn't bother me one bit." She smiled at Celeste and Adrian. "I'm busier now than I've ever been."

"Every group needs an optimist." Adrian responded.

"What could be better than time to explore this new world we're living in. Now, cheer up and let's order. I'm starved."

Adrian turned to face Sabrina, a wistful smile on his face. "I only wish I had your enthusiasm. I'm dreading this next phase, my retirement, and will put it off as long as I can."

Her arm draped over Adrian's shoulders; Sabrina gave him a hug. "It must be awful to be fearful about what's next. Cheer up Adrian. The boomers are setting their own pace for what it means to be over 60."

A pang of jealousy stabbed through Celeste as she watched him soften. Why couldn't she find the right words with Adrian? Instead they'd end up in a squabble. With women like Sabrina, the old Adrian she knew and adored returned. Or was it just with Sabrina? They seemed familiar with each other. Was she being naive?

Celeste addressed the group. "I agree with Sabrina. Let's get started." She gestured to their young waiter with spiked hair. "I'll have the pan-seared scallops with basmati rice. What about you, Adrian?"

A big smile was pasted on Adrian's face as he caught the young man's attention. "Give me the New York steak, medium rare with baked potato. And sour cream on the side. Sabrina's the one who's starving. Why don't you order next?"

"Friday night for me is pasta. What do you recommend?" Sabrina gave the waiter a dazzling smile.

The young man straightened up and glanced at his list of specials. "Tonight, we've got linguini with a chicken and wild mushrooms sauce or penne in a fresh tomato sauce with spicy Italian sausage."

"That second one sounds great." Sabrina blinked her green eyes at him. "I just love anything hot."

Celeste turned to face Marjorie. "Life hasn't changed that much for you. You've continued heading up local charities just like you did in Toronto. I remember your name from when I was at the hospital."

Marjorie nodded. "Yes. I've been at it for a long time."

"You took over as Chair of the Heart and Stroke Foundation and it suddenly bloomed. How'd you do it?"

Marjorie smoothed her hair and folded her hands on the table. "Well, it helped that Dennis was a V.P. with Scotiabank." Her forehead wrinkled with concentration. "Let's face it. I used our connections to raise the profile of the organization. Then everyone wanted to come to our fundraising events." She sighed. "I'm hoping that I can do the same thing here. But we're not as well known."

"Well, the research money you provided for our stroke unit was very welcome," said Celeste.

"Thanks. The information in their seminars and the website sure helped us when Dennis had his heart attack. Otherwise, I might have thought he had major indigestion since we'd just come back from a restaurant."

"What happened?" Asked Sabrina with a shocked expression.

"I called the ambulance right away."

Dennis interrupted as he glanced at the table directly across from them. "Enough you two. If we start talking about each other's illnesses, we'll bore the other patrons into leaving."

"I wouldn't worry too much." Ian dropped his bored expression. "This isn't like the pubs in Britain where the other diners join in your conversation. Here in Canada, they're a little more reserved."

"Why don't you consider going on the Board at the golf club, Ian? I know they've been courting you," Dennis inquired. "I hear you're on the priority list of players."

"It doesn't have the prestige of the elite British clubs, you know." Ian's deep black eyes roamed around the room once more. "Back in Toronto, I golfed with the CEOs of some of the major corporations."

Dennis placed both hands on the table. "Come on. We're past that now. Volunteering is what's left to us. You might as well embrace it."

"Well, something a little more creative than golf then." Ian frowned. "Maybe I'll try for the Town's Waste Management Committee." He gave Dennis a challenging look.

"Those young engineers don't want advice from old guys like us." Dennis shook his head. "But, if you want to give it a try, I know a couple of people I could talk to about your background."

Ian laughed his whole-body relaxing. "Yes. Mr. Citizen of the Year should be able to pull a few strings."

"Just let me know when you're ready."

The conversation dropped off when the waiter brought their dinners. Sabrina ordered a second vodka martini. When Celeste next glanced in her direction, Sabrina was smiling at Adrian, and her eyes sparkled.

"I can't believe how much there is to do here in this small town." Sabrina said. "The Passion and Food Fundraiser this summer has asked for my help and I'm on the committee planning the Summer Music Festival. You need to get involved."

"You talking to me?" Adrian laughed. "I'm still out there Monday to Friday. If I did anything, it would be with the wineries. I'd love to see what the young ones are up to. See if I can still keep up to them."

Sabrina leaned in toward Adrian and touched her curly black mop against his dark brown hair. "I like that about you. We're only old if we begin to think that way. Boomers can still lead the way as we always have." Celeste glared at Sabrina who quickly straightened up.

Celeste put her arm through Adrian's and squeezed his hand. "It's so good to have you home on the weekends, honey."

Disengaging himself, Adrian pushed back the cowl of hair that had fallen across his forehead. "The reality is my job's not exactly easy. I used to manage a group of professional hospital managers. Now I'm the hired gun easing them out the door."

The group fell silent and continued to eat.

"So, what's our plan for the summer?" asked Dennis.

Adrian perked up. "I'm waiting to see what the Jazz Festival at the Riverview Winery is like. I hear from the local guys at the golf club that it's rather good. Why don't we go as a group?" He glanced around the table.

Sabrina's face was alive with excitement, both hands fluttering. "Great idea. We'll have a picnic. I'll order the curried chicken and barbequed wings and the other girls can bring the salads and desserts."

"Wait a minute there, Sabrina," said Marjorie. "It's a little early to be ordering the food when we're still in May. The concert's not until the first week of July.

*   *   *

On the way home, Adrian drove in silence not looking in her direction. He had been more distant with Celeste over the past few months. He seemed preoccupied and less attentive. Partly that was his nature when immersed in work; however lately he'd shared less and less with her. She had begun to worry about the gulf between them which seemed to only widen the more he was away.

She needed to find things they could do together when he retired. Celeste got along well with Marjorie and hoped to interest her in a tennis game. It was something she and Adrian used to do together. On the other hand, she had little in common with Sabrina.

That's probably why she found her behavior tonight mystifying. Her extreme attention to Adrian was so out of place. When he had the time, golf had become Adrian's main hobby since they moved. But was that the only reason he now insisted on socializing with the guys from the golf club, and, of course, their wives? She felt a creepy sensation engulf her shoulders and neck. It wasn't her imagination. She needed to pay closer attention in future to what was going on between Adrian and Sabrina.

Chapter Two

Celeste

Oscar Peterson's *Anything Goes* echoed into the kitchen from their new doorbell. She could thank Adrian's ingenuity for the music. Celeste placed the two china cups she carried onto her flowered tray and hurried to open the door for Marjorie. She looked forward to these coffee sessions the two of them had been having over the past few weeks. Marjorie understood her frustrations with being forced into retirement. Or at least she listened.

"Great outfit." Celeste said.

Marjorie smoothed the skirt of her yellow sundress and handed Celeste a bunch of pink tulips. "I found these blooming in my front garden this morning and knew you'd enjoy them."

"Thanks. They're very cheerful. I'll find a vase for them." Celeste carried them into the kitchen while Marjorie followed.

"We'll sit on the patio. I want to feel some of that early sunlight on my face."

Leaving the kitchen through the French patio doors, they entered her lush back garden. Marjorie said. "I really admire your house, especially those bay windows in the living room. And your

Victorian furniture sets it off exactly right. Your garden is so lush, it could be in a magazine."

Celeste set the vase of tulips on her white wicker table. Her face broke into a smile and she readjusted the cushions on the loveseat. "Thanks. We brought most of the furniture with us from Toronto." She settled into one of the chairs and sighed. "I keep thinking if it hadn't been for Hollinger's arrival at the hospital, I'd still be working. The weekly presentations I did for my two medical wards. I miss those." She lifted the coffee urn, held it high over each of the cups in turn and poured to within an inch of the top. They sat in a comfortable silence as she became absorbed in adding just the right amount of cream and sugar.

After taking a sip of hot coffee, Marjorie set the cup down, her face a mask of concern. "You know I can understand your frustration after years of recognition from your old boss. Especially since the new CEO replaced you with that young woman barely in her thirties. What was her name again?"

"Jennifer." Celeste set down her coffee cup. "Apparently, she was one of the new interns he hired at his last position and two years ago, when he joined our hospital, he brought her with him."

"What about Adrian? Didn't he work there, too?" Marjorie waited for a response.

"Yeah. Fortunately, he'd left a year after I got laid off to set up his own business. As one of the senior managers, he guessed more layoffs were coming." Celeste took a dainty bite out of her caramel biscotti. "They paid him out during one of their restructuring efforts. Quite a large chunk of money. He invested some of it in his current business."

"Now that you've mentioned Adrian, how are things with the two of you?" Marjorie asked.

Celeste sighed. "I didn't believe Sabrina could be that brazen. Doesn't she realize how obvious she is? Leaning her head against Adrian's, as if they were lovers. You were there. Didn't you see them. I can't believe it's my husband she's so enamored with."

"Oh, Celeste. How hurtful for you." Marjorie said. There was a long pause. "Has he acted this way with others?"

Celeste dropped her head, deep in thought. "I don't think so. We don't communicate anymore. It's not like it used to be."

"How long has this been going on—with the two of you, that is?"

After another long silence, Celeste responded. "A long time now. It started after I lost my job."

Marjorie touched her hand. "What happened? What's different?"

Celeste said. "I'm different.

Marjorie dropped her eyes for a moment and then fixed them back on Celeste. "What's happened lately to change him?"

"Well, he's still away so much, it's hard to tell." Celeste hesitated. "Really when he is here, he's just not interested in me. And we quarrel over petty things, like what to watch on TV or which movies we'll go to see. It was never like that before."

Celeste twisted the creamy linen napkin in her hands. Tears stung her eyes and she bit her lower lip. "I thought we'd be so happy here. We could start again."

Placing her hand over Celeste's, Marjorie kept her voice soft. "Men are more insecure about getting old than women are. Do you think he just enjoyed the extra attention she was pouring on?"

"Well. That's true with Adrian. I know that, however Sabrina's not just joking around. She's lost any interest in poor Ian and he's not even aware of it—or doesn't care. We saw that at the Bistro."

"Then Sabrina's your problem." Marjorie pushed back her chair and began to carry dishes into the kitchen. "Why don't I hold a coffee party just for us three women? You and I will find some way to confront Sabrina. She won't be able to ignore it with both of us there."

Celeste grinned. "That would be wonderful. I'll wear my new rose sleeveless dress and gobs of makeup. I'm not about to let that bitch upstage me again." She wiped her eyes with the napkin before discarding it beside her cup. "Thanks for letting me talk. It means so much."

*   *   *

Settled on the brocade sofa in Marjorie's front room, Celeste shrank back against the cushions. When she heard the door chimes ring in the quiet room, she stared at Marjorie. Was she ready for this? Sabrina was known to be feisty and would certainly fight back.

Marjorie patted her hand. "Relax. We'll just ease into the topic after the normal chit chat." She rose and made her way to the front door. Within minutes, Sabrina and Celeste were seated in the living room while Marjorie poured the coffee.

"Sabrina, I'm so glad you could fit my little event into your schedule." Marjorie exclaimed. "Help yourself to cream and sugar, Celeste. Sabrina, I know you drink yours black." She paused. "I love the vibrant red of your Capri suit."

Sabrina glanced warily around the room. "It's just the three of us I see." She hesitated. Of course, I like the idea of us girls getting to know each other better." She gracefully relaxed against the back of the sofa next to Celeste.

"We were just discussing our working lives in Toronto, weren't we Celeste?" Marjorie took the chair directly across from them and passed a plate of goodies. "Have a cinnamon twist or chocolate croissant."

Sabrina grabbed a croissant then picked up her coffee taking a gulp. "I rarely ever think about work now that it's over with. The lure of stocks and bonds doesn't hold me anymore. I don't miss the vultures circling around my old office door. Surely you don't want to go back to wiping up the blood and listening to people in pain, Celeste?"

As she shifted forward on the sofa, Celeste stammered. "Of--- course I miss it. The hospital was my life for so long. I miss the other girls. With Adrian away so much—there's a gap in my life."

Sabrina stared at Celeste. "Where does Adrian go so frequently? I thought most consultants just used that title as a cover up. You mean you think he really works during those trips?"

Celeste's mouth dropped. Marjorie was quick to jump in. "Enough Sabrina. No need to start suspicions about Adrian's behaviour without any facts." Her eyes narrowed. "Since you mentioned him, we've noticed your growing interest in his every move."

"Humph," said Sabrina. "So that's what this sudden desire to include me in your little circle is about. I wondered, Marjorie, what you were up to." Sabrina's eyes glittered, and she rose standing over Marjorie.

"Don't be too hasty." Marjorie said. "If the six of us are going to continue as a group, we need to know about hidden agendas. And yours is pretty obvious."

Sabrina turned to glare at Celeste. "You're just jealous because Adrian finds me exciting and he's bored with you. Well, my behavior isn't any concern to Ian. He's too secure with himself to make a fuss over a harmless flirtation." She grabbed her clutch purse from the table. Then flounced across the room and left the house, slamming the front door.

Searing stabs of pain hit Celeste. Her suspicions had been true. She felt the tears roll down her face. "Well, at least now we know where she's coming from," she mumbled.

She and Adrian had had so many fulfilling years together even when wrapped up in their different careers. What had happened to them? Were their animated discussions about health care the only thing they had shared?

Marjorie spoke firmly and gently. "We still don't know where Adrian stands in all this. He may accept her attention without understanding what the consequences might be."

"How do I find out what he's thinking?" Celeste's plaintive voice rang across the silent room.

Marjorie held Celeste's gaze. "You'll simply have to ask him." Her matter-of-fact tone had a calming effect.

Celeste squirmed. Could she do it?

Chapter Three

Adrian

Adrian glanced down the long mahogany bar in the Portland Crowne Plaza looking for someone whom he might coax to join him in a scotch. What about that sexy woman with the long brown hair and tight black dress? Just as he was about to head in her direction, she was joined by a blond man in his mid-forties who draped his arm possessively over her shoulder. Adrian wrapped his hands around the cold glass. Maybe he was losing it. His life had become bleak nights in business hotels and long days around boardroom tables where he listened to desperate plans for dealing with cuts to budgets.

He could have invited Celeste on this business trip. She had lots of time on her hands. However, she'd spend the days shopping and want him to entertain her at night. The truth was they had less and less to talk about. Her excitement about her work life while they lived in Toronto had disappeared in her new surroundings. No. What he needed was some new stimulation. His face relaxed as he ordered a second drink. Maybe he needed someone like sexy Sabrina to spice up his life. Her warmth and friendly joking would cheer him up right now. He didn't know whether he should take her seriously. She was fun though. He'd make sure she and Ian got invited to all the summer events.

As he finished his second drink, he glanced around once more, squared his shoulders, and headed toward the bank of elevators. He might as well watch some TV and see what was happening in the world. His presentation for tomorrow was on his laptop and he knew every line of it by now. After all, this was just one more hospital attempting to squeeze more services out of a fixed budget. Very little of the innovative stuff in technology he loved to do was welcome anymore. Maybe he should think about retirement. With no hobbies except the occasional game of golf, it was really no solution. Taking off his shoes, he lay on the bed restlessly clicking from one channel to the next.

He glanced at the phone in surprise when it rang. On the fourth ring, he swung his feet to the floor and picked it up. It had better not be the hospital Board Chair yet again. His voice was hesitant. "Hello."

"Hi, honey." Celeste's voice was warm and clear. "I wanted to see how your day went. Is this one of your four-day trips or are you coming back tomorrow?"

Adrian frowned. Was she checking up on him or was it just a coincidence? He forced a cheerful response. "Celeste, this is a surprise. I thought you were used to my being away during the week by now."

After a short silence, Celeste responded. "Well, I was thinking about what we could do this weekend. What would you like to do?"

After he eased himself into the chair next to the desk, Adrian picked up a pen and doodled on the hotel notepad. "I thought we'd get together again, just the six of us for another Friday night dinner. Or would you rather have the group over for a barbeque on Saturday night?"

"Well, whatever you'd like to do, honey. It's okay with me." Her voice rose. "If it's at our place, I'd prefer just Marjorie and Dennis."

"I don't know what you have against Ian and Sabrina? Ian's one of my golf partners and I definitely wouldn't want to leave him out." He paused. "Sabrina adds life to the party don't you think?"

"Sabrina and I don't see eye to eye." Her voice sounded clipped. He waited through her long pause. "We had a blow up earlier this week at Marjorie's." Celeste continued. "How about we skip them this time?"

Adrian gritted his teeth. "Damn it. We were getting along so well with the four of them. Why can't you women try to get along? I don't want the dinner without Ian and Sabrina, so think about it. We'll talk tomorrow." He was already on his feet ready to hang up.

Celeste spoke slowly and deliberately. "We always end up doing what you want. So, I might as well give in now. You can go ahead and invite the guys. I'll be seeing Marjorie and will let her know but I refuse to call Sabrina. Goodbye." He heard the phone click off.

Pulling off his clothes, Adrian crawled into bed. Now what was that all about? He liked to joke around with Sabrina but that was as far as it went. At least for now it was. He chuckled to himself before he drifted off to sleep.

Chapter Four
Sabrina

After roaring out of the driveway at Marjorie's, Sabrina headed onto the main street, eager to get home. She was glad they had invested the money from the sale of their property in Toronto on an upscale townhouse in Old Towne overlooking Lake Ontario. Their view of the lake was spectacular, and they could enjoy late lunches at Queen's Landing Hotel down the road. She'd challenged the agent about how Re-Max got away with charging such exorbitant prices way out in the country. She loved the summer parties with the other owners, many of whom also came from across the lake in Toronto. Ian enjoyed getting his feet into an advocacy role when the group dug into some of the local politics. The others wanted the local boat enterprise directly across from them shut down. She could tell it satisfied his need to know what these Niagara-on-the Lake people were about.

What was wrong with Marjorie? Attacking her like that. She'd expected some push back from Celeste who clung to Adrian tightly. Marjorie was more sophisticated and already had her own followers in town. No jealousy from her. She snickered. But then, who'd be interested in her husband anyway? Dennis was too uptight and too private school to suit Sabrina's taste. Now Adrian was another story. His sexuality was right out there in the restless way he looked at women and dressed in his edgy outfits. She couldn't really imagine him and Celeste together. Her anxious looks every time Adrian criticized Celeste gave away her neediness. Sabrina slowed down and pulled into her parking spot under the rear balcony of the complex.

She'd have to be careful when Ian was around though. Her husband's normally suspicious nature was easily aroused, and she still needed their relationship. What the hell. She was only looking for a little fun. Something to spice up her long days alone which extended into the evenings when Ian was hanging around the Sailing Club with his buddies. His Jag was parked next to her space, so he was obviously at home. As she opened the front door, Sabrina dropped her keys on the hall table, and strolled into the family room where she knew she'd find Ian in front of the TV. With a smile pasted on her face, she dropped onto the sofa next to him.

"Let's go out to lunch today, darling. I just don't feel like cooking."

Ian turned and put his arm around her shoulders. "Dearest, when do you ever feel like cooking?" Not expecting a response, his eyes took in her red suit. "What's the occasion for a new outfit? Can us retirees still afford your expensive tastes?"

Sabrina face brightened. "As long as my investments are doing well, I plan to spend the gains. We've got no one to pass the money on to anyway."

Sighing, Ian responded. "Yeah. Do you ever regret not having kids? I know we were both too busy working over the years to give it any serious consideration."

Surprised at the earnest look on his face, Sabrina took her time to answer. "Occasionally. Photos of my former teams' grandchildren were so cute. However, it would only make us seem old, don't you think? Having grandchildren, that is."

Ian brushed both hands over his stylish black hair. "You're right. My appearance fools most people who don't know me. Let's try the new place, the Gordon House, out near The Village. The guys tell me the food is good."

"I don't think they're open for lunch during the week. We could go to Queen's Landing if the patio is open, or maybe the other one across from the Shaw. Zee's, I think it's called."

Ian turned off the TV and jumped to his feet. "Come on." He reached down to help Sabrina. "The patio, it is then. I'll just grab a sweater to throw over my shoulders. What about you?"

She rose quickly and stumbled in her strappy three-inch heels. "No. Not while I've got this little red jacket." She closed the door behind them, and Ian locked it. They strolled up the street toward the restaurant holding hands. Sabrina gave Ian another of her brilliant smiles. "What do you think about our four new friends?" Sabrina glanced at him while she continued to walk straight ahead. "Should we plan on next Friday night, same place, with the group?"

Ian stopped a confused look on his face. "What friends are you talking about?"

Sabrina tugged on his hand and continued. "You know. Adrian and Dennis from your golf club and their wives."

Ian frowned, his steps slowing. "Oh, yeah. The jokers from the Bistro night. I do like Dennis. Bankers learn to listen to all types of people and get them to bare their souls. He'd be interested in my *Save the Shoreline* group. Celeste is okay, too. Adrian though is pretty egotistical." He frowned. "What is it he really does anyway? What's this consultant thing?"

Sabrina held her breath for a moment. "He's in health care or something similar. Well, think about it. It could become a regular event for us." She hesitated. "I don't want another Friday night staring at TV. I'm just saying if you're interested, I'll arrange it."

Ian held the door for her as they entered the restaurant. "Can't we leave it open for now? We'll see if any better offers come up."

Sabrina forced a smile and led the way onto the patio in the bright sunlight. She chose a table under an umbrella, near the railing which overlooked the lake. "This is a wonderful view." Removing her jacket, she crossed her arms rubbing long fingers across her shoulders. "The sun feels so great this time of year."

She'd find some way to get an invitation out of Marjorie before the weekend. She was quick to forgive and wouldn't stay mad at Sabrina for long. She relaxed and lifted her first glass of Chardonnay. The thought of seeing Adrian again caused an excited tremor to travel through her thighs. Too bad about Celeste. You could never take away another woman's husband. It took two. Sabrina knew she would be ready to play when the right signal came from Adrian.

Chapter Five

Celeste

After she stepped out of her shower, Celeste gazed into the mirror. She stared at the tense face which looked back at her and gently kneaded her temples to chase away her sudden throbbing headache. They were becoming more and more frequent and usually arose after a row with Adrian. Turning away from the mirror, Celeste pulled on her robe and began to pace. The phone call last night had begun with good intentions. She wasn't spying on Adrian. How could she from so far away? Or was she? Doubt flooded through her as she entered the kitchen, poured a cup of coffee, and climbed onto the bar stool at the island. After she picked up the phone, she dialed Marjorie's number. Because there was no way around it, she decided it was time to get this weekends' social occasion under way.

Celeste leaned both elbows on the counter. "Hi. Marjorie. It's just me bothering you again."

"Celeste. Good to hear from you." Concern was evident in Marjorie's response. "You sound so stressed. Are you having a bad day?"

Tears stung the back of Celeste's eyes. "I don't know why I let Adrian get to me so. I called him yesterday at the hotel. It didn't go well." She wiped her eyes with the back of her hand. "It wasn't all doom and gloom. He suggested that I invite you and Dennis to a barbecue on Saturday night." She hesitated and then blurted out the rest of the message. "He can cook outside on the deck, and we'll eat in the dining room. It's late May and the evenings are still chilly. What do you think?"

After a moment of silence, Marjorie said. "That's great. We'd love to come. But does he expect Sabrina and Ian to be included? That could be a little uncomfortable for you after the last blow up."

Celeste forced her voice to sound cheerful. "I left it up to him to contact Ian. With Sabrina's active social life, maybe they'll have another engagement. At least I can hope so."

"Well, if you are okay with that, sure we'll come." Marjorie's vibrant laugh came over the phone. "Wait a minute. I'd better check first with Dennis. His only activity is golf and it's too early for sailing. However, he's managed to get himself on one of the Town's volunteer committees. It's something to do with an economic development plan."

"I'm glad to hear about it. He seemed a little disappointed when I raised the question about how retirement was going the other night." Celeste was surprised at the blunt edge to her voice. "I can empathize with his thoughts."

Marjorie's warm tone was soothing. "Have you thought anymore about volunteer work? The Heart and Stroke Foundation would love to have you. Also, I hear there's a vacancy on the Hospital Auxiliary."

Celeste frowned and crunched up her nose. "Thanks, not for me. The women in the auxiliary at UHN were ancient. And my experience doesn't really fit with the Heart and Stroke mandate. That's mainly fundraising. I've thought about some type of contract work, but it would probably involve frontline work on weekends and then Adrian and I would never see each other."

Marjorie gave a deep sigh. "Just don't forget to look after yourself. Living your life to appease Adrian could backfire."

Celeste tapped her finger against the phone. "I don't know what you mean by that. I've always had my own life under control. I do what I want regardless of Adrian."

Marjorie's response this time was firm. "It's just Celeste you are sounding so sad and angry lately. I'm only trying to help you. If these conversations aren't any help tell me what you want me to say."

"I'm so sorry, Marjorie. It was stupid of me." Celeste sighed. "Your advice does help. I'm just sensitive about Adrian right now."

"It's good to express your frustration. Just remember I'm just the observer." Marjorie's warm tone returned. "I've got to go now. I'm speaking at a luncheon in twenty minutes."

"Goodbye then. Let me know when you've talked to Dennis about Saturday." Celeste dropped the phone into the cradle and stared at it in silence. What would she do with the rest of the day?

Her current life was so different from the past twenty years at the hospital. The excitement she had felt the day Gail Smythe called her into her cramped office outside the main nursing station on 4B, pushed a pile of papers onto the floor and told her to take a seat. Celeste's hard work had paid off. She was the new Nurse Manager for two clinical wards which included a nice salary bump. The best part for her was she'd oversee training all new recruits, a role she loved. Celeste felt her face flush as she grabbed Gail's hand in gratitude.

After she completed rounds on the surgical ward, Celeste entered the staff room and blushed at the crowd of other Nurse Managers waiting to greet her. Wow. News spread fast in hospitals. It was part of being a somewhat closed community. Her best friend, Susan Spence, had put her arm around Celeste and led her up to the table to cut the chocolate cake decorated with candles and iced pink roses.

"The best part, Celeste, is that you'll be going to the management team meetings with Adrian whom I know you have your eyes on." Susan laughed.

Celeste shook her head. "You're imagining things which don't exist. Adrian doesn't want to know anyone who's not on the senior executive team."

The others laughed, finished their cake, and dwindled away back to their regular activities. Celeste had hung back daydreaming about the day Adrian's deep blue eyes had stared into hers over the main desk at the nursing station. That's when he told her about the award she'd be given by the CEO.

Chapter Six

Celeste

Celeste's concentration was broken by the sudden noise from the phone. Standing in their spare bedroom where she worked, she dropped the brush onto the tray of watercolors. Damn it. She is wiping both hands on her smock and hurried into the main bedroom to pick up the cordless phone. "Hello." She fumbled the receiver and dropped it on the counter.

After a moment of silence, Marjorie responded. "Did I get you from something? You sound rushed."

Celeste sighed. It's okay. I thought it was Adrian. I'm glad it's you, Marjorie." Celeste took a deep breath. "That was clumsy, I guess. I'm trying to get back into painting. What's up?"

"Dennis and I would love to come to your barbeque on Saturday night." Marjorie sounded cheerful. "Would you like me to bring a dish? I could do a green salad."

"That would be great." Celeste said. "Adrian's confirmed that Ian and Sabrina will be there. I should be out shopping. I couldn't get enthused about dinner until I knew for sure you two would come. Besides your salad, we'll have steak, baked potatoes, and a dessert of some kind. I'm not sure what yet."

"I've been thinking more about how to deal with Sabrina." Marjorie hesitated.

"Okay. What's our plan this time?" Celeste gave a tight laugh.

"The guys can cook outside while we're in the kitchen and then we'll move into your dining room. You can set it up in advance with place cards. Put Adrian at one end and Sabrina at the other. What do you think?"

Celeste sighed. "Yeah. It might work. Certainly, worth a try. But it doesn't really fix the problem."

"Well, that could take some time. Let's do what we can right now." Changing the topic, Marjorie inquired. "Have you thought anymore about what you want to do with your time?"

"Haven't found anything which really interests me. What about Dennis? Has his town committee work helped with his depression?" Celeste asked.

"Well, he's not depressed exactly. It's more like he's lived with a huge disappointment since he had to leave work. I still say that men have a much harder time adjusting to retirement than we do."

"What does he want to do? Not go back to work, I assume." Celeste asked.

"No. He knows he can't do that. He talks about sailing to Bermuda and back. That's totally unrealistic with his health problems."

"He seems to enjoy the other two guys when we get together. So that's good." Celeste felt more cheerful. It was great to discuss someone else's problem for a change.

"Yes. He's become fond of Ian. For some reason, his quirky nature appeals to Dennis." Marjorie laughed.

Celeste laughed with her. "I'm beginning to look forward to Saturday night. I'd like to see Sabrina squirming when we keep her and Adrian apart. I'd better go and finish my artwork. See you then."

Adrian had arrived home in good spirits for once. He'd even given Celeste an awfully long kiss in the front hall after the taxi dropped him off. He was now sweeping the patio and checking out the barbecue.

As she opened the screen door, Celeste called to him. "Adrian, I'm going out to Costco. I'll pick up the rib-eye steaks you like and see what they have for desserts."

Adrian waved his hand from behind the barbecue. "Why don't you get the desserts at The Pastry House. They're spectacular."

Celeste forced a smile. Adrian still liked to direct. "Sure. By the way, did you get confirmation from Ian they were coming for sure? Remember. You wondered if he'd checked the date with Sabrina."

"Don't worry. Sabrina called me right back to say they wouldn't miss it. She even cancelled their other engagement." Celeste withdrew and headed to the car her forehead in a deep frown. It seemed she wouldn't shake Sabrina so easily.

Choosing the steaks was easy. Costco always had good meat. As she entered The Pastry Shop, Celeste breathed in the wonderful smells of fresh bread and cinnamon buns. She decided to splurge on a Belgian chocolate sin cake. The women would love it.

"I'll take that one." She pointed to a beautiful specimen in the showcase.

Satisfied, Celeste was in a good mood on the drive home. After she fussed in the kitchen for the next hour, she had the appetizers ready by five and concentrated on setting the table in the dining room. With her good china and wine glasses on the table, she carefully arranged the place cards and stepped back to admire her work. The effect was good although a little formal. She tensed when she heard Adrian's footsteps on the kitchen tiles, she held her breath. Would he make a fuss?

As he entered the dining room, Adrian stood by the doorway. "What are you doing with these white cards? This is supposed to be a barbecue, not a dinner at the Four Points Sheraton. What's wrong with you this evening?"

While tears blinded her eyes, Celeste ran from the room. When she'd regained composure, she moved to the living room and waited for Adrian to join her on the sofa. She should have anticipated his anger.

Adrian stood in front of her his body rigid. "Is this some kind of a joke? We've never used place cards before. They'll think we're putting on airs."

"Stop this right now, Adrian." Celeste glared at him. She'd decided to stand her ground. "I've just got time to change before the guests arrive. Do you want them to see us arguing when they're looking forward to an evening out?" She stood up and headed upstairs to the bedroom.

"Okay. You're right. I'll need time to put on a fresh shirt and pants. We'll talk about this tomorrow." Adrian followed her and began to rummage through his side of the closet. He ignored Celeste, giving her room to select just the right dress. That rose silk one would be nice, he murmured.

After they got dressed, the two of them sat silently on opposite ends of the sofa waiting for the doorbell. Celeste was relieved when he made no further attempt to talk to her. She knew the company would stimulate him and the argument would be forgotten. However, this tension wasn't helpful to their relationship.

Marjorie and Dennis were the first to arrive. Celeste greeted them and led them into the living room. She offered them Camembert spring rolls with blueberry sauce on small plates while Adrian fetched a Chivas Regal scotch for both he and Dennis and Chardonnay for her and Marjorie.

"So, Adrian, where did your travels take you this week?" Marjorie inquired.

"Back to Portland, Oregon. I've a big contract there for the next month. The usual hospital stuff." Adrian's face became animated once again. He loved to talk about his work.

Dennis set his scotch back on the coffee table. "It must be nice to have a regular job."

"Yes. But it's getting harder and harder to satisfy those hospital CEO's. There are fewer and fewer cost-saving experiments around."

"I'm having fun with my volunteer work with the town committee." Dennis chuckled. "Believe me, attempts to come up with ideas to bring new businesses which aren't tourism or wineries isn't easy."

Marjorie sighed. "It's the same with fundraising. We've done it all before and we're competing with the special events hosted by the wineries during the summer. They have so many luncheons, dinners and even concerts going on."

"Well, why don't you join them?" Celeste face felt flushed. It was probably the wine. "Have an extravagant celebration with great food and lots of wine at one of the major hotels."

"Celeste, I keep saying you'd be perfect in fundraising. Especially with associations which have a health-related theme." Marjorie said.

The doorbell chimed and Adrian rushed to respond. Celeste heard the excitement in his voice as he greeted Ian and Sabrina and urged them to join the group while he got drinks. She nibbled at her bottom lip.

"Why don't you have a seat? We've just started the spring rolls." Celeste ushered them to chairs. "I'll bring yours." She glanced at Sabrina, noting the shiny pink top over tight black pants.

"Wonderful of you to have us, Celeste. What a good start to the summer season. I guess we're next to host, Ian." Sabrina exclaimed.

Ian was still looking around the room. "Nice place you've got here. Any problems with the builder?"

Adrian's forehead wrinkled. "I don't know. We're second owners. The roof made it through the big storm we had last month. That's a good sign. The winds from across the river were scary though. It's was too close for our liking."

While Adrian went back out to check the steaks, Celeste removed the dirty dishes to the kitchen. She smiled at the guests. "Let's go into the dining room. The steaks are almost ready."

As they entered, she was aware Sabrina remained standing in the doorway. "Oh. This is special, Celeste. Place cards even. Who would have expected that?" She rolled her eyes. She then proceeded to the head of the table and dropped into her chair.

Adrian placed a steak on each guest's plate according to their earlier requests. He waited until everyone was seated, poured the wine, and gave Celeste one last glare before he sat down at his end. "I'm glad at least you've shortened the table. Otherwise I could barely see Sabrina and Ian at the far side."

Ian gave Sabrina a puzzled look and shrugged. "What's the big deal?"

Sabrina gave him a big smile and touched his hand. "Nothing to worry about, dear." She turned toward Dennis next to her and started an animated discussion about his new committee.

Adrian played the perfect host, checked with each guest about more steak or vegetables and filled glasses as soon as people emptied them. "More wine, Ian or are you the driver tonight?"

Ian nodded. "One more of that red won't hurt. Sabrina can drive back for a change."

Adrian got up and moved around the table with the bottle. "Dennis can I fill your glass? You look a little dry."

Celeste stood and reached the glass over to him and set it down. "I'm on my way to get the dessert and coffee now, so you're on your own." She returned in a few minutes with small plates with slices of chocolate cake.

"That cake is so pretty and it's delicious with the stenciled chocolate fans on top." Marjorie exclaimed. "Wherever did you get it?"

"The Pastry House on Mary Street." Celeste nodded in Adrian's direction. "His idea."

After setting down her dessert fork and finishing her coffee, Sabrina excused herself for the bathroom. On her return she stopped at the end of the table. "Adrian, you promised to show me that painting by Novak you bought at the art auction. You know how art is my passion. If you're finished, can we do that now?"

In his haste to join her, Adrian caught his foot behind the table leg and stumbled to his feet. "Damn." He stood up straight. "Of course. This is a perfectly good time. Just follow me into the den."

Celeste and Marjorie exchanged glances. "I'll help you take the dishes into the kitchen," said Marjorie. She picked up a few plates and headed in that direction while Celeste followed. They saw Dennis and Ian head towards the back deck for some fresh air.

Celeste clenched her teeth. "Okay. How long do I leave them in the den alone?"

Marjorie put her hand on Celeste's shoulder. "I know how this must feel for you. Give them a little space and then I'll barge in and ask to see the same painting. This is worse than I imagined."

Clenching her hands by her sides, Celeste frowned. "I can't believe it. I could just rush over there and pull Sabrina's hair out. I'm not usually like this. It's just that she's so brazen."

"And Adrian does seem smitten." Marjorie said. "I thought men got over these infatuations in their mid-fifties. I know Dennis did. He has no interest in anyone else now. My main problem is getting some free time for myself."

As Celeste started to head out of the kitchen, Marjorie grabbed her arm. "You stay here. I'll go see what I can do."

Celeste's eyes narrowed and her face turned red. "Okay. I can't stand here with them alone together a minute longer."

Time dragged while Celeste waited in the middle of the kitchen doorway to see who would come out of the den first. She bit her fingertips. Then she saw Marjorie arm in arm with Adrian move into the living room, to study the painting on the wall beside the fireplace.

Sabrina trailed out after them and looked around. "Where's Ian? It's getting late and I think we should go now. Can you call him?" She looked directly at Celeste.

"He's on the deck with Dennis. Go get him yourself while I finish cleaning up." Celeste jerked her head in the direction of the patio door.

From the kitchen, Celeste could hear Adrian saying goodbye to the guests. She knew Marjorie would understand why she didn't join them. Maybe Adrian would go straight to bed and they could avoid another one of their rows. But then perhaps he didn't notice her agitation. She couldn't be so lucky. Celeste heard his footsteps headed toward the kitchen.

She turned to face him and forced a smile. "Did you enjoy the dinner?"

Adrian's face softened in a smile; his eyes bright. "They're great company. We should do this more often. Sabrina's so enthusiastic and I've caught on to Ian's dry sense of humour. He's so British." He hesitated. "You don't look like you had a good time. What's up?"

Gritting her teeth, Celeste stared at him. How could he be so unaware? Overwhelmed with fatigue, she decided to let it go. "Let's leave the dishes for the morning. I'd like to sit outside for a while."

He followed her out to the lounge chairs, and they sat quietly and watched the stars overhead. "Remember how after long hours at the hospital, we'd dream about how wonderful living out here would be."

Celeste managed a smile. She was surprised he'd even joined her. "And is it? Does this lifestyle work for you?"

"Yes and no." Adrian's face turned serious. "Sometimes I miss the energy and the buzz of the city. What about you?"

"I love this pretty town. I feel lucky to live here. But I wasn't ready to leave work. I miss the sense of achievement when patients got better and left for home. I miss the camaraderie of my team. I often feel adrift and don't know what to do about it."

He placed his hand over hers. "I'm sorry that you're unhappy."

She leaned toward Adrian. "Thanks for listening to me."

Chapter Seven

Adrian

Adrian gave Celeste a quick kiss on the cheek, picked up his briefcase and headed towards his car. He'd put his suitcase in the trunk earlier and was anxious to be on his way. God, he hoped she wouldn't find some excuse to delay him this time. The flight to Oregon would leave in two hours and traffic was bound to be hectic on a Monday morning. There were times when a taxi made more sense.

Guilt washed over him when he recalled the hurried conversation, he'd had with Sabrina on Saturday night before they were interrupted by Marjorie. Adrian had been shocked at first when he realized she was proposing to join him in Portland this coming week. She'd tell Ian she was going on a shopping trip to Boston with her girlfriends. Although flattered, Adrian knew the risks. He didn't want to lose Celeste. She didn't need to know about this fling. She'd just become so predictable and therefore boring. After he pulled into the Valet parking lot at the airport, he handed over the keys, grabbed his bags and jumped on the bus which was just leaving for the departure gate.

He hurried down the narrow aisle to his seat in business class and pulled out his laptop so he could concentrate on the presentation he'd be giving in a few hours. Business came first. He'd have to think about Sabrina later.

*   *   *

Adrian stood at the head of the boardroom table beside James Reid, the CEO. He could feel the sweat beads across his forehead. What was the matter with him? He wasn't usually nervous, and he'd faced these senior hospital managers before. After turning his head to the side, he caught the CEO's steely eyes and realized that he was supposed to be speaking. His focus brought rapidly back to the slides on the screen, he took a deep breath. He knew this material and had given most of it to the last group he'd been hired to lead. It seemed he'd become the expert on managing change in hospital environments. The tension in the room was getting to him.

"Since James has already explained to all of you what we want to achieve here, I'll just briefly go over the strategy and then I'll be happy to take your questions." He listened for the usual excited buzz in the room, and knew he was on the right track.

By lunch time, he'd finished the discussion. He'd used his slides to lay out the amalgamation of several departments which had been proposed. The positions which would be phased out over the next year were clearly outlined on the chart. Many of these employees were close to retirement and some bridge funding would be available until they were eligible for pensions. His transparency as he laid out the facts had been well received. Satisfied, he turned the meeting back to James. Free to leave, he hummed quietly while he strolled back to his hotel room and sat at his desk where he stared at the phone. His heartbeat rapidly as he dialed the number Sabrina had given him. What would he say if Ian answered?

"Hello. Is this who I think it is?" Sabrina purred into the phone.

"You guessed right. It's me. I've had you on my mind all day." He paused. "Can you talk, or is Ian around?"

"Sure, I'm fine. Ian's at a Town Hall meeting again this afternoon. Believe me it's great to have him out of the house for a change." Sabrina paused. "I've told him I'll be in Boston shopping on Thursday and will return Friday night."

Adrian stood up, almost jerking the phone off the desk. "It's set then. You're really coming to Portland. I'm glad you can stay overnight?"

"I thought for the first time, we'd better both be home for the weekend." She laughed softly. "We can fly back on Friday night and pick up our own cars at the airport."

With a shaking hand, Adrian picked up a pen. "Okay. What flight will you be on and when does it get here? I'll take a cab to pick you up."

Silence again from Sabrina. "Well, are you excited? You do want me to come, don't you?"

He took a couple of deep breaths. "When we talked on Saturday night, I didn't know if you meant it. You could have been teasing me. Of course, I want you to come."

"I'll be in Portland by five in the afternoon on Thursday then." Her voice was husky with promise. "Great if you can you make it to the airport to meet me?"

Adrian felt a nervous thrill run up his leg and into his groin. "Don't worry, Sabrina. I'll be there. I'll be thinking about nothing else for the next two days."

Sabrina whispered into the phone. "I can't wait. Look, Ian just came in the front door, so I must run sweetie."

With the line dead, Adrian stared at the phone and then dropped it as though he'd been scorched. The reality of what he had just done made him jittery. He'd been in a couple of short-term affairs since he'd been married. The opportunities were there since hospitals were mainly staffed with women. They were nothing quite like this. Not with anyone whom Celeste would know.

He changed into black pants and a silk shirt for dinner. James would pick him up at six for a visit to his golf club. The dinner would take his mind off Sabrina for a while at least. Adrian waited for him in the hotel lounge. He sipped a scotch on the rocks and just before the agreed time went out to the front steps.

James drove up and parked just outside the door promptly at six. "There you are Adrian. Sorry you had to wait but the meeting went on much longer than I expected."

Adrian opened the passenger door and slid into the sleek black leather seat of the CEOs' Cadillac. "I was tired of my room and decided to people watch for a while in the bar."

"It seems the managers group really liked you. Your talk opened them up to face some fears. They raised lots of questions and a couple of them had good suggestions. I'm impressed."

"Yeah. I try to break the tension and get them to talk to each other rather than dwelling on who might be left out of a job. They'll find that out soon enough."

The car pulled into the driveway of a grey stone building with a backdrop of huge stretches of emerald green grass. Tonight, was dinner only then they had golf games set up at this club for all the managers on Friday. He'd be expected to play which would give him an excuse not to spend the day with Sabrina in case she got too clingy.

Over dinner the two of them discussed more of their strategy for the downsizing which was to come. Adrian had learned from other jobs it was better to spend his time with the leaders rather than those who wouldn't make it. He felt for them however there was nothing more he could do about the final plan. James dropped him off at his hotel at ten. The message light was on when he entered his room. Checking it he heard Celeste's voice saying she'd call him again on Wednesday. He'd better call her first so she wouldn't call him back on Thursday night. This was getting complicated. He crawled into bed and immediately fell asleep.

The next three days were packed full of meetings. The managers were getting jittery again as more and more details about their future became clear. Adrian always found this part difficult. He reassured himself he was only the instrument. It wasn't his decision to cut staff. His excitement increased all Thursday afternoon and he was anxious for the meeting to end. Not wanting to be late, he grabbed his briefcase as soon as it did, ran out the door and hailed a cab to the airport. Sabrina was one of the first passengers to exit the arrivals lounge. She had on a pencil-thin black skirt and an slinky silk blouse through which he could make out her firm breasts.

He walked towards her. "Sabrina, you made it. I kept thinking you'd cancel. It's great to see you." He put his arm around her waist and picked up her overnight bag.

Sabrina touched his hand. "I'm so excited to be here with you. It'll be our first night alone together."

"We can grab a downtown limousine over by the stand and you can check in at the hotel while I make a dinner reservation. Let me know what you feel like eating?" Adrian hustled her downstairs and out the door.

Settled in the limo, Sabrina pressed against him and ran her finger down the side of his face and over to his throat. "I've been dreaming about this all week. Let's find a small Italian restaurant. Something intimate."

Adrian began to feel hot and resisted any further advances. "There's a good one a few blocks from the hotel. Carpaccio's. The concierge recommended it to me." He paid the driver and followed her into the hotel. "I'll ask them to make the reservation and wait for you in the bar while you get checked in."

Sabrina flashed him a big smile. "You can come up with me if you like."

"They know I checked in alone. Let's keep things private. I don't want to complicate our lives." He squeezed her hand and turned towards the lounge.

Sipping his scotch, Adrian felt a chill across his shoulders. What if someone from the hospital ran into him with Sabrina? She looked nothing like how he'd described Celeste. What was he thinking? Then, what was taking her so long? He'd loved the smoothness of her skin in the limo. He watched as she walked into the lounge and saw other men stare. Yes, she was something. She'd changed into a silky black dress which showed a glimpse of cleavage and gave her a mysterious look. He left his drink unfinished and took her hand to lead her out into the quiet street.

Outside the restaurant, they studied the menu together and he pulled her into a brief embrace, kissing her on the cheek and then lightly on the lips. Her warmth surrounded him as she leaned against him. She gave him a teasing look. "Are you sure we need dinner?"

He chuckled. "Come on. I hear they have a great Pino Grigio or Chianti Classico." He opened the door for them to enter. "We'd like a table in the alcove for two."

Their host led the way. "Yes, sir. I think you'll like this one. Very private."

After two glasses of wine each, both were relaxed and chatted easily about things to see and do in Portland. They avoided any reference to their hometown.

"What will you do tomorrow while I'm at my business meetings?" Adrian asked.

"I do need to shop so Ian won't be suspicious. Besides, I can use a few new outfits for fall. And the hotel recommended a cute little restaurant on Winston Street for lunch."

"Didn't you enjoy your veal chop with linguine? Adrian gestured at her unfinished meal.

"Yes. It was wonderful; I'm too excited to eat right now." She gave him a coy smile. "How was your steak?"

"I was ravenous. You can tell by my plate. Do you want dessert or a liqueur?"

Sabrina gazed into his eyes. "No. Let's go back to the hotel. I just want to be with you."

Adrian dropped his fork and signaled to the waiter for the bill. As soon as he'd finished paying, he stood and pulled her chair back to help her get up. "I've asked the waiter to call a cab. Since it's a nice night, we can wait outside."

The cab ride was short, and they were soon back at the entrance of the hotel. "Would you like to stop in the bar for a night cap?"

Sabrina smiled again. "No. I want us to go to your room. What are you waiting for?" She grabbed his hand.

He flushed and led her to the elevator. His nervousness had increased over dinner. It had been a while since he'd been with another woman. What was wrong with him? She was obviously ready. "Lead the way my love. I've been waiting for this all evening."

Chapter Eight

Adrian

Adrian closed the hotel door quietly as they entered the room. Her face flushed from the wine; Sabrina looked even more sultry than usual as she wrapped both arms around him pressing her full breasts against his chest. "I've wanted to get you alone for a long time. I could tell we'd be good together," she purred.

His breath coming in gasps, Adrian kissed her neck several times and moved down to curve of each breast. Sabrina pulled him even closer and then, dropping her hands, she hooked her thumbs into the top of his belt. He stepped back and yanked off his jacket and tie, dropping them on the floor. Draping his arm around her waist and he slowly moved her towards the bed. She turned her back and reached for her zipper which he pulled down for her so she could remove her dress. While she was undressing, he undid his belt and removed pants and shirt. After throwing back the sheets, they slid onto the bed and wrapped their bodies around each other, sighing and moving to get comfortable.

Adrian was surprised at how quickly he was ready. No Viagra needed here. To increase her pleasure, he stroked the silky skin of her stomach and continued down to her thighs before he rolled on top of her. She moaned and dug her fingers into his buttocks pulling him closer. Using a strong rhythm, he continued breathing heavily as he went deeper to make sure that she was satisfied. With her hands on his back, his own sexual tension continued to build. Only when he felt her climax did he allow his whole body to relax.

Sabrina touched his chest gently. "That was wonderful, my darling. Was it for you?"

Adrian turned onto his side and pulled her body against his, softly kissing her shoulder. "Better than I could have imagined." He felt more tenderness towards her than he expected and was reluctant to let her go.

They dozed for a while before he heard Sabrina sigh and felt her sit up. "I hate to leave you when there might be more to look forward to. Just as I told you earlier, I promised to call Ian tonight when I got back to my room. His suspicions are easily aroused. We don't want that complication."

Adrian swung his feet over the side of the bed and put on his shorts. "I know we agreed to be careful and to keep things secret. I'll take you to the door when you're ready." In the dim light, he watched her dress and followed her to the door. He gave her a light kiss then she was gone. Adrian was glad now that she was just two rooms down the hall.

Sprawled back on the bed with his head against the pillows, Adrian flicked from channel to channel trying to find something to catch his attention. The night had been a surprise for him, and an experience he would relive in his daydreams. Sabrina was so much more a sexual match for him. With Celeste, he felt the need to coax and pamper to get her into the mood. But then, maybe he wasn't being fair. This was just all so new for him, so intense.

*   *   *

Waking from a sound sleep, Adrian reached over to the bedside table to turn off the alarm. He'd rolled over to doze for a while when the sharp ring of the phone startled him. He forced

47

himself to sit up and grabbed the receiver. "Hello." He mumbled. His voice sounded hoarse to his own ears.

"Hi, honey. I'm sorry to wake you." There was a pause. "You said you'd call last night."

God! It was Celeste. Why didn't he call her like he intended? He swung his feet over the side of the bed, with his head down. "That's okay. I'm sorry about last night. James and I were out late talking business over dinner, and I was so tired when I got back that I forgot." The excuse sounded lame even to him.

After a long silence, he heard Celeste's anxious voice. "I wanted to know if you'll be back tonight. We're supposed to meet the group at Bistro 77 again."

Sharp pangs of guilt ripped through him. "Yes. Of course, I'll be there. My plane gets in at 5:00. I'll take a cab from the airport, as usual. You can spend your time choosing a sexy outfit."

Celeste gave a brief laugh. "I'm not so sure that I'd call it sexy. I'd planned to wear that new white sundress. You know the one with the pink and red flowers."

Adrian sighed with relief. "That sounds great. I'll look forward to the group after a day of confrontation with the hospital staff. We've scheduled meetings with the managers who'll be part of the new organization. Workshops in career planning for those who won't."

Celeste's voice had fallen again. "I know what that's like. We'll talk about it when you get home. Bye for now."

After replacing the receiver in the cradle, Adrian looked at the clock again and hurried into the shower. He couldn't afford to be late. Thank goodness he wouldn't be seeing Sabrina again until tonight. How could he have been so stupid not calling Celeste? He guessed that it was just avoidance. Much like he felt this morning, not really wanting to return to the hospital, knowing what he would confront with anxious staff. Maybe this second career wasn't such a good idea.

He checked his appearance in the mirror. Light blue short sleeved shirt, with open collar tucked into tan pants. He grabbed his summer weight blue blazer and briefcase and headed out to the elevator. As usual, he dressed down for these sessions. Staff would find him more approachable and he would provide what reassurance he could. As he passed Sabrina's door, he prayed she wouldn't open it. He couldn't afford the distraction. She'd said that she intended to sleep late, have a leisurely breakfast and shop until late afternoon. He'd see her at the airport.

*   *   *

It was late when the cab dropped him off at departures. He couldn't afford to miss this plane, so he broke into a fast walk across the airport lounge. James had left him alone with the managers who would be receiving packages for the last hour and they had poured out their anxieties in waves. His own anxiety increased as two of them followed him out the door as he headed for the airport. What more could he do for them? When he approached the line-up for check-ins, he smiled. Sabrina was waiting for him at the end with her boarding pass in hand.

Adrian waved at her and shrugged his shoulders. He was glad the check-in was efficient this time and he was able to catch up with Sabrina, grab her hand and head to the security check together. "I hope it won't be a strip search this time out."

Sabrina smiled. "I wouldn't mind if you did it; then it would just delay us getting on board."

They got through quickly and were soon walking through the loading ramp onto the plane. Sabrina had insisted on changing her ticket to business class so they could be seated together. Once they found their seats, she squeezed his hand. "You're right about the extra space in business. And I can see you need to relax." She patted his arm.

Adrian let out his breath. "You're right. I am tense. The meeting this afternoon was difficult."

"Sit back and relax. I won't even bother you until they come with the drinks."

He closed his eyes and leaned back against the seat. "Just give me a few minutes and then I'll be ready to be more social."

The clanking of the drink cart awoke him from a doze. He turned toward Sabrina who was flipping through a fashion magazine. "Thanks for being so considerate. What will you have?"

"I feel like scotch on the rocks for a change. Maybe it'll calm me. I'm not good at flying." Sabrina replied.

Adrian ordered two from the attendant, passed Sabrina hers and took a long sip from his glass. "Did you remember to call Ian? I forgot to call Celeste, so she called me this morning and she was pissed."

"Yes. I called him as soon as I got back to my room. I woke him up. However, he sounded relieved."

"Did it go well then?" Adrian asked.

Sabrina scrunched up her nose. "Not exactly. I tried to sound excited about the shops in Boston, but I don't think he was buying it. He questions everything. Just his nature, I guess."

Adrian took her hand in his and held it. "Maybe I can reassure him. He's a good golfer and seems to enjoy a game with Dennis and me. I'll set something up tonight at the dinner."

"That's thoughtful of you." Sabrina ran her fingers up his arm. "Just don't get too chummy with him."

Adrian chuckled as he pulled her closer looking into her eyes. "You're the one I want to be chummy with. Don't you know that?"

Sabrina relaxed. "This is like being an actress. We'll all be together tonight and we'll both behave as though nothing has changed."

*   *   *

As he walked up his cobblestone driveway of his house, Adrian felt twinges of guilt. Would he be able to hide how he felt about Sabrina from Celeste tonight? He should be good at that with all the practice with his teams. This time was different. He took a deep breath and opened the front door. "I'm home." The house was silent. Maybe she'd gone ahead with Marjorie and Dennis.

Standing at the bottom of the stairs, he tried again. "Celeste, I'm back."

He heard footsteps across the hardwood floors, then she stood at the top of the stairs. Her white dress gave her violet eyes a shine, making her look younger.

She smiled down at him. "Hi. I just finished getting dressed. I know it's a little early. Let's sit on the patio for a drink before we go."

"Sounds good. Give me a minute to change my shirt and I'll join you." Adrian climbed the stairs and gave her a light kiss on the cheek before he went into the bedroom.

One of the great things about their town was the warm spring air ideal for patios, gardens, and long strolls. As he joined Celeste, he admired their bed of pink hydrangeas. "It's peaceful out here isn't it? I need something to sooth my nerves after the week I had at the hospital."

"How are they responding to the changes?"

Adrian dropped his head. "That's just it. I don't think people ever get used to seeing their friends at work disappear one by one. Even though I provided what support I could, it was like a fog of depression drifted over them."

Celeste put a sympathetic hand over his. "I didn't know it affected you so much. You don't talk about it."

Sitting back in his chair, Adrian took a sip of his scotch. "The leaders are supposed to be the strong ones. I guess I feel that if I don't say anything it will all go away."

They shared a comfortable silence for a few moments. Adrian checked his watch. "I guess we had better be on our way. The others will be waiting."

"Okay. If you want to talk again, I'm here." Celeste picked up the glasses and led the way through the patio door.

*   *   *

Celeste entered the Bistro first. When she heard Sabrina's shrill laughter, she shrunk back.

Annoyed at her delay, Adrian pushed past her. "That sounds like our group at the back. Come on." Not wanting to be too obvious, he sat next to Dennis and gestured to Celeste to join him.

"Celeste, I see the wanderer has returned." Dennis said gesturing toward Adrian. "How about a game with Ian and me tomorrow morning?"

Shaking off his annoyance, Adrian grinned. "I'll be there at six. What time will you two old codgers show up?"

Ian bristled. "Old. Who're you talking about? He faced Adrian. "I know you got pushed out of the workforce by a young Turk just like I did. The Board was constantly seeking out new methods and new technology to increase their profits. All focus was always on the share price and what they could do to push it up."

"What are you two worried about? The new crew are young now. They'll get older, make mistakes just like us and will soon fall from grace." Dennis patted Adrian on the back. "I would love to join you tomorrow. The earlier the better for me."

"What are you up to tomorrow, Marjorie? I just finished a shopping trip so thought maybe we could do something cultural for a change. What's on at The Shaw? Have you seen anything yet?" Sabrina said.

"Dennis and I have tickets for later in the season. I love the Festival Theatre best. We enjoy sitting outside with a glass of wine during intermission. Their gardens are just so beautiful. What about trying the new Studio Theatre? I hear they have some more modern plays from Broadway. That might be a treat."

Sabrina's eyes brightened. "I'd like that."

Marjorie turned to Celeste. "You'll join us, won't you?"

Celeste frowned and then nodded. "Yes. I've nothing else to do."

Adrian ordered roast beef and Ian decided to have the same. Sabrina choose curried lamb and both Marjorie and Celeste had seafood with a cream sauce. The chatter over dinner was mainly about social events coming up over the summer. It wasn't until coffee was served that Adrian had a chance to catch Sabrina's attention. Celeste and Marjorie had gone to the lady's room.

"Sabrina, you wanted me to point out to you the nature painting done by Forsythe. He's a local artist. There's one in the reception area if you'd like to see it." He rose and headed toward the front of the restaurant with Sabrina following him.

"Do you think Ian noticed anything strange?" He said as they stared at a painting on the wall. The stark outline of the boat against the moody grey water suggested a simplicity he hadn't experienced in a long time.

"No. I was nervous when you suggested I join you for this, however he just looked bored." Sabrina slipped her arm around his waist.

Adrian jumped. "Careful. Celeste was watching everything we did." He looked directly into her eyes. "I'd like to see you again, but I don't think you'd get away with another trip right now."

Sabrina brightened. "Not likely. But I've been thinking. Niagara Falls is big enough that we could disappear there and no one who knows us would likely see us. Especially at the Marriott."

He squeezed her hand. "When?"

"Let's try for early Sunday evening. You can say you have to fly out in the afternoon? Then take the midnight flight."

"Okay. Let's get back before they get suspicious. I'll call you on Saturday to let you know if it's a go." Adrian said.

Sabrina smoothed her skirt and led the way back to the table. As they got closer, she said, perhaps too cheerily. "Forsythe is a good naturalist artist. Does he do anything else besides this nautical theme?"

"Trees and other landscapes. I didn't know that you were an admirer." Adrian slipped back into his seat next to Celeste. "He has a small shop in town. It might be fun for our group to explore more art and cultural interests."

Chapter Nine

Celeste

Celeste stood at the kitchen window and stared out into the garden. The champagne roses she planted last summer where in full bloom. As she emptied the dishwasher and stacked the clean plates, Celeste couldn't shake off twinges of anxiety. It wasn't just the long absence of Sabrina and Adrian last night that was bothering her. Now this unexplained departure. Adrian had rushed off after breakfast giving her some excuse about shipping some binders to Portland by Express Post for his meeting next week. What a weak exclamation he'd given her. He said it could take hours, so he'd pick up lunch downtown. Did he think she was stupid? She knew the hospital would usually make up the binders for him with materials he sent by email.

Could the situation be worse than she had thought? Was he having an affair? Sure, he still gave her occasional light kisses on her cheek, However, the passion wasn't there. For months, although they slept in the same bed, there was no love making. Celeste sighed deeply. She would confront him when he arrived back this afternoon. Avoiding talking about it wouldn't make it go away.

She missed Natalie since her daughter had moved to Ottawa with her father after their divorce. With his quick remarriage, it made sense for their daughter to live with him. It had been an amicable split with both feeling they'd married too young. As a single mother who worked nights and weekends, she hadn't been available to look after a small child. Ever since Celeste and Adrian married, he'd become Natalie's stepfather. She was about nine then. She and Natalie had become closer. After all, Natalie spent every summer with the two of them in Toronto until she went away to university. Not that she would confide in Natalie about the issues with Adrian. She was proud her daughter had skipped nursing and instead had been invited to teach history at a large university in Ottawa.

Celeste had decided in the spring that she'd take up tennis again now that she had the time. It seemed to her that when you retired, all you had left was time and the days were long. She'd drive over to the courts and see if it were still possible to sign up for the ladies' ladder. Adrian had taken the BMW as usual, so she pulled the older model Honda CRV out of the garage and backed down the driveway. Marjorie was right. He could be selfish. Within a few minutes, she pulled into the parking area for the town tennis courts. Pleased to see how full the lot was, Celeste took her tennis racket out of the back seat and headed for the pavilion where she knew Rosemary Swift, usually hung out. She knew that as President, Rosemary spent many long hours at the courts.

Celeste opened the door small clubhouse. "Hi. Have you given up on me yet or do I have another chance?"

Rosemary's face broke into a broad smile. "Celeste. Good to see you. It's been a while since you signed up; I just knew you'd join the competition eventually. I've watched you practicing. You're too good a player to not be drawn back to it. We need a spare on one of the women's ladders."

"How soon could I start? I'm anxious to try playing before I get cold feet."

"They have a game in half an hour. Why don't you watch the play with me until then? I'll join you on the bleachers as soon as I let them know I've found a spare," Rosemary said.

Her bum felt numb on the cold metal bench, but Celeste watched the four women in their white shorts and tops running back and forth across the court. She had a moment of doubt. Would her feet ever be that nimble again? Their easy chatter with each other reminded her of what she had been missing. Through tennis, she could get back some of that team spirit sensation.

Rosemary plunked down beside her and smiled. "You look excited. I know you'll soon be a regular. It'll only be another fifteen minutes for court 3. You'll be with Bernice, Stella and Pam."

"Well, I don't know any of them. I'm glad they're willing to have me."

"They're more than excited to have you. They thought they'd be left with a threesome." Rosemary turned toward the pavilion. "Here they come now. Let me introduce you." She jumped down and led the way toward the group.

After greetings all around, the four of them headed to the courts which were now vacant. Although she felt awkward at first, Celeste soon picked up on the play and her strong forehand was soon winning her side points. She felt energized and her feelings of uselessness drained away. That was probably why the guys played golf so much. She could taste the sense of achievement.

Her partner, Pam, was a strong player and they easily won all three sets 6-5, 6-3 and 6-2. The hour was up, and the next teams were already heading towards the courts. She walked back to the bleachers with Pam.

"You'll come again, won't you Celeste?" Pam coaxed. "You can put your name down as a spare since the teams are full and you'll get quite a few games."

"Sure. Why not?" Celeste smiled. "It's not as though I've got numerous other events pulling me away."

When the other women were off to Balzac's for a coffee, Celeste declined the invitation. She wanted to get home to see if Adrian had returned yet. The need to keep a closer eye on him had been growing for weeks now. She wondered if Ian felt the same way. After maneuvering her car off King Street and onto John, she made her way to their red brick house. Their BMW was parked in the driveway.

Celeste took a deep breath, squared her shoulders, and pulled open the door. Why was she so awful at confronting others and especially Adrian? She knew he'd be in the den. Her nature was probably due to her quiet upbringing and her father's habit of avoiding conflict.

"Well. Adrian you're back from your errands. It took you long enough."

While she stood in the doorway, Celeste watched as he snapped his head back and look at her with a defensive expression.

"Come on, hon. I wasn't gone that long." He sat back in his chair. "Besides, you were out, too."

Celeste sat across from him. "Do you remember how we used to play tennis with that club in Toronto? We both enjoyed that group so much. Well, I've signed up with the local tennis club. I need a challenge."

"Good. Don't count on me. I'm not really retired yet and I need to finish reports on nights and weekends." He stood and began to walk towards the stairs. "In fact, I'm waiting for a report from Jim he'll be sending online. I'll need to review it before dinner. Call me when you want me to turn on the barbecue."

With his back turned, Celeste gave him a dirty look. Adrian had time for everyone but her.

*   *   *

During their dinner of grilled beef spareribs and fried sweet potatoes, Celeste tried several approaches to engage him in conversation. "So, what's the plan for your next meeting in Portland? Has Jim pulled together the staff who will be staying on yet? They'll need to know how their workload will be readjusted."

Adrian pulled himself back from his daydreaming with an annoyed frown. "What's this sudden interest in my work? I've explained that I don't like to talk about it on weekends. I'll live with it when I have to live with it."

"It's just that I feel shut out of your life." Celeste swallowed hard to keep her voice calm. "We used to talk about your job.... before I retired that is. What's so different now?"

He dropped his fork with a clunk on the glass table. "Everything is different now. We're different now. Why can't you see that?"

Bewildered by his agitated manner, Celeste sat silently. "I'll get the peach tarts and coffee." She rose and carried dirty dishes into the kitchen. Tears glistened in her eyes while she filled the dishwasher. These dinners left her stomach tied in knots. Taking a deep breath, she loaded a tray and carried it back to the patio.

After breaking off pieces of the tart, he slowly put them into his mouth while gazing off into the distance. Later he sipped the coffee. "Good dinner. By the way, I'll be leaving early for Portland on Sunday. The flight goes at two since the later one was totally booked. I should have told you about it earlier."

Celeste felt her whole-body tense. Now what was this about? He always left on Sunday night so they could have dinner together first. "This is a sudden change. Is something else going on here, Adrian? I need to know."

He dropped the cup into the saucer spilling the coffee. "What's wrong with you? You're starting to question everything I do. I don't like it." He stood up and headed for the kitchen, slamming the patio door behind him.

She took her time eating her dessert and sipping the coffee which was already cold. She was confused. Was he right? Was she imagining things that weren't there? Her life had changed so much in the past month. Although she dreaded seeing Adrian right now, she put the dishes on the tray and entered the kitchen. He was in the living room with his back to her, talking into the phone. All she heard was something about see you then before he hung up.

Celeste tried to sound casual. "Did someone call? I didn't hear the phone."

With a red face, Adrian turned to her. "Are you spying on me now? Can't I even use the phone?"

She gave him a black look. "What's the big deal? Are you feeling guilty?"

"I can't even talk to you anymore." He headed for the stairs. "I'll be in my office upstairs working on my report. Don't disturb me."

Waiting until he was safely upstairs, Celeste checked the phone display. She didn't recognize the phone number and guessed it was probably a cell phone. Could it be Sabrina or was she overreacting at his new behaviour? She'd be keeping a closer eye on him from now on.

* * *

Bright sunlight gleamed on the bowl of red roses that Celeste had just placed on the glass patio table where she was preparing to serve their lunch. Since Adrian would be leaving early for Portland today, she'd picked up cold sliced ham, potato salad and his favourite rye bread. When the meal was ready, she poured two glasses of chardonnay and called to him while she carried them out.

"Hon, our lunch is waiting outside. We might as well enjoy the nice weather. You never know what Portland might be like."

She left the door open a crack so she would hear his footsteps on the kitchen floor. Yes, there it was. He must be on his way out.

"It's such a rush leaving this early. Jim will be pleased that I have time to go over the presentation for tomorrow with him before dinner." Adrian took a sip of wine. "This will relax me for the trip. My suitcase is already in the car. I'll drive to the airport this time."

"Whatever you have to do." She paused. "Marjorie has convinced me to go to the Heart and Stroke fashion show with her this week." She watched to see if he was listening. "Normally, I'm not into these charity events, but I enjoy her company and it's a chance to meet other people."

Adrian focused his attention back on her for few minutes. He had been gazing off into the distance with a strange expression. "That's good, dear. You'll want to keep busy. It's known to be a cure for depression."

"What do you mean by that?" Her head snapped back. "I'm not depressed. Why would you think that?"

He crossed both arms across his chest. "Whoa. Don't get carried away my dear. You, of all people, know that as we age idleness can lead to apathy or depression. You've read the statistics at the hospital just as I have."

Celeste glared at him. "Well, I've now got my art classes and the tennis club. I'm planning to take some new courses in the fall, too."

"What are you taking? I might be interested."

"I haven't figured that out yet. I wish they had a university closer. McMaster is so far away in Hamilton. It's probably the only one with health-related courses."

"There's also Niagara College in Buffalo." He nodded his head. "I think that's a great idea for you to research what's available locally. I remember how excited you were anytime we had expert presenters at the hospital. Let me help you clean up these dishes before I have to take off."

She filled both hands and headed for the kitchen. "Thanks. Bring the rest in and we can put them all in the dishwasher."

Later she followed Adrian out to the driveway and stood watching as his car pulled away. They'd had a decent conversation over lunch. Something that hadn't occurred in a long time. Was he trying to make up for his early departure? She returned to the house and having nothing else planned decided to sit in the garden and read until dinner. After she picked up her novel she'd dropped it on the table, as she tried to concentrate.

Something was nagging at her. It was strange that Adrian needed to leave early this time and he hadn't mentioned it when he arrived on Friday. What could he be hiding from her? The image of Sabrina and him at the restaurant last night flashed through her mind. Before she could think about the consequences, she picked up the phone and dialed. She held her breath while it rang.

"Hello."

It was Ian's voice. Celeste relaxed. At least he was home, and that meant Sabrina was almost certainly there as well. "Can I speak to Sabrina for a minute, Ian?" She'd have to think of some excuse for the call.

Ian hesitated. "She's not here right now, Celeste. She went to a local art show in Niagara Falls." Celeste could hear a note of sarcasm in his voice. "Haven't you noticed her sudden interest in art?" There was a silence. "Can I give her a message?"

"It's okay. I'll call her tomorrow about arrangements for getting together for lunch, just the three women."

"What about Adrian? Is he at home?" Ian sounded skeptical.

Celeste's heart sank. "No. He left early for Portland today."

"Some coincidence, don't you think?" Ian said with steel in his voice.

"I can't imagine what you're talking about. Anyway, I must go now, and I'll call Sabrina tomorrow." Was Ian just being his normal suspicious self? Or was something going on with the two of them? This time Celeste felt anger churning in her stomach. If Adrian was up to something, she was going to find out the very next time he came home.

Chapter Ten

Adrian

Parked at the Marriott Fallsview Hotel in Niagara Falls, Adrian looked around nervously to see if he recognized any of the cars. He knew that Celeste was beginning to get suspicious. Why should she worry? He'd go back to her when the novelty with Sabrina wore off. It's not like he was leaving for good. He admired Sabrina's skilled maneuvering of the Lexus through the lot with cars entering and exiting and smiled at her when she pulled up beside him. She stepped out of the car dressed in a shiny emerald-green dress that rippled in the light wind.

Adrian got out of his car and called to her. "Glamorous as usual, Sabrina. I don't understand why Ian would doubt your regular shopping trips." He chuckled.

She blew him a kiss. "It's not that he doubts them. He just doesn't understand why I no longer invite him to come along."

He reached her and gave a long, sensuous hug while he caressed the back of her neck. As he pulled back, he frowned. "Seriously. Ian's not giving you a hard time about being away, is he?"

"Well, over breakfast this morning, he grilled me repeatedly about exactly where I was going this afternoon." Sabrina kissed him on the cheek. "Let's check in and then I'll give you the details. We don't want other ears listening in."

Adrian grabbed a small bag from the back seat of his car. "You're right. We don't want to raise any questions. Besides, I brought a special bottle of red burgundy." His eyes glinted as he gazed at her and he could feel the excitement travel up his body. "The hotel is bound to have those plush robes."

Sabrina grabbed his hand and squeezed it while they headed into the front lobby to register. The desk clerk hardly glanced at them as Adrian filled out the registration form and passed over his credit card. The clerk handed over two access cards and said they would be in Room 702. Adrian gestured towards Sabrina and they walked to the elevator together. When the door closed, they were glad to be alone together. Adrian put both arms around Sabrina and kissed her on the lips. His hand traced down her neck to the top of her exposed breasts. He stepped back just as the door opened on their floor.

His arm around her waist, Adrian led her to the room, slid in the card and pushed the door open. Sabrina pranced across the carpet and collapsed on the bed admiring the view over the falls. "What a wonderful photo this would make in the bright sunlight. We're so lucky to live here. People travel from all over the world just to see this."

Adrian set the bag on the table, removing the bottle of wine and a small, wrapped package. He sat beside her on the bed holding the gift out for her to see.

Sabrina sat up and leaned against him, taking the gift into her hand. "This is a surprise. I didn't expect a gift. What is it?"

Adrian kissed the back of her neck. "You'll have to open it to find out."

She ripped off the paper and opened the box taking out a delicate gold chain with a love knot at the end. "I love it. Where did you get it? I haven't seen anything like this in town."

His smile broadened. "I picked it up in Portland after our last date."

She walked over to the mirror and held it up against her neck. "It's just the right length." After she placed the necklace back in its box, she dropped it into her purse. "I'll tell Ian it was part of my shopping today."

He had removed both shirt and trousers, folding, and placing them on a chair. "Let's get comfortable and enjoy our wine by the window. I've been so looking forward to us being together." He was soon standing naked while pouring the two glasses half full.

She gave a throaty laugh and pulled her dress over her head. "What happened to those luxury robes?" Kicking off her shoes, Sabrina slipped off her silver bikinis and lacy bra, throwing them on the floor. They stood by the window and toasted the falls before he closed the brocade drapes to turn the room into soft lighting.

With their glasses empty, Adrian took her by the arm and eased her towards him until bodies were clasped together. His breathing grew heavier as he traced patterns across her buttocks and shoulders. Sabrina leaned back so that he could place his lips, first on one nipple and then across to the other. He heard her gasp as he touched her lightly down the length of her body. They moved together to the bed and Adrian pulled her onto his lap while gently rubbing her breasts.

When he was sure that he was ready, Adrian threw back the comforter and sheets and they climbed into bed, still holding on to each other. "This time we're not rushed, and I can enjoy every touch."

Sabrina licked his ear while she ran her hands down his stomach. "Friday seems like a long time ago. I want you now while everything's still new."

Sabrina maneuvered herself on top of Adrian shifting up and down with a steady rhythm, both breasts gently touching his chest. He could hardly contain his excitement until she clutched his shoulders, moaned, and collapsed onto him. Rolling her over, he straddled her body and was soon able to reach a peak of tension followed by a gradual release. They lay face to face, their bodies just touching while he traced an imaginary line from her stomach to the sensitive area of her neck. As his breathing became more regular, Adrian could feel himself drift off.

*   *   *

Startled into alertness, Adrian saw Sabrina's face above him just before she kissed him on the lips. He sat up and swung both his legs over the side of the bed. His voice was groggy with sleep, "What's up?"

Sabrina playfully slapped his thigh. "If you want to catch the next flight to Portland, you'd better start moving." She rubbed her hand down the inside of his leg. "Unless you want to stay overnight, that is."

Adrian held his face in his hands for a few minutes while he cleared his head. "No. I've got to be at an important meeting at the hospital tomorrow morning. Give me a minute to shower and I'll walk you to your car." He pulled on the bathrobe lying on the chair.

"No need. I'm ready to leave now. I don't want to arouse Ian's imagination by being late. Before I left the house, he wanted to know exactly where I was going, what I planned to buy and whom I was going with. We'll talk tomorrow night. I've got to pick up a few packages before I go home." She opened the door to the hall. "I'll call you when I get a chance."

He had a quick glimpse of someone standing in the hall before the door was shoved wide open and Ian barged through, his face red with anger. "I've been sitting in that damn parking lot for the past hour waiting for you to come back. I guessed what you two were up to, then the desk clerk refused to give me your room number until I showed up with a briefcase and convinced him that I needed to deliver it."

He could see Sabrina's rigid posture as she braced herself against the doorframe. "How dare you follow me."

Ian shoved her back into the room and raised his fist while he turned on Adrian. "What the hell is going on? I've watched you playing up to my wife. Did you enjoy making fools out of Celeste and me? "He clenched and unclenched his fists, while his body shook with fury. "We'll see what she has to say when I tell her where I found the two of you."

Fear and embarrassment flooded over Adrian. He watched Sabrina and was surprised to see that she remained calm and stared coldly at Ian. He couldn't let Ian drop this on Celeste while he was away. "Sabrina, why don't you leave the two of us? Ian, we need to talk. Give me a minute to change. "It's not as bad as you think. Let's be civilized about this."

Sabrina escaped into the hall, slamming the door behind her. Ian glared at Adrian then dropped onto the settee, his back rigid. "I'll give you about five minutes."

Adrian grabbed his clothes and retreated into the bathroom. He ran a quick shower while trying to decide how to handle this situation. No matter what happened, he'd have to fly out to Portland tonight. It was obvious that he'd already missed the first flight out. The water revived him and after dressing, he returned to sit in the armchair across from Ian.

Once seated, Adrian had regained his business manner. "Look, Ian, I know that this is rotten for you and I'm sorry. We weren't thinking straight and certainly didn't mean to hurt you or Celeste."

Ian's eyes were slits that drilled into his as he responded. "Just selfish, the two of you. No thought for anyone else."

"I'm glad you're being a man about this." Adrian shifted in his seat. "I'm worried about Celeste. I've got to continue to Portland, and she'll be hurt and embarrassed to hear it from you. Can I ask you to wait until I'm back on the weekend? I'll tell her myself then. I promise." This time Adrian could see the deep hurt in Ian's eyes.

He choked out. "Why should I believe you? Tell me what trust you have built with me?"

The tension was heavier than the recent negotiations that he'd had with hospital staff. If he couldn't talk Ian into a delay in confiding what had happened, he'd have to tell Celeste by phone before he left for the airport. "It won't make things any worse if we wait. I want to save Celeste from some of the shock. I will call you as soon as she has been told."

Adrian was glad Ian had agreed to discuss the matter with him. He watched Ian as he stared down at the floor in front of him. Between the tension of waiting for Ian to speak and the fear of missing the last flight, he could hardly remain seated.

"I'm trying to think what Celeste would want." Ian said. She's the innocent party, not you. As for me, I had my suspicions for a while and needed to know; maybe she'd rather hear it from you." Ian raised his head. "I'll wait. But for the weekend only." He pulled the door open and left without a backward look at Adrian.

Adrian grabbed the small suitcase, his wallet, and keys, before he left the room. He discreetly checked for Ian in the lobby, and when he saw no one, he opened the door and ran to his car. There was no sign of either Sabrina's car or Ian's sleek Jag. Backing his car out of the lot, he headed for Highway 420 which get him to the airport. Adrian knew that it would be tight for making the last flight out tonight. There was no time for him to contemplate what the weekend would hold with Celeste or how Sabrina would react when he saw her again, and he knew that he would.

Chapter Eleven

Adrian

After a harried trip to the airport in Toronto, he'd been the last passenger loaded. It paid off to book business class since if meant they'd waited the extra time. For once, he wolfed down the microwaved meal they set on his tray. Stress did that to him. Left him with a ravenous appetite.

The hour had approached midnight when he finally closed the door to his room at the Crowne Plaza in Portland. He threw his clothes on the chair and crawled between the soft, clean sheets. When he heard the alarm ring, after what seemed like only a few hours, Adrian sat on the edge of the bed, unable to force himself to his feet. How was he going to explain what happened to Celeste? God, he hoped she wouldn't call him this morning. He needed time to get his story together.

In the taxi on the way to the hospital that morning, thoughts swirled in his head over what he could say to her. Celeste would always be important to him. She'd been his wife and partner for over twenty years. However, the excitement was no longer alive between them. Maybe they'd just been together too long. It wasn't that he disliked their lifestyle in Old Towne; he'd always been someone who sought novelty. He needed it.

The minute he walked through the hospital door and down the hall, he knew that something had happened while he was away. Staff avoided looking at him and he could see them huddled into small groups whispering amongst themselves. He felt the tension increase when he entered the boardroom to join the senior managers gathered with the CEO. Jim pulled him aside. "We just heard from Stephen's wife that he killed himself yesterday at their cottage." Jim's voice broke. "Shot himself."

Stephen was one of the middle managers who'd worked for the hospital for almost twenty-five years and hadn't taken the message well that he was being declared redundant. He knew these restructurings could result in despair and even suicide; Adrian never really got used to it. He tried to reassure people and asked them not to take it personally; but a few could see no future for themselves. Over coffee in Jim's office, they agreed on a strategy for calming the survivors. They didn't want to chance any copycat occurrences. The CEO would get them all together in the boardroom in an hour.

Adrian gave the group one of his better speeches focusing on what the future might look like for each of them individually. He outlined new opportunities that would be opening and described access to one on one personal counseling available to them. By lunchtime, at least he'd cheered them up. He watched them chatting while they joined the line for the huge buffet of roast beef, baked salmon, grilled shrimp, and gourmet salads. The good food would resolve some of the bad vibes that had circulated. As he headed back to his hotel in the late afternoon, a feeling of accomplishment washed over him.

The week ahead was filled with training sessions he'd organized on managing change to help the managers to deal with their own staff. Since they had to think about their staff's reactions, it helped those who knew Stephen to put their own grief in losing a friend behind them. Adrian left for Toronto late on Friday and arrived back home after Celeste had gone to bed. He crawled into bed careful not to wake her. The next day, even though it was Saturday, Adrian awoke at seven and told Celeste to sleep in while he picked up their breakfast from the restaurant at the nearby Pillar and Post Hotel.

After his return, he laid out the croissants, quiche, coffee, and juice, on the white linen placemats and serviettes she loved. Adrian took a deep breath and called to Celeste.

"Hon, your breakfast is ready."

The sunshine on the round kitchen dinette gave the meal a special look when she arrived and took her place. "What's this all about?" She gave him a quizzical look.

Adrian, his hand shaking, forced a smile, while he poured their coffee. "Let's just enjoy it while the food's still warm. I've got to talk to you about something, however it can wait." Adrian sipped his coffee and cut into the quiche with his fork.

He watched Celeste rub her hand across the place mat. "I haven't seen these for a while. Really. What's the special occasion?"

"Nothing. I thought they'd be a nice addition to our breakfast."

Without much conversation, the two of them ate the breakfast and she accepted a second cup of coffee. "Okay, Adrian, what's going on? What do you want to tell me?"

After he swallowed once or twice to ease his dry throat, Adrian mumbled. "It's about Sabrina."

He saw Celeste's face contort with a deep frown. "What about Sabrina?" Has something happened to her?

"Well, you must have noticed that she and I have been attracted to each other. At least, I guess that's been obvious." He hesitated until, unable to bear the silence, plunged in again. "We've been together a few times." Adrian felt the pressure build to relieve his painful guilt. He leaned forward putting both elbows on the table. "Ian found out about it and threatened to tell you."

Celeste pushed her chair back away from the table. Her face felt like it was carved in ice and her body went rigid with shock. "What do you mean by *been together?* Does that mean slept together? Is that what you're trying to tell me?"

He sighed, glad to have the confession out in the open. But after looking at Celeste, he felt the pangs of guilt bite deeper. Tears streamed down her face which left it red and blotchy. "What are you saying?" The tears stopped and her eyes became glassy. She crossed her arms. "You're a selfish liar. How could you do this to us?"

He hated to hurt Celeste like this, however she must have known their relationship was stagnant. Adrian waited and watched, in silence while she regained control.

"What are you going to do about this mess now? You said that Ian knows. Does that mean you have broken off with her?"

He thought about that for a few minutes. Could he give up Sabrina? They'd had great fun and he liked her fiery style. Adrian paused. He admitted enjoying their sensuous nights together. No, he wasn't ready to give her up. "Well, you know it's just an infatuation, Celeste. The novelty will wear itself out given time…no, I'm not ready to give it up just yet."

Celeste pulled herself up straight. "Well, then get out. I can't live with this affair."

He tried to take her hand, while she pulled it away. "Celeste don't take this so hard. We've had a good life together and why throw it all away. I'll move into the spare bedroom down the hall and I'm away most of the week anyway. Things don't need to change."

Celeste just stared at him in amazement. "Leave me alone to think about what you've done. I'm still in shock about your betrayal."

"Sure, honey. That's more like you. We can still live together and once I'm over this, we'll be a couple again. No need to overreact."

She stood there and stared at him as he put the dirty plates in the sink, walked through the living room picked up the paper on the way and left. He'd give her some time to come to her senses.

Adrian drove aimlessly around town. On a busy Saturday, Queen Street was full of shoppers. Tourists who raved about the historic brick and stucco buildings which housed shops and restaurants. Beds of red, yellow, and blue flowers lined the street with the red brick clock tower which was the centerpiece. He kept checking his cell phone. Sabrina had promised to call him as soon as she could break away from Ian. At least he knew Ian well enough to know that he wouldn't ever hit her. Exhausted from this morning's tension, he went into Balzac's, ordered a coffee, and sat by the window so he could continue to watch the people on the street. Couples of all ages passed by, as they smiled and held hands. Why couldn't he ever be satisfied like they were? His body tensed at the sound of his phone. Checking it, he saw that it was Sabrina's number.

"Well, honey. How did you make out with Celeste? Lots of tears and lamenting, I suppose."

A moment of irritation hit him. Just like Sabrina to be so callous about other people's feelings. "The scene wasn't as bad as I expected. She was shocked, of course. She'll think about what's next. What about Ian?"

"Much as I thought. Once he had time to think it over, he's decided that I should stay while we work things out. Ian doesn't take well to sudden changes in life."

As he breathed slowly and with relief, he continued. Was she willing to take the risk of losing Ian? "And what about you? What does this mean for us?"

He was surprised to hear her laugh. "We'll have to lay low for a while. Especially when we're in town because they'll both be on the watch. However, I still intend to continue my shopping trips and he can't do anything about that."

"He'd agree to that?"

Her voice was matter of fact. "He'll have no say about where I go, and he knows it."

"Celeste has already been questioning my movements, so it'll have to be Portland. My contract goes on there for another six months." He chuckled. "I guess that's the end of dinners out with the group."

He heard the tension in her voice rise for the first time. "Ian's just returned and he's in a foul mood, so I don't want him to hear me talking to anyone. I'll call you Monday night."

As he sipped his warm coffee, Adrian knew his relationship with Sabrina had changed. The excitement and intrigue were gone now they'd been caught. From now on they would be sneaking around and always be on guard. He hated when affairs deteriorated like that. For now, Sabrina was worth it.

He couldn't face Celeste over lunch and didn't want to go to the golf club in case he ran into Ian. He'd love to talk to Dennis whose calm manner tended to put him at ease, however Adrian didn't know where to find him. His laptop was still in the trunk of the car and he'd need several new presentations for next week so he might as well go to the library. The kids didn't usually flood the place until Sunday. He'd take Celeste out to dinner tonight, so she didn't have to cook. She deserved a break. His mind made up, Adrian ambled up the street to his car and headed out towards the outskirts of town.

As he left the parking lot and moved towards the front door of the library, Adrian found himself several feet behind a tall man in a camel coat. As he caught up to him, he was relieved to see that it was Dennis. "So, Dennis what are you doing here on a Saturday?"

Dennis turned and smiled. "Well, Adrian. I could ask you the same question. I'm on one of the town's volunteer committees. Community development stuff. Nothing too heavy, but it keeps me busy. What about you?"

"I needed some quiet so thought I'd hide out in the computer cubicles." He pointed at his laptop. "When is your meeting over?"

"We're done. I just put my laptop into the trunk of my car and was going to pick up a couple of books before I leave. Do you want to grab some coffee next door?"

"Sure. I'll grab a table and you can meet me there." Adrian changed direction and walked into Second Cup. It would be good to have Dennis for conversation even though he really didn't need another cup of coffee. He placed an order for a medium coffee for Dennis and a cappuccino for himself and was on his way back with them when Dennis joined him.

Dennis stirred the cream into his coffee, set the spoon on a serviette and took a sip. "The stuff they served in the meeting room was crap. I couldn't drink it. So, how's your job going in Portland? Sounds like you have your hands full with that crew."

Catching Dennis's eyes, Adrian realized that he was seriously interested in the project. They'd discussed it briefly before at one of the dinners. "We're going through a really bad spot right now. One man has committed suicide and several others are clearly on edge. Downsizing is never easy."

Dennis nodded. "As V.P. of a major bank, I saw several businesses go through it. Some of the managers don't make it and even the ones that do need support to get over the survivor guilt. Have you got a good human resource firm to back you up?"

One of the skills that Adrian took pride in was his ability to read people. He could tell Dennis genuinely empathized with his situation and it gave him some relief. He used to be able to talk to Celeste about how hard his job was. He'd had to give that up. "Yeah. We've done all that and when it gets to this point, the staff wants someone they can trust. And it helps if you've been there yourself."

"Did you get caught up in that huge restructuring of the five big hospitals on University Avenue?"

Nodding his head Adrian responded. "I was one of the casualties. A good payout for me then, with no new opportunities in hospital administration in Toronto at my level so I travel. As a matter of fact, Celeste was hit by it as well. Just before me." He felt a twinge of guilt recognizing that he had caused her to suffer again.

"How's Celeste? How come she isn't with you today? I heard her and Marjorie on the phone when I was leaving. Marjorie seemed concerned about something."

Adrian felt the hand holding his cup tremble and set it down so Dennis wouldn't notice. "She seems a little depressed lately. Maybe too much time on her hands. You know what it's like. After working so hard for so many years, you find it difficult to find satisfying hobbies."

Dennis's eyes lit up. "I certainly know that one. At the bank I was a respected advisor. On these volunteer committees, I'm just one of many former managers vying for some recognition."

He stood and pulled on his coat. "I've promised to take Marjorie out to lunch so I'd better not be late. See you at the club."

As he watched Dennis leave, Adrian felt the silence. This was the first time Dennis ever confided in him about missing his own work. He guessed they were all going through those feelings in different ways. Sabrina was the only one who seemed to be immune. She was quite good at amusing herself. He smiled. Maybe that was all he was to her. Another amusement she'd grow tired of in time. Well, short term was fine with him. He didn't intend it to go on forever.

Chapter Twelve

Sabrina

Sabrina took a deep breath and strolled into the living room where Ian was flipping channels, his face engulfed in dark clouds. She sat beside him on the sofa.

"Can't find anything to watch this morning?"

Ian gave her a black scowl and settled his gaze on a golf game in Florida. "Who were you talking to just now? I told you to stay away from Adrian."

"Of course, dear. You've made that quite clear." She settled back into the sofa and picked up a fashion magazine. "I was talking to Marjorie about a charity tea that she's heading up. I told her we'd give a small donation."

When she took a glimpse at him sideways, Sabrina could see that Ian was beginning to relax, fixated on the methodical swings of the golfers. She knew his dark mood would lift as he got over the shock. They had been married for over thirty years and had immigrated to Canada together from Britain when he was offered a good job with Ellis Don. The arthritis in his hands had caused him to retire earlier than he had anticipated leaving him to brood over the loss of status. They had come to Canada at just the right time.

Her career in the brokerage industry had accelerated leaving her more independently prosperous than she had ever expected.

Sabrina was relieved to talk with Adrian this morning to catch up after the trauma of yesterday. Although she had tried not to acknowledge it, the shock of seeing Ian as he stood there in the hotel hallway had really unnerved her. The thrills of the previous night receded as she was faced with the angry face of her husband. Sabrina had tried to stall for time to think before Ian had barged right into the room to confront Adrian. Sabrina now realized she'd lacked the ability to feel guilty about Ian's discovery of them. Instead, she'd felt only fear he'd scare Adrian away after she'd finally got him to herself. She and Ian had an understanding. At least she thought that was what it was. Normally, he let her go her own way and wasn't bothered about her flirtations. He seemed to see this as different. He must sense Adrian was a real threat.

She loved the way Adrian could take charge in any situation and showed no fear. At the same time, he was sensitive to the finer things in life like art and music. He knew how to make a woman feel special.

Sabrina chuckled to herself as she remembered frequent nights at the jazz clubs in Manchester with her sister Roxanne. Club Mecca had been their hunting grounds for single men back in the mid-70s. In fact, the club was where she had met Ian. She'd been attracted by those black eyes and his mysterious manner. Only after they were married did she find out that the mystery she loved was just his normal suspicious nature when he was in a crowded room with strangers.

Those early years in Toronto they had both been totally focused on new jobs with many demands. No time for children or trips back to England. He'd been her main support. A sudden feeling of nostalgia came over her. What could she do to make it up to him?

She moved slightly closer to Ian on the sofa. "Why don't we go out tonight to the English pub you like so much in St.

Catharines? You know. The one with breaded haddock and chunky cut chips and great coleslaw."

Ian set the remote on the coffee table and turned towards her. "You mean the Duke of York? Okay. I would like that. I don't mind driving at night."

Sabrina put her hand over his. "I'll drive back home so you can have a few extra pints. Remember the drinking and driving laws now are quite strict." She took a quick look at him and was relieved to see him relax. "Right now, I'll make up a pot of chili for lunch and we can have it with those sourdough buns that I picked up at the bakery."

Ian managed a smile although it was more like a grimace. "Sounds good." His manner turned suspicious again. "Dennis and I have a golf game on Sunday morning. Why don't you join the two of us for lunch at the club after?"

He obviously wants to know where I'll be tomorrow. Well, I guess I can't blame him. Sabrina responded. "Sure. That would be great. I didn't have anything planned." Celeste would have her eyes on Adrian, so he wouldn't be available this weekend. She might as well keep up the good work with Ian. She wasn't sure exactly what she wanted from Adrian, but he livened up her existence and, for now, she was determined to continue seeing him.

* * *

From the kitchen window, Sabrina watched Ian pack his clubs into the trunk of the car, his every movement slow and careful. In the past, he had liked the fact that she was attractive to other men. He obviously sensed this one was different. She went back to clearing up the breakfast table and mused to herself about how it would be if she and Adrian were to move in together. They'd move back to Toronto, of course. In a small town like this there would be too many opportunities to for gossip to smear them. One of those new condos on the lake would be a nice change. Just as she turned on the dishwasher, the phone rang. Checking the display, she saw Adrian's number. She was surprised to feel a tremor.

"Hi, Adrian. I was just thinking about us. How's the atmosphere at your end?" She heard a deep sigh.

"Celeste has taken it really hard. Damn Ian for being so snoopy anyway." Silence stretched the tension. "I miss you."

"I've booked another trip to Portland on Thursday so we can be together. Ian should have calmed down by then. I'll call you at your hotel to confirm. I'll travel back on Friday morning after breakfast. With us on different flights, he won't suspect anything."

"What I like about you, Sabrina, is you're so quick on your feet. Good strategy and you've thought of all the details." Adrian chuckled.

"I'm going to take a long hot bath with lots of bubbles." She added just the right sensual tone to her voice. "Wish you could join me." She was satisfied with the sharp intake of breath over the phone.

Adrian's voice had deepened. "It's a long wait until Thursday. I might be able to get away this afternoon for an hour. What do you think?"

Caution crept into Sabrina's voice. "No. Forget it. I promised to meet Ian and Dennis for lunch at the club and once his suspicions are aroused, he'll be on the alert for the next few days anyway."

"I hear you. Thursday it is then. I've slipped out for an hour to go to the library, so I'll be a good boy and return right on time. I guess I'll find out then if Celeste is planning to throw me out."

"Well, it would solve our problems, wouldn't it?"

"Only temporarily. Our circumstances would still make it difficult for the four of us to continue to live in this small town. They live for rumors here."

Sabrina set the phone down and climbed the stairs to change for lunch.

Chapter Thirteen

Celeste

On Monday morning, Celeste wandered aimlessly through their bedroom and stopped to run her hand over her favourite cherry-wood dresser. Next, she ran her hand over the smooth surface of the gleaming white Jacuzzi she'd just soaked in. Out the window, she admired the serviceberry tree full of white blooms which contrasted with the red berries of the holly bushes. The first morning she and Adrian had spent in this house, they'd enjoyed breakfast in bed while she'd admired this view. A sharp pain hit her in the gut. What would happen to her if she forced him to leave? The thought of being single again in this town full of couples didn't feel right. She'd never had to manage a house on her own. Adrian made all the decisions about what servicemen were needed, when the building structures needed repairs, and what gardeners to hire. Her responsibility was to supervise the woman who cleaned and put food on their table.

It was a big decision and Celeste needed help. Marjorie was her closest friend and would know what to do. She picked up the phone and dialed.

"Hi." She waited for the familiar voice. "I've got some wonderful summer squash soup that I picked up at the deli yesterday and some croissants. Would you be free for lunch today?"

At first there was silence. "What a surprise," said Marjorie. "Sure. I'll just finish up this paperwork for my next event and I'll be over around 12:30." She hesitated. "Is everything okay?"

Now it was Celeste's turn to pause. She couldn't keep the tension out of her voice. "Well, I have something to tell you." Silence. "I'd prefer to do it face to face."

"Mmmm. That sounds ominous, I'll be there. See you soon."

Celeste held the receiver in a tight grip until she heard only silence.

*   *   *

She set the table with her favorite yellow placemats. The soup was warming on the stove and the croissants ready for the oven. Time dragged as Celeste waited for the doorbell. Is this what it would be like if she were living alone? The silence of the house was eerie and there would be nothing to look forward to on the weekends. How had she filled her time when she was single? Of course, work sometimes took up to ten hours a day back then.

She got up from the sofa on hearing the chimes. Taking a deep breath, she strode into the hall and opened the door.

"It's great to see you." She gave Marjorie a hug, clasping her just a bit too tightly.

Marjorie followed her into the kitchen and took a seat at the table. "You're worrying me, Celeste. You seem so much more anxious than usual. What's wrong?"

Celeste ladled the soup into bowls and warmed the croissants, both of which she placed on the table. "It's Adrian again. Only worse this time." She took her seat and gestured for Marjorie to start.

"I should have known. What is it then?" Marjorie took a few mouthfuls of soup and broke off a piece of croissant.

Twisting her hands together, Celeste bit her lower lip. "He and Sabrina are...." She choked and broke into tears.

Marjorie remained calm. "What have those two been up to? Did you see them together somewhere in town?"

"Worse than we thought. Adrian has confessed to having an affair with her. And Ian caught them together." Celeste choked out.

"So, they've actually taken it that far. I can understand your distress." Marjorie moved over to Celeste's side of the table and put her arms around her. "There, now. You have friends on your side. Let's finish our lunch and then we'll talk over your options."

Returning to her seat, Marjorie sipped her soup in silence, while she kept glancing at Celeste to see how she was managing.

Celeste took a few mouthfuls and pushed the soup aside. Her croissant was untouched. She waited until Marjorie had eaten the last of the croissant. "Let's sit in the living room and I'll pour us some hot tea."

While her hands shook, Celeste carried the teacups carefully and placed them on the table. Seated beside Marjorie, she continued. "Adrian says he wants to stay. For us to be a couple. However, he plans to continue seeing Sabrina."

After she swallowed the hot tea, Marjorie set the cup back on the table. "What did you say? He really wants everything his way, doesn't he? I hope you told him to get out."

Tension filled the silence. "I'm afraid to live alone. I'm not ready. I didn't give him any answer and he left for Portland on Sunday night as usual. I need time."

Marjorie grimaced. "Get hold of yourself, Celeste. You must have been a very independent woman to hold the job you did at the hospital all those years. You'd have had to make decisions for your team."

While Celeste covered her face with both hands, Marjorie waited. "The way I see it you have two options. One you kick the bum out and make your own life. Two you let him continue living with you and become a door mat." Marjorie seemed to sense

Celeste's distress and her face softened. "I realize that you've had quite a shock. Give yourself some time to think about it. But you must decide before he returns on Friday night. And remember, I'm on your side."

*   *   *

After she saw Marjorie out, Celeste poured another cup of tea and returned to the sofa to think. She had to admit Marjorie was right. Celeste had handled much more difficult matters with her team at the hospital. She recalled one of her former patients. Alexandra, a young woman with two daughters under three, who hadn't survived her second operation for invasive breast cancer. Celeste had accompanied the doctor who gave the bad news to her husband. She'd stayed behind to help him recover from the initial tears and anger so he would have the strength to go back home to his children. She'd been able to hold things together then.

This was different. It was her loss of her primary support. What happened to her and Adrian? Over time, his feelings for her had changed. Back at UHN, when she'd enter the boardroom for biweekly quality assurance meetings, she'd see his face light up. Often, he'd gesture towards a seat he'd saved just for her. For her 40th birthday, she remembered the excitement when he told her they were going to Sabatini's, her favourite upscale Italian restaurant. After they shared an expensive bottle of Cabernet Franc, he took her hand.

"It's so great to see your face so excited and vibrant. I've got a special gift for you." He continued to hold her hand while he slid on a white gold ring with a sparkling diamond.

Celeste sighed and took another sip of tea. The romantic time seemed so long ago. She knew relationships often went through a honeymoon period, before the next get to know each other better period. Often, they ended with a comfortable take each other for granted period. Adrian seemed to hate the last part. He wasn't the type to embrace sameness. Marjorie was right, of course, about her need to decide. Really, the decision had been made for her. She hadn't had the courage to face it, but she knew her trust in him was totally broken.

On Friday night, Adrian arrived home late and headed upstairs immediately with his suitcase. She could hear him rummage around in the bedroom but ignored the noise and pretended to be watching some mindless TV program. When she finally gave up and climbed the stairs to find him, he was in his home office staring at his computer. He turned when she entered the room.

"Hi. I had a hectic week in Portland. These restructurings seem to always hit a bumpy stretch somewhere in the middle. Right now I don't know how to move it along."

"Sorry that things didn't go well for you," Celeste murmured. "I'm going to bed early to read. We'll talk in the morning."

Giving her a quizzical look, Adrian turned back to his computer screen. "Fine. See you in the morning then."

An hour later, Celeste set the book down on the bedside table, turned out the light and slid under the sheets. She tossed and turned while she listened for any sound of Adrian joining her. Eventually, she fell into a light sleep, and awakened when she felt him push the covers back. Moments later, she looked over at him from the night light in the hall could tell he was asleep with his back to her. She turned to face the wall and shortly after began to feel sleep begin to return.

When she woke, the other side of the bed was empty although she hadn't heard him get up. Since she couldn't avoid their talk any longer, Celeste took a quick shower, and dressed in white linen pants and a soft violet blouse. After that she applied eye shadow and black mascara. She was gratified to see that the colour of her blouse highlighted her eyes. For some reason, it was important for her to look good. The tension was building in her stomach as soon as she started downstairs.

From the kitchen, she could see Adrian with his head in the morning paper. She prepared their scrambled eggs, brown toast, and pineapple slices. After setting them on the table, she called Adrian and poured their coffee. His face was expressionless as he took his seat.

"Last night you mentioned you wanted to say something to me? What was it?"

Feeling more in control, Celeste responded. "Not now. Let's finish our breakfast. Then we have to talk."

The only sound she could hear was Adrian's crunch from the toast and the clang from the two forks against the plates. Both sets of eyes stayed focused on the table. After she poured a second cup of coffee, Celeste gestured toward the living room.

"Why don't you join me on the sofa?" She smoothed her hand down over her queasy stomach. "I have made a decision."

Adrian followed close behind her and dropped into his seat. He held her gaze.

"After twenty-four years of marriage, I never thought I'd have to do this. You've broken my heart and my trust." A sob caught in her throat. Forcing herself she continued. "I can't live with you under your conditions. Either you give up Sabrina or you move out. And if it's the latter, I want you out by the end of the week."

A range of emotions crossed Adrian's face, from shock and surprise, to what she hoped was a twinge of admiration at the gumption of her ability to reject his suggested resolution.

"Well, this is more like the old Celeste I knew. Why haven't you been able to assert yourself like this over the past few years?" He paused and stared across the room. "Well. Whatever this is with Sabrina, I'm not willing to give it up right now. I'll have to live through the alternative."

Hands shaking, Celeste bit her lip to stop more tears. "This is it then. I'll expect you to move by next Saturday."

Adrian glared at her in anger before he jumped to his feet. "Let's be realistic here. I've got to go back to Portland on Sunday night. How do you expect me to make those kinds of arrangements with only a week's notice? Even a landlord would do better."

Celeste stood up and faced him. "You should have thought of what would happen. Did you just expect that I'd go along with you again as usual?"

"Okay. Okay. Have it your way. I'll take next Monday off and spend tomorrow and Monday searching for a rental property in town. I'll move as soon as I get something." He headed towards the stairs. "Just remember we'll both have to watch our money from now on. Two homes to support will decrease our income."

With Adrian out of sight, Celeste held her face in both hands and sobbed quietly. She'd done the deed. She wasn't sure this was what she really wanted now that it was too late.

*   *   *

Celeste had begun to dread the wait for Friday night. She sat on the sofa and tried to read while spending every few minutes pacing to the window and back to look for Adrian's car. When she saw the headlights of his car turning into the bottom of the driveway, she took quick steps back to the sofa and picked up her book. Her back ached and the acid in her stomach burned. Was this really happening to her?

She stayed motionless as Adrian entered and dropped his suitcase on the floor. His face was grey and drawn. Obviously, this wasn't easy for him either. But he'd found a Condo unit that first weekend. The next day, she'd relented and given him a week's extension. Celeste wanted to be out of the house when he left.

"What time will the truck come tomorrow?"

Anger tightened all his facial muscles. "Look, I said that I'd move tomorrow, and I will. Don't nag me, okay." He headed upstairs.

Celeste couldn't stop her hands from shaking. She decided to give him some time to calm down. The sound of a loud bang from upstairs startled her and she climbed the staircase to peer into their bedroom. Two of his suitcases were open on the floor. Shirts and ties of every colour lay across the bed while he struggled to pack his suits.

"If I can make a suggestion, why don't you put those suits in bags and pile them on the back seat. You're not going far."

He turned towards her and glared. "I don't need any more advice from you. Why is it the man who always has to move out anyway?"

She felt the heat rise in her neck and flood into her cheeks. "Probably, because they're the ones who usually have the affairs." Celeste bit her lip. "I was trying to be helpful."

He dropped the suits on the closet floor. "I don't need your help. Go back downstairs. I'll do most of my packing tomorrow anyway." His voice softened. "What time is Marjorie picking you up?"

"Right after breakfast." The pain in his eyes was hard for her to bear. "We're going into Toronto to do some shopping." She slowly descended back down the stairs. The sound of him thrashing around as he strived to fill the suitcases drifted down.

By the time he came downstairs and rummaged around in the bar for a glass of scotch, it was dark. He sat as far from her as possible and sipped his drink. "We don't have to do this you know. We've haven't tried to resolve our problems."

"It's much too late for this kind of talk." Celeste held his gaze. "From what you've told me, you've been unhappy for some time."

"Not unhappy exactly." He frowned. "Just dissatisfied with life in general." He hesitated. "I hate getting old."

So was this what the affair was really about. A desperate attempt to hold back the aging process. Celeste got up from the sofa and headed for the stairs. Whatever it was, it was too late for them. "I'm going to bed. Tomorrow won't be easy for either of us."

She glanced at Adrian as she left. He took a large gulp of scotch and stared at the floor. "I'll sleep down here. I might as well get used to it."

Chapter Fourteen

Celeste

The sun shone through the bedroom window as Celeste made the final touches to her make-up. She grabbed a sweater before heading downstairs. With her foot on the final step, she heard the doorbell. There was still no sign of Adrian as she opened the door for Marjorie.

"You're ready to go?" Marjorie gave her a warm hug and a quizzical look.

Celeste shifted from one foot to the other. "I guess I should say goodbye to Adrian. We'll still have to see each other." She turned and walked into the kitchen.

Adrian stood at the kitchen window drinking coffee. "You're on your way?"

"Yes, Marjorie's here." Celeste kept her distance. "I'll probably be back around five. You can leave the key. I'll let you in later if you forgot anything." She turned to head back to the hall.

His voice was full of anger. "Don't forget I'm still an owner here. Until we're legally separated, I can come back in any time I want."

Celeste hurried to the front door and rushed Marjorie out and down the steps. As she settled into the passenger seat, she exhaled a deep breath. "That was harder than I expected. I was even tempted to feel sorry for him."

Marjorie gave her a hard look. "Hold on to your anger where he's concerned. Adrian's used to being the one in charge. Of course, this is hard for him."

The road had a comforting familiarity as they drove out of town onto the QEW and headed for Toronto. Marjorie was such a good friend. She didn't know anyone else who would be willing to go through this trauma with her.

"Have you told Dennis what's going on? I guess everyone will have to know soon."

Marjorie nodded. "I told him yesterday when I explained why the sudden trip to Toronto. He'd hear it from Ian soon anyway. He was the only one of our group who didn't know."

"How did he react?" Celeste asked. "I'm just wondering if our problems were obvious to everyone else except me."

The car picked up speed as they entered the main highway. "Well, he couldn't help but notice the flirtation between Adrian and Sabrina. It was so blatant. But he was surprised things had become so serious."

Celeste was quiet until they passed the outskirts of Burlington. "I've had my suspicions since he started all this travel. Mainly a growing distance between us but other times, when he made excuses for extending his time away, I knew something was wrong."

Marjorie touched her shoulder. "I know this is painful for you. But, talking about it may help."

While she turned her head back towards Marjorie, Celeste asked. "Have you and Dennis every gone through this? You seem like such a stable couple."

"No. But one of his brothers did." Her face turned serious. "Dennis and I got married young, had kids, built careers. Then we immigrated to Canada. It brought us closer having to go through the upheaval together. We needed each other."

Following a long silence, Celeste said. "Adrian loved my success at the hospital. The more ambitious I was and the more awards I got the more his eyes sparkled."

"What happened? You must have loved your ambitious side as well."

Celeste closed her eyes, struggling to remember. "I suppose you're right about the change. I've worked in health care ever since I graduated. It's all I know. Now it's gone. My career is over."

"But it doesn't have to be over." Marjorie stated. "There's volunteer work. You could set up your own consulting business. You don't have to work in a hospital."

"I'm a health caregiver." Her voice rose in alarm. "I'm not an organizer or planner like you. It's the patient care that I loved."

Marjorie replied. "I'm just throwing out suggestions. You know yourself and what works for you." Time passed quickly as they fell into a long silence. She watched Marjorie maneuver her car through heavy traffic on the Gardiner and then north on Bay Street.

Before long, Marjorie pulled the car into the parking lot at the Manulife Centre. Come on. Let's go to the Bloor Street Diner for lunch and forget about your situation for an hour."

"I'd like to be able to forget." She dabbed her eyes with a tissue choking back tears. "This morning was hell. Watching Adrian get ready to leave, I mean. I couldn't eat any breakfast and now I'm really hungry."

They were soon seated in the dining room with its crisp white tablecloths, deep rose napkins and low mood lights. Celeste was able to sit back and begin to relax for the first time. When the waiter arrived, she asked for a large glass of Chardonnay and browsed through the menu.

Marjorie ordered the same. "I love their cob salad and the omelets are the best in town. That's it. I'm having the cheddar and mushroom omelet and will think about dessert later. What about you?"

"The veal sliders with sweet potato fries appeal to me." Celeste forced a smile. "I probably won't want to eat later tonight when I get home." While they waited for their food, she glanced at the other tables full of well-dressed shoppers, who smiled and laughed with each other.

"Did you and Adrian have any children?" Marjorie asked. "We've never talked about our kids as a group."

Celeste focused back on her friend. "Not together. I have one daughter, Natalie, from an earlier marriage. Her father and I met in college and married after graduation, but it didn't last. She was twelve when I remarried, and Adrian was a good stepfather to her. Regardless, she preferred to live with us during the summer and the rest of the time with her father and his new wife in Ottawa."

Marjorie rested her chin on her fist. "Are the two of you close? She might be a comfort during the next few difficult months. Do you plan to tell her?"

Biting her lip, Celeste sighed. "I guess I've been putting it off. I keep thinking about her resentment with her father and I when we split up. It's like I'd have to admit I made another mistake."

Marjorie gave her a sympathetic smile. "I understand. But I'm sure she'd welcome your confiding in her. It could bring the two of you closer."

As she breathed out, Celeste relaxed. "I'll have to do something before her next visit. I need to get through the next few weeks first." She turned to the waiter who had arrived with their plates. "Great. Lunch looks delicious." She ate quietly for the next while lost in thought. What would this new life be like? Acquaintances she knew in town wouldn't notice anything different at first since Adrian was often away. Their group of six had seen the friction build between them. They probably knew what was going on each in their own way. But she'd always hated going to social events alone and avoided it when she was single.

With nurses as companions, there was usually someone to go out with.

"You're quiet. Am I losing you already?" Marjorie sounded concerned.

"No. You've been great. I've begun to adjust to what's ahead. I love our small community, but I also know it's very couples focused."

"Dennis and I will be there for you." Marjorie said in her regular take-charge style. "You and I need to set a weekly time for lunch or dinner together. And if you need a chaperone for socials, I'll check with Dennis to see if he's free."

Celeste chuckled. "That's true friendship. Lending me your husband. Seriously, I'll keep in touch, but I need to find activities for myself, something to excite me again." She frowned. But what was it that she wanted to do with her life? She'd been facing this inertia for some time now with no answers.

"Okay. Let's not rush things. Remember. Adrian will leave this afternoon. Give it some time." Marjorie picked up the menu. "How about splitting a piece of this chocolate raspberry torte?"

"Sure. Order it with two forks and I'll do my best." She turned to the waiter. "I'll have coffee. Strong and black."

When dessert arrived, Celeste took a small piece on her fork and nibbled at it while she watched Marjorie devour several large chunks. "We've got lots of time to fill if we want to get back home late this afternoon. Did you want to wander through Holt's? I know you have a big fundraiser dinner at Queen's Landing soon. Maybe you'll find a new outfit."

"Have at least one more bite or I'll eat it all." Marjorie licked her lips. "I love chocolate." She set down her fork. "You're right about it being too early to leave. I plan to pull out of here about 3:30 to miss the worst of the traffic. So, if you're okay about it, I'd like to check out a few dresses when we're finished here."

On the way up the two long sets of escalators into Holt's, Celeste admired the bright colours and sparkles from cosmetics and high-end clothing displayed on each floor. She would come here every Christmas to the least expensive third floor. Usually, she was able to find a great new party dress for the hospital dinner and dance. It had been exciting to surprise Adrian with her make-up professionally done up and her new outfit. She felt tears sting her eyes as they got off on the second. She wasn't surprised that Marjorie shopped on the designer floor.

"I get a small annual stipend for my charity work and spend most of it on clothes for their grand events." Marjorie shrugged. "You have to look the part to encourage the large donors you're worth their investment."

Celeste followed her from rack to rack of beautiful gowns. "With your hazel eyes, that lavender silk dress would look great."

"I'll try it, but I also like this one." Marjorie gestured to a rosy pink dress with sequined bodice. She took them both off the rack and headed toward the dressing room as a saleswoman hurried to follow her. "Why don't you choose one to try for yourself? You don't have to buy it."

She shook her head. "I'd have no use for it right now." She'd always been careful about money and felt uncomfortable even being on this floor. It was like the sales staff could just tell and didn't even offer to wait on her. She admired both gowns on Marjorie and agreed the rosy sequin one gave her more flair.

While waiting for the gown to be packaged, the two women sipped tea and sampled delicate biscuits, compliments of the store. Marjorie glanced at her watch. "They had better hurry with the wrapping. We need to head back to the parking garage soon. I haven't forgotten how bad rush hour traffic in Toronto can be."

Celeste stood and gestured at the closest saleswoman, who nodded and headed into the back room. Shortly after that the package arrived and they got on the escalator and descended past those expensive cosmetics once more.

"What a successful shopping day for me." Marjorie twirled her package. "I do miss this part of Toronto although I don't want to live here anymore. Not during retirement. Too crowded for me."

"I sometimes wonder if Adrian and I would have been happier if we hadn't left Toronto." Celeste said. "But really what changed was our jobs and we never had any control over those decisions."

*　　*　　*

Traffic on the QEW was congested but not unbearable. After last night's disturbed sleep, filled with dark dreams, Celeste was able to doze past Mississauga and into Oakville. Traffic slowed down to a crawl. "Will they ever fix this mess? With all this construction, it's a long trip between Oakville and Burlington."

"We'll be okay. We're past the worst of it. I'm glad that you were able to sleep." Marjorie said turning towards her. "You looked so tired when we left the city."

"Yes. I think reality is catching up with me." She could feel her neck stiffen and her shoulders felt tighter the closer they got towards home. Would Adrian still be there when she got back? If he were, what would she do then? She tried to go back to sleep so she wouldn't have to think about it.

The next time she woke the car had stopped. Opening her eyes, she could see the red brick of her own townhouse. She placed her hand on Marjorie's arm. "Thanks for doing this for me. I couldn't bare being in the house today while he moved out. You're such a good friend."

Marjorie covered her hand with her own. "Don't mention it. And remember that Dennis and I are around if you need someone."

As she closed the door of the car and turned toward the house, Celeste realized that she was still holding her breath. She deliberately breathed out, straightened her back, and walked to the front door. In a few minutes, she turned the key, and pushed it open. Entering the front hall, she looked around. Everything seemed the same. The furniture was all in its place, the newspaper was on the table, and as she walked into the kitchen, there were no dirty dishes in sight. She slowly mounted the stairs and climbed toward their bedroom. Walking down the hall, she noted that the guest bedroom door was open.

As she entered, she found the room barren. Adrian must have taken the furniture. The emptiness mocked her as she moved down the hall toward the master bedroom. She glanced at the bed before her eyes moved to both closet doors flung open. She stared at bare hangers lying in a pile on the floor where Adrian's clothes had hung. Throwing herself on the bed, she let free the sobs she had pushed down all day. Then she began hitting the down comforter with her fists. Sometime later, she felt herself falling into a light sleep.

When she awoke, the room was dark. When she sat up, Celeste realized her stomach was feeling hollow and empty. Still in rumpled clothes, she rolled off the bed, and made her way back downstairs and into the kitchen, putting on lights as she went. She found some frozen lasagna in the fridge to reheat in the microwave and sat at the table with it sipping a diet coke. The house was eerily quiet. Adrian was gone.

Chapter Fifteen

Celeste

Over the next week, Celeste alternated between short bursts of rage and long bouts of crying. How could that inconsiderate bastard have left her for a floozy like Sabrina? Marjorie listened to her patiently over the phone while she ranted. Towards the end of the week as she felt calmer, Marjorie talked her into attending one of the winery events in town on her own. Celeste knew that she'd have to start somewhere.

So, there she was on Friday night. Standing at the entrance of The Lower Bench Winery waiting to be ushered into the wine and cheese reception. She felt alone and lost, amidst the chatter of the crowd. Why couldn't she enjoy having her night out? Her gaze remained fixed on the other fashionably dressed couples; an envious glance seeing them together. While they proposed toasts to each other raising their glasses of Meritage or Riesling, a deep sense of melancholy engulfed her. She remained steps away from the group, a solitary figure reluctant to join them. She couldn't help but wonder what Adrian was up to. Was he spending tonight with Sabrina? Celeste sighed. What was wrong with her? It wasn't as if he hadn't frequently left her alone in the past.

She strolled to the wide glass opening where the wall completely disappeared. Celeste stared at the sheets of rain falling on rows and rows of grapevines, their heavy clusters of fruit still green. Her aloneness left her emotionally adrift. One hand pushed her damp grey hair out of her eyes as she reminisced. When she first met Adrian, how he had impressed her. As Clinical Nurse Manager at the Toronto General Hospital, her unit had won the award for best quality improvement project and he had made the presentation. They knew each other vaguely since he often represented the hospital executives at these events. But that night he sat beside her through dinner, giving compliment after compliment. He started about her great work and later moved on to her clear violet eyes. The explosion of sparkles in Celeste's stomach when she caught his gaze signaled this wasn't just a fleeting attraction for her. Following a six-month romance, they had married—but that was so many years ago.

Drawn towards the sound of chamber music somewhere behind the masses, she joined a small group crowded around a quartet. Celeste listened to the sweet sounds of the violin and flute, as she watched the four young musicians, who appeared to be lost in their own fantasies. With a pang of regret for her own lost hopes and dreams, she moved on.

Celeste returned to the entranceway intending to slip out. Caught in the crowd, she was forced to listen to a speech by one of the local politicians. She caught the thread about the benefits of future development to this town. A local man gave the usual lament on how these types of changes weren't needed in their community. Although Celeste loved living in historic Niagara-On-The-Lake, the large number of retirees meant that expectations were high and loudly expressed. Tonight, she didn't have the patience for it. She'd worked hard for any recognition which had come to her.

Breaking free from the group, her quick steps took her through the exit. She hurried to where she'd parked her car. As she pulled out of the lot, breathing a sigh of relief, Celeste congratulated herself for making it through her first night out alone.

* * *

"I'm proud of you for going to that wine reception," said Marjorie as she followed Celeste into her kitchen. "The more you find your own niche in town, the less you'll dwell on Adrian. Dennis and I are both at home tomorrow night if you want to go out to dinner somewhere."

Celeste plugged in the kettle and took out her teapot. "I don't think so." She clenched her fists. "Every time I think about doing something downtown, what comes to mind is me standing there on the main street watching Adrian and Sabrina, hands clasped coming towards me."

"Well, with the three of you living in the same town, it's likely to happen. What about Ian? With his suspicious nature, I can't believe he's not kept an eye on Sabrina."

Celeste sighed. "He seems to have taken it better than me. Especially since he discovered them. I overheard Adrian talking to her on the phone the day before he left. He checked to see if Ian was at home, so I guess she's still living with him."

"Okay. Why don't you join Dennis and me for dinner tomorrow night at our house instead? I'll cook a roast with new potatoes and baby carrots."

Celeste relaxed and smiled. "Sounds good. But let me bring the dessert."

"Sure. You know the best bakeries in Niagara." Marjorie finished her tea and stood up to leave. "I've got to be at another afternoon coffee party, but we'll look forward to seeing you at seven Sunday night."

Sunday morning, Celeste was able to relax with the paper over her second cup of coffee and even to enjoy the view of her garden through the window. Finally, she couldn't put off going out any longer and pulled on her leather jacket, picking up the car keys. At least for now she still had a car. She drove down the main street checking for familiar faces but saw no one she knew. She gave a sigh of relief. The two bakeries in town both catered to tourists with portions small and expensive. Not finding anything suitable, she headed out of town toward the one she liked on the outskirts, Chef Nina's Patisserie. As soon as she opened the bakery door, the pungent smell of chocolate and cinnamon invaded her senses. In the glass case, she saw a wonderful chocolate mousse cake which she knew Dennis would love. While they wrapped it, she ordered and ate a delicious custard fruit tart. She was starting to feel better as she left the shop.

During her drive to Marjorie and Dennis's house on the far end of Queen Street later that night, doubts crept in for Celeste. Did they really want to spend Sunday night dining with her? It was Adrian who was the entertainer in the group, who kept the conversation going and who came up with new ideas. Sometimes lately, while driving along the Niagara Parkway, she'd find herself staring at the bike path. Just beyond it lay a steep drop into the Niagara River. Her anger would build until it caused her throat to tighten and then she'd look over and feel compelled to turn the car in the direction of the river. Only thoughts of her friend and of her daughter made her shake the dark illusion away.

Her lack of confidence increased when she parked in the long driveway and wandered up to the enormous clapboard house, slate grey with bright white trim, and knocked on the solid oak door. It opened immediately into the warmth of the front hall with maple floors lit by a large crystal light fixture.

Dennis took her jacket and disappeared while Marjorie welcomed her and led her into the living room. He returned with two bottles of wine; one white and one red which he set on the table beside the three glasses. "What can I offer you or would you prefer something stronger?"

"A glass of that Merlot would be great," said Celeste. While he poured, Marjorie raised her glass as well. They nibbled at small quiches and biscuits topped with crab meat as they shared news about events in town.

"Dennis, if you'd like to carve that roast, we'll move into the dining room and I'll serve the soup."

"Sure. With this electric knife, there's nothing to it. I remember how my father struggled with our usual Sunday roast often with a knife that was dull. I've got this one." He proudly held it up for her to see.

Once they were all seated, Dennis poured another round of wine and proposed a toast while looking straight at Celeste. "To better times for some of us and good health for all."

Celeste gulped her wine and forced back tears. Why was she so sensitive about every little thing? Dennis was just trying to be kind.

"I ran into Adrian at the club yesterday over his lunch." Dennis hesitated and glanced at Celeste. "He was by himself and seemed preoccupied."

"It must be awkward between him and Ian. With them both being members, I mean." Marjorie exclaimed. "Do they avoid each other?"

"Not at all. They're both civil." Dennis said. "Ian joined another foursome and Adrian and I decided to make do with the two of us. He's a good partner."

Marjorie looked at Celeste. "You might be right in some circumstances."

Celeste could feel her cheeks heat up and her chest tighten. Her voice rose. "I'm glad he's losing some friends. And at least that's one place he can't take Sabrina."

Dennis stood. "I'm sorry, Celeste. I didn't mean to be so blunt. I'll go put the slices of beef on our plates. Marjorie, maybe you want to bring in the vegetables."

"I know you didn't mean anything, dear. I'll help you with the plates." She put her hand on Celeste's shoulder as she passed her chair. "You're right to be angry about what happened. It'll take time."

Celeste clenched her napkin and took several deep breaths before the two of them returned with the dinner. For the balance of the meal, they kept to safer conversations like Marjorie's charitable events and what activities they were interested in for the summer. When Marjorie served the chocolate cake, Dennis's face lit up.

"Wow. This is a surprise. With my heart problems, Marjorie has deprived me of such sweet delights." He nodded at Celeste. "Great choice."

"I decided that once in a while a good dessert wouldn't be the end of you," Marjorie said.

Celeste's face brightened. "Thanks for the compliment. I can use more of those." She dug her fork into the rich chocolate and savoured a piece.

Later when Marjorie retrieved Celeste's jacket and walked her to the door, Dennis had disappeared into his den to watch TV. "Glad you could come. Having a friend here motivated me to make dinner special which is a nice change."

Celeste kissed her on the cheek. "Thanks for taking care of me. I'm so lucky to have you as a friend." She opened the door and stood on the front stairs.

"I'll be over to see you again on Wednesday. Tuesday is a big event again and I need a day to prepare." Marjorie said. "Good night and don't think about that ex-husband of yours. You need to live for yourself."

On Monday, Celeste moped around the house, unable to motivate herself to attend her painting class. She just couldn't stand another enquiry about how she was making out. It seemed everyone in town wanted to talk about her and Adrian's situation. However, there was no mention made about Sabrina. They deemed to have decided she was the guilty party.

Celeste kept the door to the den, where he had removed most of the furniture, firmly closed. Dinner was frozen pasta heated up in the microwave. She tried to concentrate on the TV programs with little success. Around ten, she put on pajamas and poured one glass of white wine, sipping it slowly. She knew to watch her alcohol intake. Not wanting to end up a drunk. She'd force herself to go out tomorrow even if it meant eating lunch alone. Turning out the lights, she made her way upstairs and lay on the bed staring into the ceiling. Her throat felt tight. Was this how it would be for the rest of her life?

Her tennis game on Tuesday morning cheered Celeste and gave her some hope. She had made it to the semi-finals in the round robin and against some excellent players. Her constant need to run had eased some of the built-up tension. Later at home, after showering, she decided to treat herself. She'd go to the Cannery Restaurant at the Pillar and Post for a late lunch. Staff there was so kind and the dining room with warm brown maple and teak woodwork left her feeling cocooned. She and Adrian often went there for Thanksgiving dinner. Tears swam in Celeste's eyes for the first time that day. Damn. Why did she have to think of him?

Pulling on a deep blue linen dress, she hurried out to the car before she could change her mind. From the hotel entrance she climbed the stairs and waited for the host who led her to a nice table near the windows. Her apprehension was relieved when the young waiter brought a wine list and menu to the table and explained the specials. He is recommending the tomato bisque soup to start. She agreed and ordered a Chardonnay. While she sipped her wine, Celeste browsed through the menu and chose grilled tuna with a small green salad.

After she finished the main course, Celeste glanced around the half full dining room for the first time. She noted a mix of young couples, probably tourists, with a group of older couples who were likely locals. Her gaze stopped at a head of curly black hair highlighted against a deep gold dress. Although she could only see the woman's back, the stance was somehow familiar. Celeste raised her eyes and found herself staring at the handsome profile of Adrian's face directly across from her and only a few tables away. He was deep in conversation with Sabrina and took no notice of her.

Pangs of jealousy hit her so hard her throat clamped shut so she was unable to respond to the waiter when he returned. He was looking at her with concern and asking her if she was okay. She could only nod as he cleared away the plate. While he was gone, she grabbed her purse, threw some bills on the table, and rushed down the stairs and out the door. Reaching her car, she pulled open the front door, threw herself in and banged the steering wheel with her fists as bursts of agony came out of her mouth. The monster. Why was he doing this to her? He was ruining her life. Adrian was so engrossed in Sabrina that he didn't even realize that she was there. Tears continued to stream down her face while she sat paralyzed.

She had to get out of here. Pushing the car into reverse, she backed onto the street, tires squealing. Blinded by tears, she ran the stop sign at Victoria Street and, within a few minutes, turned left onto Niagara Stone Road. If she could just get out of town, then she'd leave them behind her. No more hurt. While she gritted her teeth, she followed the car in front of her through the little town of Virgil and back onto the faster two-lane highway. As she turned onto Queenston Road, she slowed again. Where was she going? Turmoil continued to build within her, a layer of darkness clouding her mind. Pain stabbed into her stomach which caused her to cry out. Just before her car reached Lock 3 on the Welland Canal, she turned left into a used car lot, parked, and stared gloomily into the canal. Why go on alone? No one would ever love her like Adrian once did. She felt so useless. Overwhelmed by a sudden need to take some action, she started the car up and shifted into drive. Her hands clasped the steering wheel tight while the tires gripped on the loose dirt on the banks. She closed her eyes and surged forward.

Chapter Sixteen

Celeste

As she fought her way through a dense fog, Celeste tried to focus on the voices around her. All she could see was blue sky through the circle of black boots and bare legs in cut-offs. Her skin felt wet causing her to shiver and she watched a streak of blood run down the bodice of her blue dress, and drip down her arm over her fingers. A strange man was bending over her wet and freezing body.

"Hi there. I'm glad to see you're awake. That's a good sign. You're a very lucky lady." He pointed into the crowd. "Those three young guys were riding their bicycles at the bottom on the hill when your car hit the water. They called emergency right away."

Reality hit her. She remembered putting the car into gear, stepping on the gas, and heading down the embankment towards the canal. Anger had engulfed her from the scene in the restaurant. She felt hooked by the vision of Adrian's shocked face when he heard the news. He'd pay for his insensitivity.

She remembered her hands clenched the wheel while she kept her foot on the gas. A bump caused her to open her eyes. Shock had hit her like cold wet rain as she saw from the corner of her eye, three teens in t-shirts and jeans riding down the trail towards her. God! Please don't let me hit them. It was far too late to stop.

Celeste closed her eyes and gave no reply as they loaded her into the ambulance. How could she thank them when she didn't want to be alive? When she tried to move her head, every part of her hurt. Would the pain ever go away. Thankful for the warm blankets, she tried to sleep, but the man kept shaking her.

"Sorry, but you need to stay awake now until we get to the hospital. They'll want to check you out. You've got a bad cut on your forehead. Possibly a concussion. And your arm is badly bruised and swollen."

Later in emergency, she endured the pokes and prods while they finished their tests. Celeste refused to answer any questions and pretended to be asleep while they moved her to a hospital room. When she opened her eyes, a nurse stood over her with a worried frown.

"Glad you're finally awake. We've been trying to contact your husband Adrian. There has been no response. Is there anyone else? He's the only emergency contact listed."

Celeste's eyes opened widely. "No. No. Please don't call him. I don't want to see him." She gave the woman Marjorie's number. "Please wait until tomorrow. I don't want to see anyone right now."

The nurse rubbed her hand. "Stay calm now. We've put a cold compress on your arm and have bandaged your forehead. Do you still have a headache? That might be a sign of a concussion."

Celeste grimaced. "It feels like someone's hitting me with a hammer. Ouch. The pain is worse when I move my head."

The nurse wrote something on her chart. "We'll see how the pain is later this evening. If it's no better, we'll schedule an MRI. If you suffered a concussion, the headache is likely to get worse so let me know."

The woman left the room but returned to check on Celeste in about twenty minutes. "Do you think you can sleep now? The doctor said rest is good for you."

Celeste watched the nurse walk briskly from the room towards the nursing station. *It was easy for her to tell me to sleep. What have I done? I can't even kill myself. And do I really want to live. I just don't know.* She began to feel the soothing flow of the medication as it spread through her body.

*   *   *

When she opened her eyes next, she was conscious of someone in the room. A female form stood at the foot of her bed and stared out the window. Although her vision was blurred, Celeste could make out a bright red jacket. The figure moved to the side of her bed and touched her arm. Recognition hit Celeste. Marjorie had red splotches on her cheeks and dark circles under her eyes. Celeste felt flooded with shame as she realized how she must have frightened her friend.

"Celeste, thank goodness you're awake. How could you do this to yourself? I don't know what I can do to help you?"

Celeste pushed herself up higher in the bed and winced as the pain in her head returned. She'd hoped to escape but had instead made her life worse. "I ran into Adrian and Sabrina at the restaurant and I was just so angry, living didn't seem to be worthwhile." She took a deep breath. "But I'm glad you're here."

"Oh, Celeste. Why didn't you come to me?" Marjorie sat in the chair by the bed. "I really want to help you get you over this shock."

"I know." Celeste blinked back the tears. "Seeing them together, it hit me that Adrian's not coming back. Sabrina has won. I felt so angry and alone."

"The nurse told me they've asked one of the social workers to talk to you tomorrow. I want you to agree to work with her. Just let other people help you right now."

As she watched the anxiety on Marjorie's face, Celeste agreed. "Okay. I'm not sure how it will make any difference, but I'll co-operate. That's the least I can do for you."

Marjorie twisted her hands together. "I'm going to have to tell Adrian what happened. He'll hear about it around town anyway. Do you want to see him?"

"No." The distress tightened every muscle in her body causing her more pain. "You didn't see them together at that restaurant. He was totally mesmerized by Sabrina's every word. For him, a new life has already begun, and he has no regrets about leaving our marriage behind. I could tell. I hate him."

"I'm sure that's not true, Celeste. But you need to get rid of some of your anger. It'll block you from moving forward with your own life." She patted Celeste's hand. "Take this as an opportunity to begin again, Leave the anger behind."

"The pain doesn't go away. I guess it was an attempt to escape it." Her face felt frozen. "But I knew what I was doing, and I meant to do it."

Shock registered across Marjorie's face. "Celeste don't say that. You almost killed yourself. If those three boys hadn't been there, ready, and able to pull you out of the car, you would have died."

Celeste let the tears fall. "You're right. I'll try to start again. I had a life before Adrian. I can do it again." She pulled her shoulders back and wiped her face. "Thanks, Marjorie for being here for me. I want you to go home now. Get some rest yourself."

*   *   *

As soon as Marjorie left the room, Celeste turned her head and stared out the window. Every time she closed her eyes, she saw

Sabrina's laughing face, eyes sparkling with triumph as she raised her glass of wine. Adrian looked like he'd just come from his regular hair salon visit. He seemed to be enraptured by Sabrina. How long was it since he'd looked at her like that? With a shock, she realized the distance between them had started way back when they first talked about a place to retire.

The excitement over their daughter Natalie's job offer with the University of Ottawa had left them feeling letdown and older. Up until then, they'd still had her with them during the summer. Their three-bedroom house in Etobicoke, with its landscaped grounds and pool, seemed very empty without her. Should they sell it or renovate? The red brick exterior still looked good, but inside almost every room needed repainting and the kitchen with its natural pine cupboards and beige laminate countertops was certainly dated.

One warm Sunday morning, after a leisurely brunch, Adrian paced the living room. He had that look in his eyes which let her know he had something new in mind. He grabbed both her hands in his. "Why waste more time and money on this old place? I've talked to an agent and we can get an exceptionally good price if we sell it this fall. It's far larger we need for just the two of us."

At first, his excitement didn't spill over onto her. Instead Celeste's arms and chest felt a heavy weight. Even back then, she had begun to feel frightened by change. "But where would we live? I'd hate one of those downtown condos. Remember when we had dinner with Sally and Jim from the hospital at their place?"

"Stay with me on this retirement thing, Celeste. My group at the golf club has already mapped this out and have firm plans. For example, Gerald and Maud have sold and are on their way to Victoria, B.C. How does the West Coast sound? The winters are better."

Celeste pulled back her hands. "Not for me. We'd be too far from Ottawa and I'd never get to see Natalie. Besides, I don't like the west coast. Too much rain." She watched the light drain out of Adrian's eyes.

He stood and opened the patio door beckoning her to follow to their favorite chairs. "Okay. Let's think about something closer. What weekend trips did we enjoy? There was skiing in Blue Mountains with Natalie every winter, but that's too isolated for me. How about the theatre and wineries in Niagara-on-the-Lake? You enjoyed that."

Eventually, they had decided on a couple of experimental trips to Niagara-on-the-Lake, committing some time during each to meet with real estate agents and walk through open houses. She was impressed with what this small town had to offer. Especially when they found their current house. They both fell in love with it right away. But now she wondered, had Adrian planned this town from the start. After all, he was a negotiator. Adrian was an expert in promoting trial balloons. He'd explore what he really wanted, inserted somewhere in the mix of other possibilities.

At the sound of footsteps, she turned her head to see a policewoman in full uniform who stood at the foot of her bed.

"I need to talk to you for a while, Celeste, if you feel up to it."

The nurse had warned her that the police would want a report on the incident. Sighing, she invited the woman in and answered the series of questions as best she could. When you stripped out the feelings and went with the facts, even Celeste admitted that her actions would seem overly dramatic to others. The woman made her sign the statement and mentioned that a social worker would also send them a report for their investigation.

The woman looked directly into Celeste's eyes. "I hope you are over this. It's not my business but you seem to have many things to live for. Focus on your family and put this sadness behind you."

As soon as the officer left, Celeste's pent up tears flooded down her face, and an anguished cry escaped her lips. *What did that woman know about her family? She didn't have a family anymore—except for Natalie, of course.* She hoped Adrian wouldn't tell Natalie about what she'd done. But then why would he? He'd have to admit his own guilt.

A nurse hurried into the room giving her a worried glance. "Are you all right, Mrs. Gardener? Do you want me to tell the social worker not to visit until tomorrow?"

Celeste choked back tears. "Yes. Please. That would be great. I'd just like to sleep."

The nurse took her hand. "Would you like some medication? The doctor has ordered a mild sedative which I can give you."

"Yes. I don't want to see anyone or talk to anyone right now." She closed her eyes until she heard the nurse return with her pills.

She sat up, took the water, and downed the pills.

The nurse smoothed the pillow and lowered the head of the bed. "Relax now and you'll soon be asleep. I'll close your curtains so no one will bother you."

As a grey cloud descended over her, Celeste felt defeated. She'd even failed to get rid of herself successfully. How had her life become so screwed up? Something had happened to that energetic, upbeat young woman she used to be.

Chapter Seventeen

Adrian

Forced to find a place of his own, Adrian had been fortunate enough to rent a two-bedroom unit at King's Point, an upscale condo complex right on the water. The owner would be gone overseas for one year, so the timing was great. By the end of the year, Celeste might come to her senses and he could move back home. He still needed some furniture, but he'd make do for now. He laughed to himself. After all, if he made his new home too comfortable, Sabrina might get ideas. Besides, he was still in Portland most of the week. The management team at the hospital had no idea his life had taken a turn. He'd kept them busy interviewing for the new jobs and counseling those staff who would be leaving about their career options.

He managed to get together with Sabrina when he was back in town mainly in St. Catharines or Niagara Falls. They had to be careful with Ian prowling around. He had a knack of showing up unexpectedly. With Sabrina's imagination and energy, they enjoyed romantic dinners in small off-beat cafes and when they did get a night together, the spark was still there for him. However, he still thought about Celeste; he liked her refined manners and the sensuous backrubs she had given him while on their week-end getaways. Losing her had been more painful than he'd thought and left a hole in his life. However, when he returned to his apartment late on Friday nights, he had the entire weekend to himself and could do as he pleased.

After the taxi dropped him off, he turned the key in the lock and stepped in. He could hear the phone ringing loudly. It was probably Sabrina checking to see if he were back yet so they could make plans for tomorrow. Adrian grabbed the receiver as soon as he dropped his suitcase on the floor.

"Hi." It wasn't Sabrina. He hesitated at the strange but somewhat familiar voice. "Who's calling?'

He heard the person on the other end clear her throat. "Adrian. It's me, Marjorie. I wanted to call you earlier, but Celeste wouldn't let me. She'll be leaving the hospital tomorrow, so I insisted you needed to know."

A sense of alarm crept up the back of Adrian's neck. "Tell me what? Why is Celeste in hospital? I didn't know she was sick."

"She's not sick exactly." There was another long pause. "There's no easy way to say it. Your wife tried to commit suicide. Drove her car into the canal. She's been in hospital recuperating."

Shock caused Adrian's throat to tighten. "Why didn't the hospital call me? I'd have come immediately. I'm still her husband." A strangled sound escaped from him.

A note of sympathy entered Marjorie's voice. "Well, under the circumstances she doesn't want to see you. The circumstances being Sabrina, of course. But I felt you needed to know."

Adrian sat down and shook his head. He found himself unable to respond. After a long silence, he responded. "Let's leave Sabrina out of this for now. You must know I still have feelings for Celeste. What can I do to help her?"

A deep sigh came from Marjorie. "She's agreed to see a Social Worker and I think that's best for now. I'd suggest you stay away until she has time to acknowledge and deal with her pain. Celeste's still claiming she lost control of the car, but there were witnesses who say otherwise."

"I'm shocked she went so far." For a few moments, he couldn't get anything out. "You'll keep me up-to-date then. I need to know what's happening with her. Make sure she's getting better."

"I'll do that. Now I have to go. I persuaded her to give me the key to check the house before she gets home."

After he hung up the phone, Adrian held his head in both hands. What did Celeste do to herself. He stopped. It wasn't just Celeste. It was his fault as well. He'd had no idea how fragile she'd become. This wasn't the Celeste he'd married.

Celeste didn't accept change well and the downsizing must have hit her hard. His mind went back to their first weekend away together while they still both worked at the hospital. He'd dropped into her office just off the nursing station twice on Friday afternoon to make sure no emergencies were on the horizon to delay them. They left right on time, and arrived in the resort town of Muskoka early, and dropped in at Three Men's Grill for steaks before they settled into the cottage he'd been lucky to rent from a friend for the weekend. Dappled light from the sun peaking over the horizon fell on her face. On the loft floor of the old restaurant, framed in a rustic wood, both flushed from red wine, they devoured their hamburgers. He kept reaching over to touch her hand at breaks in their talk about staff at the hospital. She'd been so beautiful then, vibrant, her eyes alive with excitement.

Saturday had been a wonderful day of boating on the clear blue lake, and later, after a dinner he cooked for them on the barbecue, they'd made love with the bedroom patio door open to the night breezes. Even then, he had known they would marry. Celeste was a different person then.

He poured a glass of scotch and took it into the bedroom to sip while he unpacked. He'd had a late meeting and was both tired and hungry. But there was no way he was in any mood for cooking. It wasn't his best skill even when he was motivated to do so. He picked up the car keys and locked the door behind him as he tried to decide where to eat. He needed a restaurant where he wouldn't run into Sabrina and Ian. Certainly not their old haunt at Bistro 77. He couldn't face them right now. He'd find some small out-of-the-way place.

Instead, he found himself on the road out of town heading towards Frado's Diner in St. Catharines. As he travelled the bridge over Lock 3, he found himself staring down at the water. The canal was black in the low lighting and he couldn't make out the banks very clearly. His mind raced ahead imagining Celeste in the cold water. He shook his head and picked up speed until he reached the parking lot beside the diner. Over a dinner of hamburger and salad, chased with another glass of scotch, he decided he needed to talk to Celeste, and soon. He'd follow Marjorie's advice and wait another week, but he needed to make sure for himself she was okay. He hardly remembered the drive home and stumbled into bed close to midnight.

Padding around his bathroom with bare feet on Saturday morning, he was grateful for the bright sunshine pouring in through the window. He took his fruit and croissants out onto the balcony and stared out over the waters of the Niagara River. The wicker chairs and round table with its glass top were a new purchase which suited him. He often ate dinner out here as well. Checking his watch, he realized he was due to play with Dennis at the golf club in half an hour. Maybe it would distract him from his thoughts of Celeste. Eagerly, he cleared up the dishes and put them in the dishwasher.

Dressed in his pale blue polo shirt and chino pants, Adrian pulled the leased Audi convertible into the parking lot and strolled into the club. He stopped at the front desk to sign in. and glanced around the room. There was Ian over in the corner talking with his new partners. Adrian pretended to be reading a brochure he'd picked up from the rack until he saw Ian head out onto the grounds. He tapped his fingers on the counter waiting for Dennis, while he watched other members walk around him and head to the back without a stop. Finally, the manager, Tim came over to him.

"Oh, Adrian, I'm so sorry. I meant to tell you I had a call from Dennis. He said to give you the message he wouldn't be able to make it today. Wasn't feeling well. He said it was probably something he ate last night." Tim looked down at his feet and then walked rapidly back to the counter to do some work.

Shock hit Adrian in the gut. It wasn't like Dennis to pass on messages rather than calling him directly. He had Adrian's number and had called him before. Of course, he would know about Celeste. What about the others? Did they avoid him, thinking it was his fault? He hurried back to the car and sat there letting the sunlight calm him before he put it into gear and backed into the street. He wondered what he would he do without the club. He'd never really had the time to develop any other hobbies.

Driving along the Niagara Parkway, he checked his watch again. Almost noon and he'd promised to call Sabrina about tonight. They always arranged to call while Ian was still at the club. He pulled into a small parking lot and dialed her number.

"Hi. I knew it was you right away. This is your usual time to call me." Sabrina purred into the phone. "I've been wondering what adventure you have planned for us tonight. I've already told Ian I'll be out at an art exhibit with the ladies."

"No objections from him? I can't believe he still trusts you." Adrian managed to keep his voice calm.

"It's not a matter of trust. He'd rather not know. Otherwise, he'd have to do something about it."

Adrian took a deep breath. "I guess by now you've heard about Celeste." He paused. "Everyone at the club seemed to know. I only heard about it from Marjorie last night."

"Oh, honey. I'm sorry you had to find out that way. I heard it from Ian and planned to tell you later tonight." The silence dragged. "Are you alright? It wasn't our fault, you know. Celeste has been depressed for some time."

The whining tone in Sabrina's voice only added to his distress. "Look, I'm not up for dinner tonight. Let's skip it. Maybe you can meet me in Portland next week or we can wait until next weekend."

"Let's not let this ruin our time together." Sabrina's reply was sharp. "She'll get over it. We have the right to be happy. Don't you agree?"

"I need some time. This isn't the end of us just a breather." Adrian's tone left no room for her pleas. "I'll call you next week." He turned off the phone and picked up speed as he entered the Parkway grateful to be alone with his thoughts.

Chapter Eighteen

Celeste

Although still feeling fragile, Celeste insisted on getting dressed to meet the Social Worker, and that they meet in her office. Marjorie had said her name was Amy Spencer. She found it humiliating enough to bare her pain to a stranger without feeling like a victim by having Ms. Spencer sit by her bedside. Her chest felt so tight she took short sharp breaths while she waited on the hard vinyl chair outside the office door. She breathed out in a gush of air when the door opened, and Ms. Spencer invited her in.

"Make yourself comfortable, Celeste. We'll talk first about how these sessions will proceed and then if you have questions, feel free to ask me anything."

Sinking into the deep green upholstered chair, Celeste gave the Social Worker a wary stare. "I guess you know this wasn't really my idea. The hospital is insisting on it."

Ms. Spencer nodded. "Well, you're here now so let's make good use of your visit. I'll only get to see you three more times before you're discharged and then it's up to you if you want to continue as an outpatient. We need to set some goals to work on."

"What did you mean about how the sessions will work?"

"It may seem hard at first, but I want you to concentrate on what you were feeling before this incident took place." A look of sympathy crossed the Social Worker's face. "I'll have to take some notes, so don't let that bother you."

Celeste's forehead was pulled into a deep frown. "What did you mean about setting goals?"

"It will depend on what you tell me about where you want to go next." She paused to give Celeste time to absorb the information. "We need to focus on the future."

Celeste responded while she relaxed against the chair back. "I'd rather talk about what's next and not the incident, as you call it."

Amy focused on Celeste's face. "Umm. However, the past can predict the future, especially if you don't acknowledge the road you just travelled on."

"But it wasn't my choice. The separation that is." Celeste clasped her hands together in agitation. "Adrian cheated on me which made it impossible for me to live with him."

Another long pause while Amy jotted down notes. "I know this is painful for you, but it would help me to know when the affair started."

Red blotches appeared on Celeste's cheeks. "I wish I knew the answer. All I know is Sabrina had been flirting with him for several months before her husband, Ian, caught them together at a hotel. Then Ian demanded Adrian tell me or he would." Celeste felt the anger rising in her throat as she was forced to think back to the betrayal. Putting her hands over her face she lowered her head.

After she moved around the desk to Celeste's side, Amy handed her a box of Kleenex. "Are you able to continue or is this enough for you today?"

Without a response to Amy's enquiry, words burst out of Celeste. "But even before the affair, Adrian was always seeking space. I tried to keep everything nice for him when he was home, but he continued to act bored and restless."

"Let's concentrate on you." Amy leaned towards Celeste. "What were you feeling back then? What was happening in your life?"

"That's just it. Nothing was happening. After I lost my job at the hospital, I just drifted." Celeste's shoulders drooped. "I guess I just waited for Adrian to come home on weekends and relied on him to entertain me."

"You seem depressed about the change in your own behaviour."

"It was so unlike me. I'm a doer. I loved the fast-paced environment at the hospital." Anger rose in her voice. "It was all taken away from me."

"Okay. Good." Amy smiled. "We have a goal for the next session. I want you to think back to when the two of you were happy and what happened to change your feelings. We can then go forward from there."

Amy rose and came over to take Celeste's hand. "You're doing well. I'll see you again on Thursday. I can come to your room unless you prefer the office."

Celeste nodded. "Oh, yes, the office. There's really no privacy on the wards. I know since I used to work there." She felt lighter as she left the office and slowly walked back to her unit.

Later in the afternoon, she confided to Marjorie what had happened. "You know Amy is really alright. I don't know why I was so resistant. I used to suggest to many of my patients to see a Social Worker when I worked at the hospital."

A smile spread across Marjorie's face. "I'm glad it worked out. I tried to get my sister-in-law to talk to one when she and Dennis's brother were splitting up, but she wouldn't hear of it. I think she felt too vulnerable."

"Well, I can decide what we work on so that helps." Celeste swung her legs over the side of the bed and moved over to sit in the chair next to Marjorie's.

"I feel better being out of bed. I'm not really sick, you know."

Marjorie took her hand. "You've had a bad time and a severe shock. Don't rush things. You can use some rest."

"I guess so. I know I'm not ready to go home yet."

"Dennis told me Adrian asked again if he could visit." Marjorie looked at Celeste as if to see her reaction.

"No. Definitely not." Celeste shook her head emphatically. "In fact, I don't want him to see me in the hospital at all. Maybe later when I'm home and don't feel so weak."

"What has the doctor said so far about when you're leaving?"

She sighed. "At least another week. Then, if all goes well, I can go home on the weekend. I think it depends on the Social Worker's report."

"I want you to tell me when you're ready. I'll make sure I'm available to pick you up. And if for any reason I can't, Dennis will do it. I don't want you going home alone."

Celeste hugged her. "You're so good to me. Like the sister I never had."

Marjorie's face turned serious. "Have you talked to your daughter? She needs to know."

As she waved her hand, Celeste answered. "No. I'm not up to doing it yet. I'll call her when I'm back home and we can have a long talk. I don't want her flying out here right now."

Sensing her agitation rising, Marjorie changed the subject. "I ran into the woman who heads up your tennis club. Rosemary. She was asking about you. Wanted to know when you'd be returning to the team."

"I don't think I'll be back this season. But it was a way to work out some of my frustration and tension. I'll probably play again."

"Well, I've got to put dinner on the table for Dennis and me." She kissed Celeste on the cheek. "I'll see you again tomorrow. Look after yourself."

After Marjorie left, she felt restless and took a walk down the long hallway stopping to check outdoors at each window. She needed to organize her thoughts for the next session with Amy. When had things started to go wrong between her and Adrian?

* * *

A deep sense of shock had engulfed her on the drive back home the Friday afternoon after they told her. She had no job. No one needed her at the hospital anymore. She was redundant. What should she tell Adrian? He was part of the senior management team so probably already sensed what was coming. Why didn't he tell her?

Her hand shook so badly she could hardly get the key into the lock on her front door. She dropped her briefcase on the hall floor, and then kicked it across the room. How could they do this to her? She was one of their most competent nurses. What about Marcia, who was chronically absent or late? She went into the den, fell into the stuffed chair, and stared at the TV, with no sound turned on. She turned her head toward the noise when she heard Adrian's footsteps in the hall. After a few moments silence, he stood in the doorway. "You're home early. I thought you'd said you decided to check in with the late shift when they arrived."

Celeste followed him into the living room and sat on the loveseat. "Come and sit beside me. I could use some sympathy."

Once settled, Adrian picked up her hand. "Okay. What's happening? It's not like you to be so dramatic."

"You must know I've been let go."

He sat back in the seat. "No. I didn't know. Just that your unit was being downsized. I didn't even think of you being one of those downsized."

Celeste's chest was so tight she could hardly get the words out. "This was my last day. Some jerk from HR walked me out of the building, after they took my Blackberry and access card."

Adrian put his arm around her shoulders. "I'm sorry, honey. I had no idea."

"Thank God the mortgage on this place is paid off. With some sprucing up we can easily sell it. Living on one salary will be a big adjustment for us."

Adrian stood and stared down at her. "You'll get another job. Nurses are always in demand. I'm sure it won't be long."

Disappointment engulfed Celeste like a grey cloud. He seemed to think this would be so easy for her. She stood and faced him. "All the hospitals are laying off right now. Especially nurse managers. They're only hiring junior nurses. That means those young women just out of college."

He had turned to leave the room. "We'll be okay for a while. Something will come up."

That was it, she remembered now. From that day, she would find him giving her strange looks from across the room. When she would ask him what the matter was, he'd force a smile and refuse to talk about it. The coldness had gradually crept in.

How could she explain this to Amy? It seemed Adrian loved her when times were good but became more and more frustrated when she became just another housewife. They'd kept the house, but it meant changes to their lifestyle. She stopped walking, stood for a minute, and then hurried back to sit on the side of her bed, wanting to be alone.

Part of it was her fault. She hadn't thought about it this way before. The loss of her job had been a blow, but she hid in her own little world and refused to try again. She'd never sent out any resumes even though Adrian nagged her constantly the first few weeks. She didn't make use of the career consultants the hospital provided for her. It was too painful to see her fellow staff members who'd also been let go. From time to time, she'd hear from other nurses who had taken jobs working in the community or in nursing homes, but she was too proud to accept a demotion.

When the same thing happened to Adrian a couple of years later, he followed through with job counseling and started his own consulting business. They'd all teased him saying consulting was a make work project, but he'd persevered and was still doing it. He'd taken control of his life. She'd wasted her time and lived a life, safe but dull. No wonder she was so anxious to see him when he'd come home on weekends. She didn't really have anything to talk about anymore. She'd let that happen to her.

Celeste crawled into bed but was wide awake. Turning on the TV, she watched the news. By the time she got out of here, she'd have a plan. Maybe Amy could help her with the plan. An hour later when she turned off the news, she felt herself falling asleep without a pill. This was progress in her new world.

*　　*　　*

Three days later, she was up and dressed early for her appointment with Amy. She was determined to tell her full story this time. Rehearsing her speech as she waited to be called into the office, Celeste felt a surge of energy. She could do this. Amy greeted her and led her to the same comfortable chair. Amy repeated their goal of exploring when Celeste's life with Adrian changed and how it happened.

Surprised at the strength of her voice, Celeste related the story of how she lost her job, Adrian's reaction, and how she felt worthless and alone. For her, this event had started the downward spiral. Amy coaxed her to continue expressing her feelings and commented on the spurts of anger this generated. By the end of the session, Amy stated, "I'll be passing my evaluation on to your doctor, to advise you're emotionally ready for discharge this weekend. However, I'd recommend our next goals should include we continue to meet every two weeks, for at least the next three to four months." She gave a card to Celeste with the date of the next appointment. "Do you agree? And have you made plans for when you return home?"

Celeste nodded. "I could use the help with my plans."

With discharge pending, she had thought this over in her own mind. "I want to take on some volunteer work. Something in health care." Although she'd resisted the idea in the past, she knew for her, doing something productive would keep her from falling back into the black hole.

Amy smiled. "I can help you with that plan since you're a former nurse. I'll ask our Director of Nursing, Diane Cunningham, to set up a meeting with you. She might have some ideas about what volunteer work the hospital has. Something which would be a match with your skills. Give yourself some time to recuperate before jumping into something new. Our next goal will be to build up your self-esteem so any new blows will be easier for you to work your way through."

"I never would have thought just talking would help me this much. Thank you for your support. I'm learning how to take control rather than falling into this awful feeling of being helpless."

"You've made great progress. However, it's important for you to continue when you're back in familiar surroundings, facing the same problems. You don't want to slip backward. Phone my secretary if you need to change the appointment. My office number is on this card." Amy stood, shook Celeste's hand, and walked her to the door. "Do you have anyone to pick you up on Saturday morning?"

"My friend, Marjorie promised to be here. I've started to look forward to going home."

Chapter Nineteen

Celeste

Amy called on Friday morning to tell Celeste her appointment with Diane Cunningham would be around two that afternoon. Amy was sorry she couldn't be at the meeting but reminded Celeste about her appointment for follow up at her office. She reassured Celeste; Diane was extremely interested in having an opportunity to meet since her previous work at a Toronto hospital would be useful. Celeste was to go to Diane's office and speak with her secretary shortly before the meeting.

Early in the afternoon, dressed in the tan linen pants and white cotton blouse which Marjorie had dropped off for her, she sat staring at the office door anxious for it to open. Part of her wanted to run away, but she knew Amy would expect her to win Diane over. The door burst open and a woman, dressed in a smart navy suit walked towards her.

"Hello." Diane smiled. "You must be Celeste. I'm so glad that Amy arranged this meeting for us. Come in."

Celeste swallowed once or twice and followed Diane into the office where she dropped into a leather chair next to the desk. "I appreciate you taking the time to meet with me."

"I'm very interested in the work you did at UHN." Diane met her eyes straight on. "You must have been an exceptional manager to get those awards that Amy told me about. We could use your expertise."

Celeste felt her face flush. "Well, it was a few years ago, but quality care was something I knew. I succeeded because of my influence with the others. Getting them to believe in it." The flow of conversation about her work was easier than Celeste expected. The excitement rose from her chest into her throat making her voice stronger.

Diane nodded. "Good motivators are hard to find. Can you send me a one- or two-page resume, so I can figure out where you'd best fit? I know you're leaving us tomorrow so if you agree, we can meet again in about two weeks to explore some volunteer opportunities we have here." She stood and came around the desk.

Celeste rose to shake the extended hand. "Great. I'll look forward to talking with you again."

"Good." Diane walked with Celeste towards the door. "I'll round up some of my nurse managers next week for a discussion. We'll see what opportunities there exist which you might find matches with your skills."

Celeste closed the door behind her feeling lighter and happier as she walked back to her room. Other people who were experts in her field saw potential in her. Holding her head up, she repeated to herself, *I can do this. I will start a new life today.*

*　　*　　*

Saturday morning while Celeste packed up her few belongings, Amy appeared in her room.

"So, how did it go?"

"Much better than I expected. Diane thinks she'll be able to find some volunteer work for me here. I used to scoff at unpaid labour, however I'd be so grateful to be working in a hospital again."

Amy grinned at her. "That's great." It looks like we still have an appointment for next Friday. I'm looking forward to seeing you again then. I've got to run this morning with so many discharges to process. Are you sure you have someone to pick you up?"

"I'm meeting Marjorie in the lobby at eleven. I'll see you Friday."

The nurse had insisted on taking Celeste downstairs in a wheelchair. After transferring herself to a hardback waiting room chair, she watched out the window. It was already eleven and no sign of Marjorie. Her stomach was getting queasy. Who else could she call?

As she continued to stare at the main door, she noticed a tall man with well-groomed brown hair who walked down the hallway towards her. When he got closer, she realized it was Dennis.

Taking her hand, he helped her up from the chair. "Celeste, I'm glad I found you. Marjorie got tied up in her meeting and called me in a panic to see if I could come. Are these your things?"

With Dennis standing so close to her, Celeste was distressed at how he'd aged. His skin was pasty white and there were dark circles under both eyes. When he reached for her bag, his hand trembled.

"It's so thoughtful of you to come for me, Dennis." She took his arm and headed for the door. "Are you feeling all right? You seem pale."

Dennis sighed. "My high blood pressure has worsened. The doctor has tried a new medication, but so far, it's no better than the last one. They're talking about doing more tests."

"Does Marjorie know?"

"About the new medication, yes. The additional tests, no. I didn't want to worry her." He continued to plod towards the parking lot.

"You'll tell her when you get the test results, won't you?"

Dennis shook his head. "We'll see how those turn out first. I hate being ill. That's why I had to leave work."

It felt good to worry about someone else for a change. Celeste insisted she load her own bag into the back seat before she climbed into the passenger's side. When they reached the house, she got out on her own before Dennis could come around to her side and carried her own bag to the door.

"Thanks, Dennis. Tell Marjorie to call me when she gets home." She hesitated. "And take care of yourself."

She stood in the open doorway and watched his car slowly back out of the driveway and into the street. She'd have to query Marjorie about Dennis's condition. What if she didn't know? Closing the door, Celeste stood and stared at the silent living room. The lack of sound was unnerving. She took a deep breath and climbed the stairs and crossed the hallway to enter her bedroom. Her dressing gown lay on the unmade bed and several of her dresses were lying on the floor near the closet where she had left them in her hurry to leave. There was no remaining sign of Adrian. This was her bedroom now

*　　*　　*

For the past two weeks, Celeste had followed a regular routine. Amy had suggested this approach to avoid a fall back into depression. After breakfast, she would go for a long walk with two other women from her neighbourhood. She'd discovered them during her first time out. She'd eat her lunch out in the garden in the sunshine. If it were raining, she'd drop into the local bakery for soup and a sandwich. Marjorie came over around two unless she had an afternoon event.

Celeste felt a sense of relief when she heard Marjorie had been the one to explain to Adrian what had happened while she was in hospital. She was so solid and compassionate. Celeste had finally worked up her courage to ask Marjorie about Dennis's health. She reassured Celeste he was being followed up closely by the doctor.

The evenings could be long, but when TV was intolerable, she'd started going to movies alone. Adrian had called and reluctantly she'd agreed to meet him for lunch on Wednesday afternoon at Zeke's across from the Shaw Festival. It wasn't likely Sabrina would show up there.

Celeste arrived a little late to make sure she wouldn't be the one left sitting alone. She took a deep breath and approached the table where Adrian was engrossed in the menu. His handsome profile gave her heart a pang.

"Sorry, I'm late. The traffic was slow."

He stood and pulled back a chair for her. "It's good to see you. I'm so glad you agreed to have lunch." After Adrian settled back into his seat, he gave her an intense look. "How are you?"

Celeste had gotten used to this question from everyone. "I'm okay." She hesitated before making up her mind to be honest with him. "I'm slowly making my way back to normal, if that's what you mean."

Adrian put his hand over hers. "I'm so sorry about what happened, Celeste. I didn't mean to hurt you. I just didn't think. It was so inconsiderate of me."

Celeste pulled her hand back and blinked her eyes. Was Adrian attempting an apology? That was a surprise.

"I've had a shock, but I'm getting over it." Looking at him more closely, she noticed the new lines in his face and his eyes had lost their light. "Marjorie and Dennis have both been good supports."

Adrian sat up straighter. "I'm glad that you've had them. They're great, those two. Dennis is still my partner at the club. I enjoy that British sense of humour of his."

They sat in silence after the waiter took their orders and delivered drinks. After taking a long sip of his scotch, Adrian cleared his throat.

"There's a reason I asked you to meet with me. I accept we're now separated; Celeste and I know why. That hasn't changed, but can't we be friends? We've shared a long history. And there's Natalie to think about."

Celeste almost dropped her wine in shook. "I hope you haven't talked to Natalie about me. I haven't worked up the courage to call her yet."

A guilty look crossed Adrian's face. "I've been calling her about every two weeks, just to keep in touch now that I'm not at the house. She asked if I'd seen you and I had to tell her. You wouldn't want me to lie, would you?"

Trust Adrian to find what sounded like a reasonable excuse for doing something behind her back. "Why didn't you just say that you'd have me call her? I wanted to tell her myself."

Their meals arrived and both picked at their plates. Another long silence dragged by. "Will you think about what I asked? I don't need an answer right now, but I hope you'll let me know."

What did he mean by friends? Celeste felt the tension building. She forced herself to stay calm. After what seemed like a reasonable amount of time, she pushed back her chair. "Thanks for the lunch. I'll call you when I'm ready to talk again. Meantime, I plan to have my own chat with Natalie on the weekend." She walked towards the door while he went to settle the bill.

*   *   *

This time when she entered the reception area to Diane's office, Celeste felt confident. She no longer felt like a patient but rather was an independent agent researching job opportunities. Diane's secretary escorted her into the office where she was warmly greeted.

"I've been busy since we last met. We held our annual retreat for our Nurse Managers a week ago. I was excited to hear from them about several new projects where they could use your help. They were impressed with your credentials."

Celeste beamed and squirmed in her chair. "That's wonderful. I've never worked as a volunteer before, but I'm excited to be involved."

"You'll be pleased then to know that these jobs are short term contracts, so they come with a per diem rate. The one that I think suits you best is a series of workshops on communications and team building for the new nurses we've hired over the past year." She handed a stack of paper to Celeste.

As she scanned through them, she noticed the assignments were all in her field. Celeste swallowed to steady her voice. "I'm extremely interested. What do you need from me next?"

"Well, we'll want to receive proposals from you on the ones which appeal to you most. We've suggested a potential per diem rate for each, but you can bid with your own rates and we'll compare yours with others."

Celeste's chest tightened. "What's the deadline for the proposals? And would I be working out of the hospital?"

Diane smiled and handed her a card. "I'm pleased to see that you're ready to get down to work. The deadline is one month from today and we have meeting rooms right here. I realize you've been out of the workforce for some time now. So, call me if you have questions."

The green walls of the corridor against the terrazzo floors were familiar to Celeste as she hurried down the hall to the entrance. Other people found it cold and alien, but to her it was home. She was pleased she would be working inside the walls of the hospital.

Natalie never expressed any desire to work in health care preferring the academic world. But it gave Celeste a warm, happy feeling. Now she had something positive to share with her daughter when she called on the weekend. Marjorie would be proud of her. She couldn't wait to tell Adrian—but that made no sense. Why would he care? She sensed he had been anxious to leave at the end of their lunch on Wednesday. What had all the talk about being friends been about? Was he feeling guilty or was he just trying to manipulate her once more? She realized then the likelihood of them getting back together was slim. Her trust was gone.

*   *   *

Saturday morning, after she finished her croissants and coffee, Celeste picked up the phone and called her daughter. Her confidence was still high.

She'd probably have to leave a message. "Hi, Natalie. This is your mother calling." She held her breath as she heard the pickup on the other end. "You're there. I expected you'd be out shopping by now. How are you dear?"

She heard a tremble in her daughter's voice. "I'm so glad you called me Mom. Why didn't you tell me what was going on? Adrian explained what happened to you, but not why."

"I've wanted to call you about the breakup but couldn't work up the courage. Separation seems so final." She waited for a response. "I know you have your own life to think about."

"But, Mom, you tried to kill yourself." Natalie choked back a sob. "It's not the separation I'm worried about. You could have confided in me if you felt so desperate. I'm here for you and I'm all grown up. You don't need to feel alone."

Subdued by the pain she heard in her daughter's voice; Celeste let the silence sit for a few minutes more. "I guess I was more depressed than I realized. Hurt and blinded by anger." She stopped. Careful here. I don't want to leave Natalie to think negatively about her stepfather. "The meetings I've had with my Social Worker helped me to see it's up to me to make my life more fulfilling."

Natalie spoke softly, "Any chance of you two getting back together?"

Celeste felt a pang hit her in the chest. "No. We agreed to separate. He's seeing someone else."

"I'm sorry. That must be awful for you. What can I do? I can't come to see you this weekend since we're in the middle of a conference and I'm a presenter, but how about next weekend?"

She took a deep breath. "I have some good news to share. That's why I'm calling you. The local hospital offered me a contract—several contracts to be more exact. By early next month, I'll be working, and I can't wait."

There was another silence. "That's great. Does that mean I can't come to visit?"

"Of course not. We should arrange something during this month before I start the job. I'll check my schedule and let you know. I'd love to see you honey."

And now saying the words, Celeste realized it was true. She missed her daughter. It would be great to have her here. After they said their goodbyes, she dawdled while cleaning up the kitchen. She'd better order a bed for the guest bedroom. Natalie would probably want to visit with Adrian as well, but Celeste would cope with her decision when the time came. This new lifestyle still meant so many adjustments.

The next time Marjorie came over to check on her, Celeste eagerly shared the news about her job.

"I knew you could do it, Celeste. This is the real woman I remember from when we first met two years ago. Hard working and serious, but always sensitive to others need."

Feeling her face flush, Celeste said. "You're the most kind and supportive friend I ever had. Anytime I can do something for you, don't hesitate to let me know."

"Thanks. Dennis and I have been through those early years of establishing ourselves in a new country. We raised our family and survived his retirement. What could possibly happen to us now?"

*   *   *

The sound of the phone on her bedside table pulled Celeste from a deep sleep. Who would be calling her so early in the morning? It was still grey outside. She switched on the light and fumbled with the receiver as she sat up in bed and gave a muffled response.

"I'm so sorry to wake you but I just got back from the hospital and needed to talk to someone. Dennis has been admitted and they think it was a heart attack." Marjorie said.

"Marjorie. Don't apologize. It's okay," Celeste stammered. "I'm your friend and you should call me. Tell me what happened."

"I don't know all the details. He went sailing with Ian yesterday morning. I guess Ian's looking for distractions since his split with Sabrina and asked Dennis to crew for him. I warned him that he's not so young and energetic as he used to be, but Dennis wanted to support Ian's little venture."

"Did it happen after he got back home?"

"Around five, I got a call from Ian to say Dennis had been taken to the hospital by ambulance from the sailing club. When they got back to the dock, Dennis seemed to have severe indigestion and later collapsed on the floor."

Fully awake now, Celeste began to pace across the bedroom floor. "Is he going to be okay? Where is he now?"

"When I got to the hospital, the doctor confirmed that it was a heart attack. They had stabilized him and would be transporting him to Hamilton General. I followed them there by car and stayed with him in emergency until about an hour ago. They suggested I get some sleep and come back tomorrow."

"You sound exhausted, Marjorie. I agree you should try to get some sleep. I'll come over tomorrow after breakfast and drive you back to Hamilton so you can relax."

"Okay. I'm very tired and will lie down for a while. Phone me before you come over and I'll make sure I'm dressed and ready to go."

Chapter Twenty

Sabrina

For weeks after Ian discovered her and Adrian in that Niagara Falls hotel, he'd sit for hours on their deck in brooding silence. She hated that. Anger and the crash of dishes thrown in frustration were more her style. Chaos was palatable and she could deal with it. After a while, she'd noticed his car often followed them on their way out of town. Sometimes she'd scrutinize other patrons in The Cannery Restaurant when she and Adrian were out for lunch and would see Ian three tables away, sitting alone. She couldn't stand it any longer.

One Friday morning at breakfast, she confronted him. "Ian, this can't go on. You know Adrian and I are seeing each other. You and I agreed we'd continue to share the house. It's less disruptive for both of us, but not the same as before."

"What was wrong with how it was before?" He gave her a defiant glare. "We always got along. I allowed you to shop as much as you wanted. It was your idea that we move here way out in the country. Maybe you're just bored."

Sabrina sighed. "It's not that simple. You and I were married for thirty years. We both had successful careers and shared the same social circle. Never any changes. I needed some excitement and Adrian brings that for me."

"You'll get tired of him." He poured them each more coffee. "Don't think I don't know this isn't the first time for either of you."

Sabrina chose to ignore his accusations. "Ian, maybe we just need some time apart, you and me. In fact, I've been looking around and have rented a small townhouse off Nassau Street. Let's try not to get on each other's nerves for the next few weeks until I can move."

Ian pushed away from the table, spilling his coffee and went to stand by the kitchen window. "Don't you think it's about time you told me you're moving? You mean you'd just leave and let me search the town for you?"

As she closed her eyes, Sabrina breathed in and counted to ten. That was how she'd handled difficult clients at the investment firm all those years. Don't blow up. Don't lecture. Stick with the facts.

"We're not good living together right now. You know that. We had our time and it worked for us for many years. Now, I want something else. What else can I say?" She stayed calm as Ian gritted his teeth, his face flushed.

"You're so selfish, Sabrina. Always were but I tolerated it when we did things together. I wonder if you ever loved me. He waited for an answer. Maybe we should have had children to create a stronger bond."

Sabrina threw her coffee mug on the ceramic floor and watched it break. How could he bring up children right now? She could feel her face hot and perspiring, her heart beating hard. "Why go over the past now? What does it matter?" She started to leave the room and then turned to him. "We've had some great times. I'm not denying that. However, right now this isn't working for us. And it wasn't just Adrian. I'm going over to the gallery to calm down. Don't follow me."

Strolling along the walkway near the Lake, Sabrina enjoyed the cool breeze on her hot face. Ian had become impossible. She was determined to spend as much time as possible with Adrian. After all, he was only home on weekends and was already getting protective about his own space. When she had her new townhouse, she'd persuade him to stay overnight. For now, though, long evenings at his King's Point condo in his bedroom which overlooked the water satisfied her. Their dinners in different restaurants kept the romance alive.

Adrian wouldn't be back until eight tonight and had asked her not to come over until nine. Since Ian knew the situation, there was no need for her to sneak around. She couldn't face going back to the house though with him in it. The empty afternoon stretched in front of her. What to do? Back in her car, she drove aimlessly along the lakeshore stopping at the small Strewn winery. Their wine was rather good, and they had great lunches. Entering the small dining room, she noted that it was full of tourists and thankfully no one she knew. She sighed and fell into one of their white wicker chairs. A good bottle of Merlot would sooth her irritated nerves. While sipping the full flavour, she decided on the curried rice noodles with basil and cashews. Why not indulge? She'd probably just go home to change for the evening and skip dinner.

When she arrived home around seven, the house was empty. There was no doubt that Ian had gone to the club for dinner. He did that more and more frequently now. She pulled on white cotton stretch pants and a tight red and white striped sweater. Fresh make-up made her eyes less tired looking. Fatigue was one of the problems with getting older. You couldn't hide your eyes. Thank goodness she didn't have far to drive. The wine was still making her feel lightheaded as she made her way into the Friday night traffic.

She had her own key to the front door of the condo building. At least Adrian had allowed that perk. As she walked down the hallway, the excitement caused her face to feel hot. The door swung open quickly at her knock and Adrian greeted her with a sensuous kiss directly on her lips. Sabrina pulled him close into her body circling his waist with both arms. I've missed you this long week. But I have good news for us. I move into my own townhouse on July 3.

Adrian took her hand and led her to the sofa where he had two glasses of brandy poured. "That was sudden wasn't it? How did Ian react?"

Sabrina gave him a cautious look. "Ian didn't take it well. But you and I have talked about it. This shouldn't be a surprise to you."

He pulled her towards him with his arm around her shoulders and nuzzled her long white neck. "I just know it's hard to find rentals in this town. I went through the search myself not too long ago." He pulled her closer and stroked her hair. "That's all. Of course, I didn't think Ian would be easy to live with under the circumstances."

When Adrian let her go, she took a long sip of brandy. "We'll have two open houses to celebrate now. I don't think we toasted your new apartment." She raised her glass. "To us and our new freedom." She took another long drink to finish the glass.

She watched Adrian's face darken with annoyance. "Take it easy. From your flushed face, I'd say you've already had a few too many toasts this afternoon. "He touched his glass to hers and took a small sip himself.

"What's up with you? You never used to mind what I drank."

His face cleared. "I guess I'm just tense from work. But I don't like to see you driving after so many. One day you'll get stopped."

"Once I'm in my own place, there will be no need to go home. I'd love waking up with you."

His eyes engaged hers and his voice returned to his teasing manner. "Let's go to the bedroom and watch the sunset. I enjoy golden reflection on your bare skin."

Sabrina gave her throaty laugh, grabbed his hand, and led the way.

* * *

On edge all through breakfast, Sabrina pretended to be cutting roses in their front garden. She knew Ian was upstairs changing into his waterproof shorts and jacket. He was crewing for a buddy from the Niagara-on-the-Lake Yacht Club for the day. Something he hadn't done for at least ten years since he had his own boat. Normally, she would have been concerned. However, it gave her a perfect opportunity to move to her new house without Ian following her around while she packed. The movers were booked for one that afternoon, so she would be busy placing tags on all the boxes most of the morning. She'd better start with her closets. While engrossed in packing, she heard the front door close behind Ian.

Hours later, she closed the last box and sat on the bed. Shortly after the doorbell rang. Sabrina wiped the perspiration off her face, still dressed in denim shorts and a low-neck tee shirt. She ran down the stairs to let the men into the front hall. Lunch would have to wait.

"Hi. I'm Greg. He strode into the living room and surveyed the furniture with its jigsaw puzzle of tags. "Do we take everything, lady?" He swept his hand over the assembled pieces.

Heat rose Sabrina's neck and into her cheeks. "They're clearly marked. See right there. I've put the room name and the address on all the items you're to load, just like your supervisor told me."

The man threw his hands into the air. "Sorry. Whatever you say."

"Joe, we can load from the living room first starting with the sofa. We'll do the bedrooms next."

Taking deep breaths, she climbed the stairs again to their bedroom and threw some things she wanted to take with her in the car, into a small suitcase. Jewellery, cash and other valuables, plus a change of clothes. No way did she want to be seen out for lunch in this outfit.

It would have been impossible for her to consult Ian about the furniture. He was so unrealistic. She'd taken only the things she'd need to set up the new place—most of the living room furniture, except for the TV and a leather reclining chair that he loved. From the master bedroom, she'd tagged the all the bedroom furniture. After all it was part of a set. There was always the guest bedroom furniture that he could move into their old room.

When the truck finally left the driveway at 4:30, she was tense with apprehension. Ian said he'd be back around 5. Her suitcase in one hand and the car keys in the other, she ran to her car and followed the truck down the street to Bayberry Lane. How excited she'd been when her agent called to say this townhouse was for rent. With a one-year lease in hand, she'd been able to move forward with her plans.

The movers had told her it would be another three hours for them to unload and unpack. Once they got started, she changed to go to Ginger's Restaurant down the road for lunch. She took her cell phone with her in case they needed her back.

The white leather booths in Ginger's were highlighted by the pale green checkered tablecloths with the pink rose bud on each table. Sun streamed in the large front windows and raised Sabrina's mood which had sunk as the day progressed. God, she hated moving. The disruption would go on for days. Sighing, she perused the menu and was pleasantly surprised to see the variety of dishes.

She smiled at the waiter. "I'll have the bacon wrapped grilled chicken on focaccia and the mixed greens."

"Will that be all, madam?"

"Oh. You can bring me a half-litre of the pinot gris" What was the sense of her ordering two glasses separately?

She gave the waiter another smile when he brought her plate. Then, as soon as he turned his back, she grabbed the sandwich in both hands and took a huge bite. All that packing and moving had made her ravenous. The first glass of wine disappeared in three swallows and she sat back to relax and watch the traffic stream by on the street. The cell phone which she had laid by her plate buzzed.

Annoyed, she picked it up and pressed talk. "Yes."

"It's me, Greg, the mover."

"What do you want now?"

"Mrs. McNally, we need you back here so we can finish the downstairs. You didn't tell us where to place the living room furniture. We're finished upstairs."

"I'll be there shortly. In the meantime, unpack the kitchen."

Finished with her sandwich, Sabrina savoured the last drop of wine, and waved at the waiter for the bill. She glanced at the amount and threw some bills on the table including a generous tip. He'd been quick and that was important right now.

As she walked past the sofa on the front sidewalk, and entered her new home, she felt a sense of freedom. Having her own space again was a good feeling. She sorted out for the men where she wanted the remaining furniture and watched them empty the final boxes. Handing them a cheque, she wished them well on their way out.

Her mood stayed bright while she surveyed the chaos in the living room and kitchen. She'd have this sorted out before the weekend and could have Adrian pick her up here. What a relief that would be. He's been a little testy about her drinking lately. She'd have to watch her consumption when they were together. Why didn't he realize that she'd always enjoyed a drink or two? Adrian was the type of guy who'd down two glasses of scotch and that was it. He had no need for more. The obvious solution was for her to have a couple before he picked her up and then drink lightly at the restaurant. Once they were settled back here, he'd be too mellow to notice a nightcap.

Chapter Twenty-One
Adrian

A glance in the mirror assured Adrian that the new blue silk shirt tucked into his white chinos set off his recent tan. The bedroom in his apartment was spacious and the furniture from the house fit in nicely. But something was missing. Celeste had such a great touch with accessories. A small painting here, a vase there and the whole room came to life. He guessed that was another thing he'd have to learn. Surprised, he felt a sudden need to talk with her, then shook his head.

He would be picking Sabrina up at her place in fifteen minutes. During the drive to Treadwell's in Port Dalhousie, he intended to explain to her his need not to rush things. He was still getting used to living alone. Each time he returned from Portland, the emptiness of the apartment when he opened the door was haunting. Adrian had been relieved when Sabrina left Ian and there was no longer any need to sneak around. Now it was just like being on a date. Still they preferred to go out of town so as not to run into their former spouses.

He'd left the BMW for Celeste out of guilt, but eventually replaced their older Toyota Rav4 with this leased Audi. During the drive to Sabrina's rented townhouse, he thought back to their last romantic dinner. The thrill of feeling her lightly run her hand over his inner thigh under the table. She'd kept it there while they toasted their freedom. He frowned. There had been a few too many toasts during the evening and he'd been concerned about driving back from the Falls. What if they were stopped? He'd control things a little better tonight.

The door swung open quickly after his knock. She must have watched him drive up.

"Come in, sweetie. I'm almost ready." Sabrina grabbed his hand. "I've just got to work a little longer on this hair."

"Well, you look great to me." He gave an admiring look taking in her tight coral sundress and almost bare shoulders. Her black curls with silver highlights seemed to invite him to run his hands through it.

He sat on the sofa flipping through TV channels while she climbed the stairs to the upstairs rooms. "Don't be too long. Our reservation is for seven and you know what the traffic is like in Port Dalhousie in early summer."

Sabrina's voice rang down from above. "Just give me a few more minutes. I want to look beautiful for my lover."

Adrian suppressed a laugh. "Your lover wants to make sure that we're back in time for a night cap later." Although living alone left him feeling lonely at times, being single again had its benefits. He hoped she wouldn't bring up again the discussion about when they would live together.

Sabrina descended the stairs with an ivory shawl thrown over her shoulders and a small rhinestone barrette in her hair. "Okay. Let's go. I don't want you stewing over the drive."

On the way to the restaurant, they touched hands playfully and smiled into each other's eyes. He shared with her a few funny episodes from his week in Portland. Not that there were many such incidents to share. The tension from staff, uncertain about their future, had gotten to him and he'd be glad when this contract was completed in July. He parked the car, opened the door for her and they walked to the restaurant holding hands.

The intimate dining room overlooking Lake Ontario thrilled him. He loved this spot. "We'll have a bottle of the 2007 Peninsula Ridge Shiraz to start," Adrian said to the waiter.

"That sounds pricey. What are we celebrating?" Sabrina asked.

Adrian placed his hand over hers. "The sunset is beautiful and I'm simply happy tonight. What more do we need to celebrate?"

Glass after glass, the wine disappeared. Adrian continued to savour his steak, cooked to perfection. When Sabrina finished her last glass and gave him an inquiring look, he responded. "That's it for me since I'm driving. If you would like something else, go ahead. I'm paying this time."

The smile left Sabrina's face. "Don't be a spoiler, dear. How about one more glass each?"

Adrian called the waiter over to the table. "The lady will have another glass of red."

"Would madam like the same wine or something else?" He stood waiting.

"Make it a Cabernet Franc from the same winery. And make it a half liter." Sabrina glared at Adrian in defiance. He wondered if her voice carried over to the next table. "Don't worry, dear. I intend to drink them both."

Adrian ignored the taunt and turned to the waiter. "We'll also have two Crème Brule and coffee for me."

Sabrina met his challenge. "I'll just have my wine with the dessert, thank you." Her voice was raised even louder.

Heads turned from the table beside them to see what the noise was about. Adrian ignored them and continued to eat his dinner. He's noticed that lately Sabrina had gotten loud in her demeanor after a few drinks. This was a new side of her that he didn't particularly like. He'd wait to talk to her about it when they got back tonight. He'd probably be staying over anyway.

Sabrina drank the first glass of wine in three swallows and then sipped the second while eating dessert. The look of annoyance faded from her face. "Ian tells me that he's taken up sailing again. I told him that he's too old to manage a boat on his own, but he says Dennis is helping him."

It was Adrian's turn to be annoyed. Why was she bringing up Ian again? Couldn't they leave their ex-spouses out of this? "When were you talking to Ian?"

Sabrina tilted her head and glanced at him. "Well, honey, we have business to discuss. Most of our investments are joint."

"Of course. But what I meant was since when are you interested in his social life?"

"Just a comment and no need for you to be so cold about it." She sat back in her chair.

Why were they quarrelling again? It was spoiling his good mood and he knew it wasn't all her fault. He smiled and held out his hand to her. "Sabrina, I don't want to argue over these petty things. I'm sorry if what I said sounded like a lecture. Old habits from work projects, I guess. What I'm really concerned about is both of those guys are too old to be sailing."

Her face softened and she touched his hand running one finger up his arm. "We'll make up later over a strong brandy on the patio. I'm looking forward to it."

Adrian's eyes brightened. I'm looking forward to sharing that large queen-sized bed with you and whatever else you care to offer. That silky skin against his. Her sensuous red lips. He felt the heat rising. "I'll ask for the bill." He waved at the waiter who was soon at their table.

Sabrina watched him return the credit card to his wallet and stand waiting for her. She wobbled to her feet. "I can't wait. Let's drive fast."

One hand on the wheel, Adrian used his free hand to trace a pattern down her arm, past the fingers and along her thigh to the knee.

She caught his hand and held it there. "That's nice. I've missed you. I want us to spend the whole day together tomorrow."

"Ummm. We'll see. Right now, I just want to keep the car on the road." Reluctantly, he pulled back his hand, but smiled at her, his eyes playful. He pulled his breath in sharply when he felt her hand explore his inner thigh.

"Thank you. That feels wonderful, honey. We're almost home so I'd better drive slowly from here."

Sabrina threw her head back in a deep laugh. "I knew that I could get your attention. Wait until I undress you."

Adrian pulled into her driveway, walked around to open her door and they headed into her house with his arm around her. Whatever he had wanted to say would wait. Kicking off their shoes in the hallway, they fondled each other on the way up the stairs into her bedroom where they fell on the bed.

Pushing him onto his back, Sabrina began to unbutton his shirt running her hands over his hard stomach. "You've been working out in Portland. That's one benefit of hotel living."

Adrian sat up and nestled her against his chest, kissing her curls and each cheek. "There's no one to play with on the road." His lips covered hers, moving slowly, his tongue gently touching hers. He moved away long enough to open the back of her dress. She stood and helped him remove it, then pulled down the zipper of his pants.

Back in bed, they made love gently and slowly, with all the lights on to enhance the sensation. When they were spent, he nestled her back against him, enjoying her musky scent as sleep engulfed him.

Chapter Twenty-Two

Celeste

As she yanked the car door open and got in, Celeste reminded herself to drive slowly. Tourists flooded the streets in town this time of year and she didn't want to hit anyone. Her shoulders and neck felt tense from tossing and turning last night. She could only think about Marjorie in that large house alone. What was usually a fifteen-minute trip seemed to take forever. Finally, she pulled into the buff flagstone driveway, parked, and hurried to the front door. The sound of the doorbell echoed through the front hall while she pushed the button. She waited. Nothing. Celeste turned to go; convinced Marjorie had already left for the hospital. The heavy door groaned as it moved inside, and she swiveled her head back just in time to see Marjorie standing there. How pale her complexion looked, face drawn into a sad frown, her brown hair tangled and uncombed. She looked so different from the friend she knew.

"Thank goodness I caught you." Celeste followed Marjorie into the house, along the hall and into the living room. "Sorry I forgot to phone first, but I'm here to drive you to the hospital when you're ready to go."

"I didn't fall asleep until four this morning. I'm just so worried about Dennis."

Celeste looked around at the magazines on the floor. Dirty cups and plates sat on the coffee table beside a pile of newspapers, still folded. "Tell me what's happening with Dennis. What does his doctor say about his condition?"

"He called an hour ago to tell me they've scheduled Dennis for a bypass operation next week. They want to do some more tests before they proceed. Apparently, he didn't have a good night." She hesitated. "I'm worried."

Marjorie's shaking shoulders and loud sobs caused Celeste to rush over and put both arms around her. "Dennis was doing so well. His depression seemed to lighten with his weekly sailing trips, and he enjoyed working with the town. Now this."

"I bet you haven't eaten. Let's sit at your kitchen table and I'll make you some tea and toast."

Marjorie rose and followed slowly behind Celeste. "Okay. But no toast. I'll have two chocolate croissants with my tea. That will make me feel better."

After she busied herself with the cups and saucers, Celeste piled all the dirty dishes from the sink into the dishwasher. Settled at the table with their tea, she noted with relief Marjorie seemed calmer.

"Dennis has been my friend and companion for so long, through so much. We married young and he struggled to build a career with the bank while I raised the two kids. Then with his promotion to the executive, there came the long work hours and the stress of a large staff group. I thought when he retired, it would be easier."

"Where are the children now? Wouldn't they be a help?"

"I've called Simon and Janet, but both have their own families to consider. Besides, they live in Vancouver. Right now, they're waiting to hear what the doctor says before they come."

They sat in comfortable silence for a while. "When do you want to go to the hospital?"

"That's why I told you to call first. When I talked to the doctor he said to stay at home for now and rest. The nurses finally got Dennis to sleep and don't want him disturbed right now. They'll call me if there is any change. I'm going to try to get a few more hours of sleep myself.

"Would you like me to come back later?"

"No. I'll drive to the hospital this afternoon. It's best that I have the car there so I can stay late. Thanks for thinking of me." Marjorie drank the last of her tea. "By the way, when do you start your new job?"

"Not for another month, but I'm working on several project plans to send to them. That's what I'll be spending my time on today when I get back. My previous job at UHN has made this easy for me."

"I'm glad that you've got a job to look forward to." Marjorie pushed herself up from the table and followed Celeste to the door.

Celeste pulled Marjorie into her arms for a hug. "You take care of yourself. Let me know if there is anything I can do. I feel helpless."

For the first time today, she saw a smile flit across Marjorie's face. "I know that I can count on you. Let's just pray Dennis gets better."

* * *

Working on her project proposals, Celeste was once more immersed in her former hospital life. How thrilled she had been back then when her supervisor, Anne Westbury, called her into the office to tell Celeste about her promotion to Nurse Manager for two nursing units of thirty staff each. By the end of the year, she improved the morale and through working with the two team leads had implemented totally new processes which had supported the nurses in their new focus on patient care.

That was what she needed to do here. But she didn't know the staff. Even during her brief time in hospital, she noted how demotivated many of them were. Their attitudes would make things more difficult. Halfway through the plan, she jumped when the phone beside her rang. She recognized Marjorie's number. Maybe she had some news.

"Hello," Celeste said.

"I'm glad I caught you at home. I just came back from the hospital and a meeting with Dennis's surgeon. He told us the tests show extensive damage to arteries. The operation is his only chance. They've moved his surgery up to next Monday morning and want him to stay in hospital until he's fully recovered from it."

Based on what Dennis had told Celeste, she wasn't surprised at this news, however, her spirits dropped. Bypass surgery was still a major operation and Dennis was no longer young.

The phone went silent. Then she heard Marjorie's solemn voice. "Sometimes, any action the doctors suggest is good. Recuperation will be slow, but once he's over rehab he can go back to everything he did before."

Celeste knew Marjorie's anxiety was based on her fear of losing Dennis. "What about you? You need to take care of yourself while you're waiting for him to come home."

Marjorie sighed. "You're right. I could use some company. Why don't we go to the Oban Inn for lunch? It'll cheer me up."

"I'll pick you up in an hour." It was so like Marjorie to pick a restaurant that Adrian hadn't liked. So thoughtful.

"I can meet you there." Marjorie's voice had become calmer.

Celeste gripped the phone. "No. You'll be doing enough driving up to Hamilton and back every day. I'll drive you to the hospital on the morning of the operation. I don't want you driving when you're feeling anxious."

"Okay. You're probably right. I'll be changed and ready to go when you get here."

On the drive over to Marjorie's house, Celeste gazed at the lush green hedges, and rows of beautiful red and pink roses in full bloom in the yards of the houses on Queen Street. With the sunroof open, she breathed in the fresh air. How wonderful it must be to live this close to the lake. She hadn't felt this alive for an awfully long time.

Over lunch, Marjorie seemed tired and lethargic. "Dennis has been my main support for the past forty years. How will I live without him?"

Celeste shook her head. "Don't even think that way. He can survive this operation. Many people have and are now living a pretty normal life."

"I hear you." Marjorie breathed in deeply. "But I've never seen him look so unwell. He can barely raise his arm to pick up anything. Mostly, he just wants to sleep."

"Maybe Ian could cheer him up. Have you kept him up-to-date?"

"Yes, Ian has visited him, and it did help for a while. Adrian called me to express his concern and said he planned to visit this week. He heard about it at the club."

"I'm glad. Dennis needs their support."

Celeste noticed Marjorie had set her fork back on the table with only a few bites taken. "That's a great Sunshine Salad. The peaches and almond slices look fresh. Don't you like it?"

Marjorie sipped her glass of Riesling. Picking up her fork, she managed to eat a couple of mouthfuls. "I'm trying, but my appetite is gone."

"My salad with avocados and shrimp is delicious. I'll finish it in no time if you'd like to go."

Marjorie shook her head and ate a little more. "I'm enjoying the sunroom full of people. They do their best at the hospital, but everything is so sterile looking, and the rooms are small. Sitting in that hard chair right beside the bed while Dennis sleeps is difficult."

"You've just spent too much time there lately. At least they have a visitor's room with TV on his floor, so you could have a break while he sleeps. Do you want me to drive you tomorrow?"

"No. You've your own work to do. It's important to me you succeed with this new job. It will make me feel good." They sat in silence. "I'll let you drive me on Monday morning when he has the operation. I'll be too nervous, and we have to leave incredibly early."

Celeste put her hand over Marjorie's. "Sure. How about I pick you up at six?"

"That's good. He must be in the operating room by eight. I want to hold his hand before he goes in."

Celeste swallowed hard. So much worry for her friend. She'd hate to see Adrian go through this even though they were separated. He was still her husband.

Chapter Twenty-Three

Adrian

Adrian wandered onto his balcony carrying a glass of scotch and slumped into a chair. He couldn't believe what he had just heard. Right now, Dennis lay in a hospital bed recuperating from a heart attack. The manager said the ambulance raced in to pick him up while he was still laying right on the floor of the club house. He hadn't seen very much of Dennis since the break-up. His friend became more and more uneasy with Adrian since he and Marjorie were supporting Celeste. The six of them enjoyed a great summer together, but now everything was falling apart.

He rested his face in both hands for a few minutes. They were all getting older. Some mornings, he felt so stiff he found the walk to the bathroom onerous. But he'd never really been ill. Working in hospitals, he'd taken the advice of professionals. Preventative health care was the best investment. For the past ten years, he'd made an annual physical exam a priority. On the other hand, he'd noticed Celeste, even during their early marriage, was subject to occasional depressions she tried to ignore. These episodes worsened when she faced downsizing at her hospital.

With Sabrina, her energy level was high, and she enjoyed life—but maybe too much. Heavy drinking was the other area their age group worried about. He'd laughed about Ian's pessimistic attitude to life in the past. However, maybe there was more to it. Adrian avoided asking Sabrina anything about her husband's health.

He pulled his cell phone out of his pocket. Then dialed Marjorie's number. At the sound of her voice, he immediately responded.

"Marjorie, this is Adrian. I just heard about Dennis and wanted to let you know I'm concerned about him. How's he doing?"

"Thanks for asking." Marjorie sighed. "He's still pretty weak. They'll keep him in hospital until after the operation and rehab. His bypass surgery is scheduled for next Monday."

"I'd like to stop in to see him but wanted to know if he's allowed visitors."

"Yes. He's on the surgery floor right now so it's okay. After the operation, he'll be in intensive care for at least four or five days." Marjorie sighed again, even more deeply. "I miss him so much at home. The house feels so empty. I hate eating alone."

Adrian closed his eyes. He knew those feelings. "I'll go to see him tonight then. Will you be there? If so, we can talk more before I leave."

"I'll be there after seven. The nurses insist I have a break between visits. See you then."

Adrian gulped down the rest of his drink and returned to the kitchen. He'd have time to make a grilled cheese sandwich and green salad before he left for the hospital.

The QEW was busy as usual. It was one of those highways which never seemed to sleep. He paid special attention to his driving knowing anxiety could cause accidents. Within an hour, he turned onto the Burlington Street exit, travelled through the old industrial area with closed steel factories and entered downtown Hamilton. What a distance for Marjorie to drive, sometimes twice a day. No wonder she sounded tired. Maybe Celeste was helping her out. He didn't want to ask.

Standing in the doorway of Dennis's hospital room, Adrian took in the pale, tired figure lying in the narrow bed. He now knew what a heart attack could do to a man. He walked up to the side of the bed. Dennis turned his head and Adrian saw a quick welcome in his eyes.

"Adrian, this is a surprise. Have a seat. Marjorie isn't here yet."

The hand that gestured toward the chair trembled. This was worse than he expected. With a pang, Adrian realized how much he'd missed Dennis's friendship.

"I hear you've been having a bad time of it. Sailing takes more energy from us old guys than we have to give right now. We're all getting older."

Dennis gave a grimace and attempted to smile. "You look rather good to me. I guess I'm the one getting older and just didn't want to accept it. But I have no choice now."

Adrian patted Dennis on the arm. "They can do wonders for heart problems now. With a good doctor, you'll get through this okay. Don't worry."

Dennis turned his head to the side and fell into a deep silence for several minutes. Facing Adrian again, he confided. "I haven't told Marjorie yet, but they're only giving me a 50/50 chance of surviving this. One artery is eighty percent blocked."

Dropping his head, Adrian rubbed Dennis's hand. "Let me know if there's anything I can do. You'll want to be rested for the operation."

"Just keep an eye on Marjorie for me. She tries to hide it, but I know the stress is getting to her." He closed his eyes. "I'm going to try a brief nap before she gets here. Thanks for coming to see me. I appreciate it."

After watching until Dennis's breath slowed, Adrian walked into the hall. He'd wait in the visitor's room until Marjorie arrived so he could have a chance to talk to her. Dennis's deteriorated condition had unnerved him. He thumbed through a magazine while he waited but found he couldn't concentrate. Relief flooded through him when Marjorie dragged herself into the room and fell into a chair. She gave him a tired smile.

"Traffic was worse than usual in Hamilton and it's usually pretty bad. We need to have a good hospital in Niagara with a cardiac program."

Glad for the chance to do something, Adrian went to stand by her chair. "Have you been in to see Dennis yet?"

"I tried, but he's asleep. I don't like to wake him since he doesn't sleep well at night."

"Yeah. I know. He was dozing off when I left him, but we did get to talk for a few minutes. He's worried about you."

Marjorie pulled herself upright in her chair. "I'll be fine. The drive takes its toll, but I'd only fret if I didn't see him every day. Sometimes, Celeste brings me to provide a break."

Adrian dropped into the chair beside her. How dedicated the two partners were to each other. He could tell it would be a great loss to Marjorie if she lost Dennis. He knew they'd been married for close to forty years, but they were still so committed to each other. Adrian gave a deep sigh. That level of commitment was not something he'd ever given to any woman. Not even Celeste. Maybe they should have tried harder to make a go of their marriage. He'd call her when he got home tonight. Find out if they could at least start again as friends?

Marjorie stood and smoothed her skirt. "I'm going in to see him now. I'll probably be here until late. He'll have the surgery on Monday morning. I'll call you as soon as I know something."

"Okay. Remember, if there's anything I can do, let me know. I promised Dennis I'd look after you until he's well." He smiled and followed her out of the room, continuing down the hall to the parking lot. He didn't want to tell her what Dennis said about his chances.

By the time he was back in his living room, it was ten. He'd call Celeste tomorrow. Marjorie said Celeste hadn't started her new job yet, so she'd probably be at home. When he awoke, it was dark, and he'd fallen asleep on the sofa again. As he headed into the bedroom, he noticed that the red light on his answering machine was blinking. No doubt it was Sabrina, but he didn't want to talk to her right now.

*   *   *

His thoughts kept drifting back to their first year in this town. He'd especially loved the Sunday afternoon picnics they'd started that summer, above the power boat clubhouse along The Parkway. His mind brought back an image of Celeste dozing on a blanket in the long silvery green grass and he wondered what had changed them. He'd imagined he knew everything about his wife but stared at this new person who had become a mystery to him. How could he figure her out? What clues was she leaving him? Back when he proposed to a young energetic nurse who laughed easily and often, he couldn't have even considered ending up like they had.

Now he often saw a deep frown cross her face before she erupted into a sudden burst of anger. He felt the pain. Partly, it was his fault. His lack of attention. He'd lost her somewhere and didn't know the route back.

His cloud of depression gradually lifted as Adrian sat on the balcony as he sipped his coffee and savoured a fresh bagel covered with cream cheese. He'd checked the message this morning and, as expected, it was Sabrina wanting to know if he was free for dinner tonight. He didn't respond, leaving her to think he was still in Portland.

After filling the dishwasher, Adrian dropped into his favourite armchair and picked up the phone. Celeste had agreed he could take the den furniture. He was surprised when she answered on the first ring.

"Celeste, it's Adrian. Don't hang up. I just want to talk to you for a few minutes."

After a moments silence, she responded. "I'm really busy today. What did you want?"

"I need to know how you are. I worry about you alone in our old house. I know that you sometimes get depressed and I can't forget about you being in hospital."

"I'm fine now, no thanks to you. In fact, I'll be starting a job with the same hospital in St. Catharines at the beginning of next month."

He paused. "Celeste, can't we try to be friends? I know I hurt you, but we did have twenty-five years together."

Her response was still cold. "I thought you'd forgotten all about our marriage."

Adrian took a deep breath. "It's hard to talk about this over the phone. Couldn't we just go out for dinner one night? I know you always liked the restaurant at Peller's Estate Winery. How about it?"

There was a long silence. "Adrian, I'm sure you know just how sick Dennis is. I'm helping Marjorie as best I can right now and don't have much extra time. Maybe after he's well again I could reconsider your offer. But not now."

He gripped the phone with relief. "That sounds rather good to me. You pick the restaurant and give me a call when you're ready. In the meantime, I'm spending lots of time in Portland working."

"Okay. I've got to go now. Thanks for calling to see how I am."

Adrian still held the phone after he heard her hang up. Surprised, he watched his hand trembling. It was so good to hear her voice. He wondered why he hadn't appreciated Celeste before all this happened?

Chapter Twenty-Four

Celeste

Loud music blared from her radio and pulled Celeste out of a deep sleep. She and Marjorie had talked late into the night. She was surprised to see how fearful Marjorie was about Dennis's operation. Celeste glanced at the clock and realized she'd have to get up. She promised to pick Marjorie up at six, so they'd be at the hospital with plenty of time. Of course, she'd want to visit with Dennis before he went into surgery this morning at eight.

When she arrived at Marjorie's house, her friend was already outside standing on the front step with a small tote bag in hand. Before Celeste could even get out of the car, Marjorie ran to it and opened the passenger door.

"I just have this awful feeling, Celeste. The sooner we get there, the better I'll know what to expect."

"Take it easy. The hospital staff will take good care of Dennis." She smiled to reassure her friend. "But you're right. He'll be eager to see you. After all, you're the most important person in his life."

Marjorie relaxed as she settled back into the seat. "I'll just feel better being there. Seeing him again."

"Well, you have a rest now. I'll do the driving and we both know the route pretty well by now."

Celeste looked over at Marjorie a few minutes later and was relieved to find her sleeping.

As she pulled into the hospital parking lot, she was happy to see lots of empty spaces. It paid to arrive early since many operations were scheduled on Mondays. Marjorie was awake and seemed to be calmer.

Celeste touched her arm. "We're here in good time. Let's go straight to his room."

After she closed her own door, Celeste moved around to assist Marjorie with the passenger door, but she was already out and standing on the concrete. "Okay. I know how anxious you are so let's go to his room right now."

They found Dennis in the hallway outside his room. He lay on a stretcher with a blue cap on his head, but he was awake. Celeste noted he was attached to a cardiac monitor with his intravenous line already inserted.

The nurse who just finished taking his blood pressure smiled at them. "Mrs. Mercer, you can have some time with him before we put him to sleep. I'll be back." Just before she left, the intravenous pump began to beep loudly, and she stopped to make an adjustment.

Celeste followed Marjorie to his side. "Hi, Dennis. You're looking bright for this early in the morning."

He smiled. "Thanks. Let's just hope you can say the same later."

"I'll leave the two of you alone. Marjorie, you'll find me in the visitors' room if you need me."

She walked into the dreary room, let out a deep breath and pushed the pile of magazines off the chair. Dennis looked so white and drained lying on the gurney. This surgery had to work. How would Marjorie cope if it didn't? As a nurse, she was realistic enough to know the large risks involved. She slumped into the chair and picked up a Time magazine. The time dragged past and when she next looked at the door, a nurse was beckoning to her.

"Your friend has gone to the waiting room outside the surgical recovery area. Would you like to join her? You can follow me."

Wordlessly, Celeste trailed behind the nurse through several hallways. Marjorie sat in a rigid grey vinyl chair; her hands clasped. Celeste dropped into the chair next to her friend and put her hand over Marjorie's squeezing it. "Are you okay?"

"He looked so fragile. My strong man brought down to this." She bowed her head, her face strained.

Celeste put her arms around Marjorie. "They'll do the best they can for him. These doctors are experts, and they do this operation several times every week."

Marjorie rested her face in her hands. "I'll try to relax. It's just so hard."

Two hours later, having received no word from any staff, the two of them paced up and down the hall outside the recovery room. A woman dressed in a volunteer's uniform did her best to reassure them regarding the patient's progress. Marjorie began pacing the floor of the small hallway outside the waiting area while she stared at the swinging doors of the operating room. The volunteer tried to reassure her. "Please have a seat, Mrs. Mercer. I promise to let you know as soon as one of them comes out."

A short while later, the doors did open, and a young man in blue scrubs and red plaid head gear walked directly to her. "Mrs. Mercer, please come and sit down." As he motioned her to a group of chairs in an alcove outside the main waiting room, his face was grave. Celeste followed and stood by Marjorie's chair. He sat next to Marjorie and took her hands into his.

"He didn't make it." He paused at her outcry. "I'm so sorry. So many things can happen with open heart surgery. When we went to restart his heart, without the electrical system, it wouldn't restart. His heart disease must have started a long time back."

Celeste stood rigid with shock while Marjorie collapsed, her head falling almost into her lap. "No. I don't believe you. It's not possible." The agony in her voice trailed off to a subdued tone. "He was supposed to get well. He's worked so hard. He doesn't deserve this." Her body twisted in agony as the tears came.

The doctor nodded to the nurse at the doorway and took his leave.

The nurse entered and attempted to calm Marjorie. The sobbing had stopped but her whole body continued to shudder. "I can't go on without him."

Celeste took the chair next to Marjorie and put both arms around her. "Cry as long as you want to. It'll make you feel better." She continued to hold her friend. The nurse excused herself, to return shortly with a warm blanket and some hot tea.

"Can I call the Chaplain for you? She is a great help to family members who suffer a great loss." When there was no response from the two women, she left a card on the table.

After a long while, the shaking stopped. She pulled back. "Thanks, Celeste. For being with me." The muscles in her face were tight, her eyes glazed. "I want to see him. Even if it's the last time. You need to get them to take me to him?"

"The Chaplain can help you with this. I'll call her now."

Celeste forced herself to think back to her nursing days. Dennis's body would be taken directly from the OR to the hospital morgue. The nurses would then prepare the body for the Coroner.

She didn't want to take Marjorie down there. She'd have to ask the chaplain for help in what to do next. "Wait here. I'll be right back."

The Head Nurse recognized her right away from her visits and asked if she could help. When Celeste explained what Marjorie wanted, the nurse said the body would still have the iv and endotracheal tube in place. She advised, "the nursing supervisor would go with her if Marjorie still wanted to go into the OR recovery room. We'd keep it brief. However, it might be better if she waited to see him in the morgue. Has she said what funeral home she prefers?"

"I'll ask her about which funeral home. She needs closure. Maybe saying a last goodbye to her husband is what will work." Celeste nodded her head. "Of course, I'll go along with her. 'll also take her back home afterwards, so she's not left alone."

As Celeste stood outside the morgue, waiting for Marjorie to return, she began to feel a deep chill roll over her. Dennis was gone. What if it had been Adrian? Would she care? A sharp pain hit her in the gut. She admitted her feelings for Adrian hadn't totally died. They were married a long time and shared so much including raising her daughter. The relationship was over for her, but she probably needed closure too. Maybe she would see him again just to say goodbye.

*   *   *

When Marjorie returned to the hall, she was calmer, more subdued but listless. "I remember now he said the Clarkson Funeral Home. He liked it when he went with a friend from the golf club."

Celeste took her by the arm and led her to the car. Marjorie passively followed. Once seated, she laid her head against the soft leather and closed her eyes.

Celeste got into the driver's side and turned on the car. "Make yourself comfortable, Marjorie. It would be good for you to sleep for a while. It's a long drive and we can talk when we get to your place."

Celeste took her silence for consent, put the car into gear and drove out of the lot and onto the busy street. With the emphasis now on helping her friend, she almost forgot her own depression. As bad as it was, separation wasn't nearly as final as death. Even for her, it was hard to wrap her head around the fact she wouldn't see Dennis alive again. Surprised, Celeste found herself super alert on the drive home. Almost as if she would never sleep. Perhaps it was just the experience of death so close. Even during her work in the hospital, although she witnessed many deaths, she didn't think about it as something which related to her. However, the six of them were now entering into that final phase. She hesitated. There were only five of them now. Sure, she could live another twenty years or maybe even more. But, when you are young, the thought of dying seems so out there in the distant horizon. She'd always thought, it couldn't happen to me. She knew now, it could.

As she entered Marjorie's driveway, this morning seemed so far away. She felt the first pangs of hunger and realized that neither of them had eaten since their quick breakfast. She helped her friend out of the car, fumbled for the keys, and pushed open the door so they could enter.

"I'm starving, Marjorie." Celeste led her to the sofa and watched her fall into the seat. "Let me heat up some of your soup and I'll make us some sandwiches. Would you like that?"

"Thanks. I don't have any appetite, but you go ahead. I don't want to be letting you go hungry in my home." Marjorie pushed herself to her feet. "I'll just get changed into something comfortable. Maybe my old pants and a summer sweater. Then I'll join you." She moved in slow motion toward the stairs. "I may not eat but I do feel up to a talk."

"Okay. I'll have everything ready when you get back." Celeste watched with concern as Marjorie gently pulled herself up the stairs. Time stretched while she waited for her friend to return. With the soup on the burner, she placed dishes and cutlery on a tray. It was after six and the cool air on the patio would be good for them both. She opened the fridge for a full bottle of chardonnay and took two glasses off the shelf to set up outside.

Settled in the garden with their wine and a hot bowl of soup, Marjorie seemed to come back to life. "I've called Simon and Janet to tell them the bad news about their Dad. They were shocked. Of course, they'll both come to be with me. Simon will arrive tomorrow sometime and Janet the next morning. They want to help me plan the funeral. I guess we'll plan to have it on Friday. No point in waiting." She gave a deep sigh.

Celeste let out a deep breath. "I'm glad you'll have their help with the details. Did Dennis say what he wanted?"

"Oh, yes. He wanted to have a small funeral here in Niagara-on-the-Lake. His body is to be cremated." Marjorie hesitated. "I'm not sure that I agree with him on that one." They sat in silence.

"It would be nice to have a real body to visit. But, either way, I can't talk to him anymore. That's what I'll miss the most."

"Well, you have me. Anytime you feel lonely, call. I'll come over or you come to me."

Marjorie smiled for the first time that day. "I'll remember that. You're so good to me, Celeste. I'm glad I have friends here in town."

"Okay. I'm going to get our sandwiches now and I want you to try to eat some of it—even if it seems like a lot." She took the empty soup bowls and headed toward the kitchen.

When she returned, Marjorie was gazing out over her garden and seemed at peace. "I guess I can expect both good times and dark days. Right now, I'm happy to be home in my own garden. Even if it is alone." She wiped away a tear. "Spending your life in a hospital room or nursing home isn't pleasant. At least he's spared from living that way."

They ate silently while Celeste kept both their glasses full. Later, over coffee, Marjorie talked about the struggles Dennis went through to adjust to retirement. He'd been forced out of the bank by the Board who sought to recruit a new vibrant generation of leaders. This new group although faster, made more mistakes than older crowd.

For the first time, Celeste confided to Marjorie how devastated she had been when told she was no longer needed in her job. You could be a super star one day and then phased out a few months later in this new economy. After she finished off the last of the bottle of wine, Celeste cleaned up and sent Marjorie back up to her room for a rest. Marjorie had given her a key in case she lost her own. Soon after, she locked the door, got into her car, and headed for home still immersed in the past.

Adrian had just become incredibly quiet after he announced he was leaving his job at the hospital. He pretended to the world the displacement didn't matter. He'd do just as well as a consultant and could find his own work. But Celeste knew it shook him. He'd worked long and hard to get onto the senior team and would have felt betrayed. Why was he so closed with his feelings? Maybe this breakup could have been avoided if he'd confided in her what his restlessness was about. She sighed. It was all much too late now.

Chapter Twenty-Five

Celeste

Nervousness washed over Celeste, as she sorted through the dresses in her closet. What to wear for this dinner? She wanted to look sophisticated but not sexy. It wouldn't be good for Adrian to get the wrong message. When she phoned him about Dennis, he'd brought up the question about them going out to dinner and suggested Friday. She agreed if they went to somewhere in Niagara Falls where they were unlikely to see anyone they knew. She still couldn't bear having her friends see them together after what happened.

Gritting her teeth, she pulled a pink sundress with small white polka dots out of the closet and zipped it open. Checking herself out in the mirror, she noted that it complimented her silvery grey hair. A touch of rose lipstick would bring some colour to her pale face. This would have to do. She noted the skirt fell just below her knees showing off her tanned legs. They'd agreed to meet at the restaurant, so she got into her car allowing lots of time in case the traffic was heavy.

As she stood inside the front entrance of Casa Mia, waiting for the host to return from seating another couple, a feeling of loneliness and vulnerability hit her. He'd been dismissive when she stated she was waiting for someone. Celeste hadn't felt this way since years ago when she was single and dating. There was no sign of Adrian, although he was usually precise about time. While standing there, she gazed at the expanse of white linen tablecloths and crystal glasses. Adrian had always been good at choosing romantic places when he wanted to be persuasive.

While waiting, she stood by the window where she could watch the parking lot. She stared for several minutes at a man of medium build with a handsome dark head of hair coming up the pathway. Her interest was aroused. It wasn't until he reached the front door, with his deep blue eyes looking straight at her through the glass, that she recognized her ex-husband.

Adrian joined her. "I'm sorry to keep you waiting. The traffic from the airport was hell."

Celeste felt heat creep up her neck into her cheeks. "That's okay. I just got here myself." She stood there at a loss for words. This felt so strange.

The tension was relieved by the host who gave her a smile. "This must be your friend." At her nod, he continued. "Allow me to take you to a seat near the piano."

Once seated, the silence dragged. The waiter discreetly set menu's in front of them and took their drink orders. While they waited, Celeste noticed Adrian looked as stressed as she felt. He looked grateful when she smiled. "I'm glad you suggested dinner here. I know that you must be as shocked to hear about Dennis as I was."

With a deep sigh, Adrian sat back in his chair. "When I saw him at the hospital the other day, he didn't look good. But I thought he'd pull through. I couldn't get him off my mind all night. It wasn't just Dennis. Some of it was selfishness. I realized I was worried about how long I'd have."

She nodded. "I know. I felt the same way. I've put that thought aside. I need to concentrate on helping Marjorie with her grief."

"You realize it could on for six months to a year."

"Yes. I'm prepared for the time commitment. Marjorie helped me when I needed it and she's my closest friend."

Adrian drained his scotch surprised her by and ordered the tortellini pasta special for both of them.

"What else have you been up to since we last talked?"

Celeste smiled. He seemed to be genuinely interested. "Well, I've been asked to take on some projects for the Queenston Street hospital site in St. Catharines. It fits well with what I did before at UHN. I'm looking forward to teaching the first workshop in two weeks."

He put his hand over hers. "That's great, Celeste. I'm happy for you."

She pulled her hand away and sat back. "Thanks. I'm extremely excited about it. Even with the weird way it came about. When I was in hospital, I mean."

He bowed his head. "I'm so sorry, Celeste about what happened. I didn't really think through the consequences."

The tension was broken when their waiter arrived with the meals.

Celeste let out her breath. "Let's talk about you. How'd your work go in Portland?" She watched his face relax as he regained composure. While he continued, she picked at her food.

"The management team is finally pulling together. We're at the phase where they need to interview and hire the staff who will remain with the hospital so I can see the end in sight."

"What will you do after the project is over?"

Adrian appeared surprised at her interest. "I'm talking to several other potential clients, mainly in the U.S. so I don't know where I'll be working next. New York State might be nice for a change. Maybe even Buffalo."

He signed the credit card slip and handed the bill back. He waited until the waiter was several feet away before he turned back to Celeste. "I miss you. I think about you all the time when I'm out there in Portland. Could we maybe try again?"

She could feel the tears stinging the sides of her eyes. Why now? "Look, Adrian, my main job right now is to support Marjorie through her loss. This isn't a good time to talk about us. I've struggled, but now I'm learning to like life as a single person again. In fact, in many ways, I'm enjoying it."

"I know right now isn't the time. But will you think about at least having another dinner out. We could meet again at Casa Mia in a couple of weeks. That's all I'm asking."

This was new to her. Adrian, asking for her forgiveness. The pleading looks in his eyes appeared to be genuine. How could she say no?

She took a deep breath. "I still need more time to think about us. Can you call me in two weeks, and I'll let you know how I feel then?"

I smile brightened Adrian's face. "I'll do it. I'll call. You take care of Marjorie and let her know I'll be in touch. I now know the importance of being there for your friends."

He followed her out to her car and opened the door for her. She slid into the driver's seat and waved to him while she pulled into the street.

She didn't know what she should make of this new Adrian. He appeared genuine and contrite; however, the Adrian she knew was a master of manipulation. There was no doubt he wanted to continue dining out with her, but that didn't mean commitment. She was flattered but cautious. The pain from the break-up was still much too fresh for her. She'd take her time and keep some distance so as not to fall into any of his traps.

*   *   *

Driving up the narrow-broken pavement into the main section of the quaint small town, Celeste turned to check out her friend.

Marjorie's head drooped towards her lap, her mouth partly open, eyes closed, a soft snore just audible.

Celeste sighed. Thank goodness she'd finally slept. This escape weekend might be just what Marjorie needed. At least for this weekend, she wouldn't be reminded about the empty bed, the breakfast for one and the silence.

It had been a month since Dennis's funeral but in her mind, Celeste could still hear her friend's scream of agony when the young man in scrubs and red headgear came out of the operating room towards her, shaking his head and said those words, "I'm sorry Mrs. Mercer." She knew instantly, there would be no long period of recuperation for Dennis.

Celeste brushed back her streaked grey hair. She'd talked to her tennis group about how to help her friend. The usual cruise stories came up, but Marjorie would hate the crowds of people right now. A week of sun and sand surrounded by young couples and excited children would just make her lonely for her own son and daughter, already back on the West coast. One of the quiet ones, usually the last to speak up said, "I know what would work for me. The Glen Eden on Lake Simcoe offers wellness weekends. They promise pampering you haven't dreamed of yet."

Marjorie was the type to cater to her friends, oblivious of her own needs. Now she couldn't even care for herself. Maybe this would work for her. When she arrived at the house that morning, Celeste had coaxed until Marjorie dressed for lunch while she made some soup. When she returned, Celeste had laid a brochure at Marjorie's plate beside the bowl of clam chowder.

Marjorie seated herself. "Good for you, Celeste. You deserve to get away. You shouldn't spend all your time looking after me."

Celeste shook her head. "It's for both of us. I wouldn't relax knowing you were alone here."

*　　*　　*

The sprawling manor house with its deep green shutters they'd seen in the brochure rose ahead, at the dead end of the road. Solid oak double doors where softened by woven grass baskets on each side, stuffed with red and pink begonias. She pulled into the car park which overlooked the rushing water from the old dam, sat back and relaxed for the first time that day.

In the lobby, a young man in a soft green uniform took their bags and waited until the desk clerk secured their reservation and the key was in Celeste's hand.

"Follow me. You're on the main floor with a lake view. Our Program Director will take you up to see the facilities when you've had time to refresh. Just ring the front desk."

As soon as the door closed, Marjorie lay down on the bed and closed her eyes.

Still determined to cheer her up, Celeste said. "How about a spa treatment after we change, or should I order a pot of tea?"

Marjorie sighed and sat up. "I'd like to sit somewhere outdoors. We can enjoy the last of the sunlight. Maybe tea on the veranda would be nice."

Celeste relaxed. "I'm going to change into fresh pants and shirt. Then I'll find out if they'll serve us refreshments out there."

The two of them were barely seated in the white wicker chairs, when the waitress arrived and set a tray with blue and white teapot, cup and saucer, cream, and sugar on the glass table.

"Shall I bring a full tea tray of dainties or would you prefer a plate of our sugar cookies?"

Marjorie forced a smile. "I'll have the cookies. I can always eat cookies."

"You can give me the same. I'll save my appetite for dinner."

Marjorie remained quiet and subdued over dinner that night, so Celeste let her be. Instead she watched the people at other tables, mostly mid-forty couples who appeared to be thrilled with their weekend breakaway. Some held hands across the table, others clinked glasses and most laughed with each other. She felt a pang of regret. Would she ever feel that excitement again? Pulled back by Marjorie's voice, she asked.

"What were you saying? I was listening in on the couple next to us."

Marjorie looked surprised. "So was I. The young man with the wavy brown hair reminds me of Dennis. When we first met at a charity event, I was attracted to his wonderful mop of hair." She blinked back a tear.

"Sounds like good memories for you." Celeste encouraged.

"Philanthropy was something he kept up through all his year in business. At University and later in business, he had to be at the top. Nothing else would satisfy him. He still remembered those who needed help or a hand up."

"You told me about his Citizen of the Year award. When did he get it?"

"When he was VP at Scotia MacLeod, they were encouraged to take on community activities. The year before he retired, he contributed the most funds to charities through recruiting staff to participate in fundraising golf tournaments."

"No wonder both Ian and Adrian wanted to golf with him. They'll never find a better partner."

"Well, he received special recognition through the Citizen of the Year Award from his firm for all the money he raised."

"What about Simon and Janet? Are either of them like their father?"

Marjorie contemplated. "Probably Janet. She's someone who can talk to anyone and genuinely find them interesting."

Celeste remembered the conversation she'd had with Janet at the funeral. She said he was the best father she could have ever asked for. She knew he had a terribly busy job with late hours but from the time she and Simon were small, he'd read a bedtime story to them almost every night. Unlike with her teenage friends, her family continued to take holidays together across Europe until she went away to college. Even then, with every phone call, he'd want to know what she was learning and who were the best professors. She never worried her parents would divorce like so many other families since they still seemed so in love.

Marjorie continued. "Simon's like me. I find working a room a chore and prepare in advance for what I'll talk about. However, he was close to his father. Dennis took him sailing regularly during his teen years. It helped build up Simon's confidence."

Celeste laughed. "You're so good at it. I've watched you in action with the hospital crowd."

A sigh escaped from Marjorie. "They were one of the hardest groups to prepare for. I don't really understand all that much about health issues. So, I talked about what I know. Mainly investments but they seemed fascinated."

"Because it's something they don't know. Doctors and nurses aren't generally good businesspeople."

Noticing Marjorie seemed livelier, Celeste signaled the waiter to bring another round of wine.

"As I mentioned before, Dennis struggled with retirement. Although he was sixty-five, he wanted to continue working. He was forced out through an internal restructuring."

"Sounds just like the hospital."

"His volunteer work with the town was so important to him. His eyes would sparkle when he came back from a meeting and told me about all the stuff going on behind the scenes."

"He'd have been great on a hospital board." Celeste squared her shoulders. "They need strong problem solvers like him."

After a long pause, Marjorie continued. "He felt able to contribute again and seemed to be thriving so what happened?"

Celeste waited until new drinks were served and took a long sip. "How much damage did the earlier heart attack do? Second heart attacks hit people harder."

Marjorie bowed her head. "He didn't really give me the details. At the time, I was so relieved when the doctor told me he would be okay, I didn't ask for more. Obviously, I should have."

"Celeste patted her hand. "You did everything you could. When I saw the two of you together, I knew you were a committed couple."

"Dennis hid a lot from me. He didn't like to talk about any weaknesses. I'd ask him about his doctor's appointments, and he'd assure me everything was going well. That is, until just before the recent attack, thanks to you."

"What did I do?"

"Something you said to him, made him tell me about his low energy and feelings of dizziness. I got him to the doctor right away, but it was too late. All they could do was change his medications and give him some cardio exercises."

"I'm sorry."

"It's okay. It feels good to talk about it. About him. He was such a good man and a good husband."

"You'll always have those memories."

As she looked around, Celeste noticed they were the last two people in the restaurant. "Shall we go up now, or would you like a nightcap at the small bar across from the reception area?"

"Let's go up." Marjorie rubbed her eyes. "I think I could sleep now."

Chapter Twenty-Six

Celeste

Thinking back, Marjorie had made it through the funeral in better shape than Celeste had expected. Thankfully, both kids were there to support her, and Simon had stayed on for the rest of the week. She noticed that Ian and Sabrina arrived and left together. Celeste managed to keep moving through the crowd and avoided speaking to either of them. She nodded at Adrian, but both had kept their distance. He'd arrived alone and went directly to speak with Marjorie who held on to his extended hand.

That visit was great for Marjorie, but Simon returned to Vancouver on the weekend. Today, Celeste was on her way to pick her up for lunch at the Riverbend Inn.

She stood shifting from one foot to the other while waiting for Marjorie to respond to the doorbell. When the door opened, her friend was dressed in her red and brown paisley dress with harvest gold sandals. She looked smart and her face was relaxed.

"I knew that you'd be on time, so I'm dressed and ready to go."

"Great. I thought you'd enjoy lunch in the lovely small dining room at Riverbend Inn. What do you think?"

"Well, that's as good as any. As I told you, I don't have much appetite right now, but it's good to get out of the house."

Celeste opened the car door for her and then returned to the driver's seat. "That's what I like to hear. At least once a week, you need to have an excuse for a good hot lunch. I don't want to watch you fading away."

The sound of Marjorie's chuckle made Celeste's day. "There's not much fear of that." She patted one sizeable hip.

When they reached their table, the windows looked out on a vineyard, stretching out before them. Celeste glanced around the intimate dining room and not seeing anyone she knew, she relaxed.

Over lunch, Celeste kept the conversation on Marjorie. "So, when do you have to go back to that high-pressure role with the Heart and Stroke Foundation?"

Marjorie thoughtfully chewed her salad. "I should be there right now. They have a major fundraising event planned for next month and, after all, it was heart disease that took Dennis. However, they made me promise to take a month off. Apparently, the doctor said something about needing to avoid stress."

Celeste leaned towards her friend. "That makes sense to me. Stress is one of the risk factors, as you know. When did you last see your family doctor?"

A brief smile drifted over Marjorie's face. "You don't need to worry about me. I have a regular annual check-up but it's not due until the fall."

Not ready to give up, Celeste continued. "These aren't normal circumstances. Don't let depression become a regular part of your life like I did. I'm so grateful that you talked me into seeing the social worker at the hospital."

"Well, you'd lived through quite a shock." Marjorie sighed. "Okay, I see what you mean. I'm not sleeping well and have no appetite so if that continues; I'll call her and book an appointment."

"Just don't put it off too long, is all I ask." Celeste frowned. "It gets harder and harder to make that call when you lose motivation." Celeste shivered thinking back to a time of deep shadows for her.

Marjorie nodded. "I'll keep that in mind. How's your new job going?"

"I start in two weeks and can't wait." Celeste smiled. "You know, it was easy writing up the project plan because I love working on quality assurance and patient safety. They're things I know about."

Marjorie's forehead wrinkled and her eyes looked like spears. "The hospital could have used some of your expertise before they let Dennis die."

Since she realized Marjorie had to let out some of her anger, Celeste didn't respond but inside she cringed. They both ate in silence while the waitress poured more coffee. She was pleased to see that Marjorie had eaten most of her chocolate truffle cake.

Celeste sat forward once more, "I'd like to get your advice on something personal, if you feel up to it."

Marjorie brightened. "Of course. What is it?"

"I went out to dinner with Adrian recently and was surprised to find he wants some kind of friendship with me."

"Hmm. Friendship is it? Well he can be very charming. The last time this happened, you said it was his guilt talking. Have things changed for him?"

"Yes. At least I think so. For one thing, we went out on a Friday night and for another, I got the sense that the fling with Sabrina is cooling."

"What makes you think so?"

"Well, from his conversation, he's spent more and more time in Portland this past month. He's also been researching several new projects in the U.S., on the East Coast. Believe me I know that those are avoidance techniques for Adrian."

Marjorie nodded. "You know him better than anyone. What does that mean for you? Could you forgive and forget, after what happened? Do you want him back?"

A deep sigh rose from the bottom of Celeste's chest and she sat back. "No. At least not right now. I've lost both trust and respect for him. I guess I'm flattered he wants to see me."

Marjorie looked thoughtful. "Why don't you try friendship out for a while and see how you feel then. It can't hurt if you know what you're doing. When it feels uncomfortable, it's the time to call it quits with him."

"Thanks for the advice. I can always trust your feedback. I must admit I still can't stand to see Sabrina without getting angry. I do my best to avoid her."

"I don't blame you. Adrian may have been less than an attentive husband, but it was Sabrina who pushed for the affair. However, both she and Ian came to the funeral and gave me their regards. I must give them credit for having the guts to do that. I can appreciate Ian was Dennis's friend. He seemed shocked to hear what happened."

"I've avoided Ian since the affair. I know that's probably not fair to him. I know he was just the messenger, but I can't face him without the conversation including something about Sabrina."

"From Ian's behavior at the funeral, the way he looked at her, I'd say he wants her back.

"She just uses him. Probably has for years." Marjorie scrunched up her nose. "From the time I first met them, I thought their marriage was a mismatch. They're both power seekers, but she's more self-centered."

They left the table and headed back to the parking lot. After she headed into Marjorie's driveway, Celeste turned to her.

"Let's continue doing this every Friday. When I start work, I'll just let them know that I'll be working at home one day a week."

Marjorie gave her a grateful smile. "Are you sure that you can afford the time?"

"Yes. I enjoy your company and value your advice."

"Time is what I have lots of right now." She pressed the fingertips of each hand along the sides of her forehead for a minute. "The other board members were right about me taking time off. Right now, I wouldn't be able to concentrate and I never know when I'll burst into tears."

Celeste gave her a hug before Marjorie got out of the car. "Don't forget to make that doctor's appointment. I'll see you next Friday around the same time. You pick the restaurant."

Chapter Twenty-Seven

Adrian

The flight back from Portland had been delayed by weather on Friday night, and most of the airport limousines pulled away before Adrian got in line. After a twenty-minute wait, he was able to flag one down and settled into the seat to relax. With the anxious questions from the team of managers at the hospital still circling in his mind, he found it hard to concentrate on the chitchat from the driver.

"It must be nice in Niagara-on-the-Lake in the summer. You're lucky to live there."

Adrian made a non-descript response. "Hmm. I enjoy it."

He was sure everyone said that to the guy. He pretended to be scrolling through his Blackberry although he had nothing scheduled for the weekend. Traffic on the QEW was awful. By the time the car pulled into the driveway of his condo, he was gritting his teeth. Grabbing the door handle, he jumped out and stood by the back of the car waiting for his suitcase. He forced a smile at the driver, pushed some cash into his hand and started up the walkway.

At his unit door, he fumbled for his keys, swung it open and hunched his shoulders, squeezing his eyes shut, at the loud sound of the phone. His suitcase fell over as he dropped it on the floor.

"Damn." He picked up the receiver. "Who is this?" Although he'd already guessed.

Sabrina breathed into the phone. "Don't you sound in a good mood? Did someone spill a drink on you in the plane?"

"Sorry to be so abrupt. Both the plane and the cab were both late and I just got in."

"On such a beautiful warm summer night, I thought you'd like me to pick you up for a light dinner on the terrace at Queen's Landing."

Adrian dropped onto the sofa, carrying the phone with him. "I wouldn't be good company tonight. We'd probably quarrel."

"Oh, come on, Adrian. We used to go out every Friday night. What's wrong with you? Ever since Dennis died, you've been different."

Adrian could feel the heat rise his chest and into his neck muscles. Why was Sabrina always pushing him? He pulled off his tie, but it didn't help. "Not tonight. I'm only tired and it has nothing to do with Dennis."

"Ian has been brooding ever since Dennis died. He feels guilty for taking Dennis sailing. Seems to think he caused the heart attack. Even though he didn't know Dennis wasn't well."

Adrian wasn't in the mood for Sabrina's chatter. "So, you and Ian are talking again. What's up with him these days?"

He could hear the smirk in Sabrina's voice. "Are you jealous?" When he didn't respond, she continued. "We run into each other around town all the time. Don't worry. He's still pretty angry at me for what happened." She paused. "I think it's more about my moving out than about you and me as a couple."

Why did Sabrina keep doing that? He'd never said they were a couple. His voice rose. "I keep telling you, I'm not ready to settle down with anyone. Right now, I have my condo and you have the townhouse. Sure, we enjoy going out together for dinner or a few drinks. Let's keep it that way."

Her voice was full of ice. "You make that quite clear, Adrian. You always need space—whatever that means. But you don't mind making love with the moonlight shining over the bed."

He heard his teeth grinding. "Give it a rest for tonight. I'm not up to it." He took some deep breaths, feeling his jaw clench. How could he satisfy her? "What about dinner at Vineland Estates tomorrow night? We can sit on the terrace so you can look out over the vineyards. You'll like the atmosphere there."

Sabrina softened. "That's more like it. I'll go to The Old Winery bar tonight by myself and listen to some jazz. Maybe there'll be some action there. What time tomorrow?"

"I've got tons of work to finish in the afternoon, so I'll pick you up at six. It'll take us at least forty minutes from here to get to the restaurant along the QEW."

After the phone went dead, Adrian wiped his forehand with one hand and went into the bedroom to change. He'd phone for one of those specialty thin crust pizzas from Stone Road Grill. That would be great with a glass of Merlot. He opened the bar fridge and pulled out a bottle.

He'd given up flicking through the channels for something to watch when the pizza arrived and after paying the young guy who delivered it, he strolled onto the deck to eat and watch the lake.

His mind kept returning to Dennis. Although they weren't particularly close, he'd considered Dennis a friend and missed the camaraderie. But it was the relationship Dennis had with Marjorie which impressed him the most. Their devotion to each other had been evident to everyone who knew them. He heard this remark over and over at the funeral. He now realized the closeness was what he wanted with Celeste. Now when it was too late. But was it? Could he win her back? Could he find some special event in town to intrigue her enough to go out with him once more?

What about the secret dinner in white which Dennis had told him about last summer? The event was invitational only and usually held in August at an unknown location. He and Marjorie enjoyed the mystery and elegance, and they went to all kinds of special occasions. Dennis said it was fashioned after Diner En Blanc which originated in Paris, France and recently has popped up several places in North America including New York City. Spontaneous communal dining out in the open was the draw, the tables were all in white with crystal candle sticks and wine glasses. Couples also dressed in white, gathered an hour early with gourmet picnic baskets and waited for the signal from the event host to begin dinner. Diners were to decorate each of the tables, but he'd get one of the flower shops to put something together. The dinner was bound to be fun and it might break the ice with Celeste. He'd call her tomorrow.

Savouring the last sip of wine, he began to relax for the first time today. Maybe an early night was what he needed. He loaded the tray with his dishes and walked into the small kitchen where he filled the dishwasher. Although he didn't usually like to eat alone, tonight it had worked for him.

The next morning, after a light breakfast, he turned on his laptop and began to edit the draft report he had prepared for the hospital Board and CEO. Although he had written many of these reports, every one of them was different. Recommendations depended so much on the personalities and the local culture and economy in which the hospital was located. He was on his fourth version and it still didn't feel right. An hour later, he turned the computer off and closed the lid. He stretched, picked up the keys from the kitchen counter and left for his morning walk.

The worn path along the waterfront was empty so he could take his time to feel the light breeze, watching the blue water and the cloudless sky. The white sails of several small boats cruised past. He'd loved this condo location from the time they moved to the town, but Celeste wanted a house. He admitted their secluded location off Charlotte Street had its benefits. The Rand Estate protected them from the traffic noise, and they were five minutes from downtown.

After he returned to his apartment, he sat with eyes locked on the phone. Should he call Celeste now or would she think he was being pushy. He sighed and picked up the receiver to dial.

She sounded surprised. "Hello"

"I know you said not to call for a few weeks, but I heard about a wonderful summer event in town which I thought you'd enjoy. I couldn't wait to tell you about it. Tickets are hard to get so I took a chance."

Her voice sounded curious. "Have we been before, or is this something new?"

"As a matter of fact, Dennis told me he read an article about it from last summer. It's one of those experiential dinners called Diner En Blanc. We'd make or buy a gourmet picnic dinner, dress all in white and join a table of eight for an outdoor meal on white tablecloths under candlelight. We can pretend we're just starting out."

He relaxed when she laughed into the phone. "That does sound like fun. When is it and who are we having dinner with?"

"On August 1st. I'll put our names forward on the list at the golf club to join a table. Otherwise, we have to make up our own table of eight which might be difficult." Adrian bit his lip. What made him say such a stupid thing?

Celeste sucked in her breath and remained silent. "Yes. I'd like that. August gives me lots of time to find an outfit. Maybe the evening will even inspire me to start a new painting."

Adrian let out his breath. "Wonderful. I'll send you the instructions online. The notice says to dress elegantly, but you look great in anything."

She laughed. "I'll never get used to all this flattery. I'm picking Marjorie up for an art show in Grimsby this afternoon, so we'll talk later."

"Bye. I'm on my way over to the club for lunch and will meet up with my group there. I've put my name down to join a foursome and we play at two." He hesitated. "I'll call you before I go back to Portland on Sunday night."

Chapter Twenty-Eight

Sabrina

Why do they make these bar chairs so uncomfortable? Sabrina squirmed in her seat. She glanced over at the young man beside her, dressed in tight pants and silk shirt. He hung over a striking young woman wearing the latest slinky black dress, the top covered in sequins. She realized her mistake. The chairs weren't built for her age group. The young people here were constantly in motion and barely sat still for ten minutes. A deep sigh escaped. She'd been one of them in her younger days back in Toronto. She'd thought this turquoise silk blouse tucked into a straight-cut ivory pants looked sexy before she got here. But she couldn't compete. At least the music was worth it.

She finished her third glass of Cabernet Franc and played with the plate of deep-fried shrimps that she'd ordered in place of dinner. What was up with Adrian? They'd been so close, going everywhere together on weekends, she'd never had to worry about a night out alone. The skills she'd learned as a single woman had long escaped her. Watching a crowd flirt with each other was not her idea of fun. He'd been cold with her tonight on the phone and if she hadn't pushed, she would probably not have seen him this weekend at all. No doubt Dennis's death had affected the whole group, but it seemed to hit him more than the rest.

"Ready for a refill?" The waiter's smile seemed genuine, but she'd had enough of this scene.

"No. That's it for tonight. I've got an early morning tomorrow." Who was she kidding? She had nothing planned for tomorrow until the dinner and Adrian wouldn't be picking her up until six. Normally, she and Ian would have gone to the golf club or Queen's Landing for lunch giving her time to relax in the afternoon and plan an exquisite outfit for dinner.

What would she wear tomorrow night? Adrian had seen most of her outfits and she didn't have time to shop for anything new. She'd need to spend some time checking through her closet after breakfast tomorrow morning. After signing for the bill, she hopped off the stool, gave the room one last look and left.

The slow line of traffic on Niagara Stone Road left no gaps. Sabrina was getting impatient and finally pushed her way in forcing a BMW to come to a sharp stop honking as he did so. Maybe she had cut that a little too close. Ian usually drove when they'd been drinking. Oh well, she didn't have far to go to the townhouse on Bayberry.

Sabrina realized her hands felt a little unsteady, as she parked in the driveway and let herself in, and threw her purse on the side table. She listlessly, dropped onto the sofa and turned on the TV clicking from one channel to another. Nothing held her interest, so she tried music instead. Still not able to settle, she poured a brandy from the decanter in the living room. This time, Sabrina sipped it slowly and when she began to feel sleepy, she climbed the stairs to her bedroom. Staring at the phone, she decided against another call to Adrian. He'd only be abrupt, and his mood would spoil tomorrow night. As she crawled under the Egyptian cotton sheets, she thought back to how much more fun the spring had been with the six of them doing stuff together. She had to admit it was partly her fault it didn't last.

*   *   *

Sabrina glanced in the mirror one last time, pushed a few stray hairs back into place and decided it was the best she could do. She was dissatisfied with the clinging nylon dress in its multitude of geometric colours which she'd bought in Portland. The outfit had looked great in the shop and the saleswoman had admired it on her. She added a wide camel leather belt and was impressed with the change. Part way down the stairs, the doorbell rang. Sabrina slowed her steps. It wouldn't do to seem too eager to greet him.

Taking a deep breath, she opened the door. "Adrian, you're right on time. Do you want to come in for a quick drink or should we be on our way?" She watched his face relax.

"Let's leave now so we don't feel rushed. It's always fun to wander around the winery if we're early." He took both her hands in his. "You look great as usual."

Sabrina rewarded him with a big smile. Obviously, he didn't remember she'd shown the dress to him. "You've forgotten. I picked it up in Portland on one of our excursions. This is the first time I've worn it."

She could see that Adrian was striving to be social during the drive and his conversation made her feel better. Maybe it was only a passing phase with him, and he'd be back to normal once the shock was over. He'd booked their table in the alcove overlooking the vineyard which she loved. As soon as the waiter arrived, he ordered a bottle of Chardonnay for them. Did he always order for women? She hadn't noticed before.

"How's the job in Portland coming along? You've certainly been giving them their money's worth based on your time." Sabrina mentally kicked herself. She reminded herself not to be so confrontational. The evening had started out so well. "I mean do you plan to wind it up soon?"

Not wanting to spoil his good mood, Adrian let her comments pass. "I'm almost finished the final report, so I'll meet my deadlines. I'm searching for other contracts and have seen some which interest me in New York."

Sabrina sat up straighter. "Do you mean upper New York State, like Buffalo? It would be nice to have you closer for a change."

"Well. No. One of the hospitals who contacted me is in New York City and one is in New Jersey, so I'd be away more." He smiled. "Less flying time. But I'd still keep my condo here for later when I really retire."

Anger crept up Sabrina's neck causing her to gulp down her wine. She held out the glass for more. Not wanting to spoil a romantic evening, she swallowed her sarcastic words and remained silent.

Adrian lifted his glass. "Let's not talk about work. What are your plans for the summer?"

"Ian's friends at the club have been telling him about a special event in town on August 3. Something called Diner En Blanc which is an elegant outdoor picnic. I thought you might want to go with me. I've already got the menu planned."

She was surprised at Adrian's reaction. He took a long drink, set the glass on the table, and squeezed his eyes shut for a moment. "Impossible for me. That's in the middle of the week and I'll be away."

Sabrina's lips turned down. "Well, it's right after a holiday weekend. Couldn't you get away longer just this once?"

He smiled and seemed to have regained his good humour. "It's not a holiday in the U.S. They don't acknowledge any Canadian holidays and I already have a meeting booked."

Sabrina stuck out her lower lip and glared. "Well, never mind. I didn't really want to go anyway. It's really just a glorified picnic and, besides, what a mess if it rains."

The waiter brought their plates and set them on the table. Adrian had ordered his usual medium-rare steak with seasonal vegetables. Sabrina smiled at her own dish of shrimp with lime chili in beurre blanc and picked up her fork to taste a small piece.

"This is delicious. I'm so glad that you remembered how much I liked this dining room. The wineries have the best food in the Region."

Adrian smiled. "I can always count on you to cheer up when a gourmet dish is set in front of you. Let's enjoy the evening, Sabrina. No more fights. No more challenges."

On the drive back home, Sabrina reclined the seat and relaxed. It was so nice to have someone else behind the wheel after a dinner out. She wondered how Ian had done it all those years. But then, he wasn't a big drinker.

"Are you coming in tonight?"

"After that long drive, I don't feel up to staying over. I think we should call it a night."

Deep wrinkles settled across her forehead and her mouth closed into a tight line. She'd felt this tension more and more lately. Well, at least he'd made a special effort tonight and she'd enjoyed herself. Better not to make a scene and scare him off again.

She reached across the console and pulled him towards her, touched her lips to his and then sensually ventured with her tongue into his open mouth. His arms pulled her tightly into an embrace and she heard his breathe quicken. So, he could still be aroused when his guard was down. She released him, opened the door, and slid her legs out of the car and stood there.

She turned to smile at him. "Until the next time, then."

She waited while Adrian got out of the car and walked with her to the front door. After a thoughtful kiss on the lips, he turned and left. Sabrina watched him all the way back to the car then put the key in the lock and let herself in.

* * *

Since Adrian would be out of town, Sabrina decided she'd coax Ian into attending the Dinner En Blanc with her. It was worth a call to Ian since he'd mentioned it to her in the first place. After all, everyone would be there, and she didn't want to hear about if from others. She just had to be at that dinner.

"Hi, Ian, it's Sabrina. I'm happy to catch you at home for a change. How have things been going with you?"

"This is a surprise." She could hear him turn off the TV. "My own wife worried about me. What do you want from me, Sabrina?"

She took a deep breath. "Do you remember that Dinner En Blanc you mentioned to me earlier? You heard about it from Dennis. It was an outdoor affair in town, everyone dressed in white, linen tablecloths, candles, gleaming silver and loads of gourmet food prepared by the wives. He said people at the club raved about it. Why don't we go this year?"

"What's the matter? Adrian didn't offer to take you?"

She cringed at his sarcasm. That was one thing with Ian. You could never fool him.

"You know he's in Portland. I just wondered if you would still like to go with me. I'm definitely going, even if it's alone, but thought it would be nicer to have company."

The silence dragged. "I hear there are several tables being organized with club members and I guess I could add us. If they wouldn't make you too uncomfortable, that is."

Sabrina scrunched up her nose. Those old biddies would be digging at her out of curiosity; however, she really didn't want to go alone. Which was worse? She hummed to herself and tapped the table.

"Sure, that would be great. See if you can find a group willing to take us. However, if not, would you still come?"

She felt a moment of guilt at his deep silence. Relief flowed through her when his voice came back with a cheerful note.

"Of course, I'll go to dinner with you. We were married a long time so what's another dinner out together."

"Great." Sabrina's spirits picked up. She knew white suited her. And she'd have time to shop for a new outfit right here in town. "I'll meet you at your place—our old place, that is."

*   *   *

The next two weeks speed by in a daze of shopping and planning for the event. Her assignment was to find silver candlesticks, white candles, and a centerpiece for the table. The other women had already divided up the menu and Ian ordered their wine. An hour before going over to Ian's, she paced her bedroom in her white chiffon dress that just touched her ankles. Was it too dressy? She hadn't felt comfortable asking the other women what they planned to wear. It would have opened the door for other questions. Finally, she added a soft coral lipstick and some peach blush. It would have to do. She took her time walking down the stairs, picked up her white clutch purse from the hall table and left.

Ian answered the door dressed in white summer wool pants and a short sleeve shirt. She had to admit the white made an attractive contrast against his olive skin and black hair. He'd always been a careful dresser.

Sabrina smiled and gave him a peck on the cheek. "Your outfit reminds me of our days back at the Royal Yacht Club in Toronto. Ready, Commander?"

He frowned and smoothed back his hair. But she could tell that he was pleased.

"Let's go then. The call has gone out to the table captains. The dinner will be on the main street in town like last year. Several others are already on their way over to start decorating the tables."

Sabrina loved the confusion which unfolded before them when they arrived on the scene. People carrying picnic baskets or pulling coolers of food. All the tables had white cloths, and women were setting them up with silver cutlery. She'd bought a centerpiece built up from white roses and carnations surrounded by green ferns and ivy which looked wonderful in the middle of the table. Ian lit the candles which added to the effect.

For Sabrina, it began as a fairy-tale evening. Ian had behaved as though nothing had changed. After a few initial barbs, the women went on to other gossip and the men checked her out with secret glances. The tables sparkled in the white environment. She suspected most of the food had been purchased from local caterers and it was of a high standard. She'd savoured the baked salmon, roast chicken in wine and rare beef tenderloin. While slowly nibbling the variety of desserts with her coffee, she glanced around the other diners nearby.

After dinner, she excused herself to wander between some of the other tables. She stopped to chat with people she recognized along the way and enjoyed herself until her eyes latched onto Adrian's familiar figure. That wavy dark hair and blue eyes couldn't be missed. She stood there in shock. What was he doing here? Her heart thudded heavily, and she could feel heat climb up her neck. How dare he lie to her? Adrian had to know he would be coming here when she asked him about it.

Then across from him she made out Celeste dressed in a silk v- neck dress with a white rose in her hair. Her face froze when she watched Celeste laugh and raise her wine glass in a toast with him.

Sabrina felt the adrenaline rush into her shoulders and chest. She'd make him pay for making a fool of her. What was going on between the two of them anyway? Pushing back her shoulders, Sabrina marched directly over to their table. She ignored the shocked looks on the faces of the other couples when she pushed those next to Adrian aside to stand right over him. Two wine glasses fell over and one broke into several pieces.

"And what kind of story were you telling me about how you'd be out of town? When we were out for dinner the other night, you didn't mention you were dating Celeste did you?"

Adrian got up. "Calm down, Sabrina. You and I can discuss this later. For now, I'll walk you back to your table." He glanced over at Celeste and shook his head.

Sabrina felt a flood of satisfaction when she saw how flushed and annoyed, he was. She'd hit him were it hurt this time and he deserved every bit of it. She checked out Celeste hoping she'd be humiliated as well. Instead she was surprised at Celeste's determined expression. She lowered her eyes, her shoulders tense but she didn't make any effort to leave the table.

Adrian's hand squeezed her arm tighter and tighter as he followed her back towards her place with Ian's group. "Swallowing his anger, he growled, "This is it Sabrina. I don't ever want to see you again. What were you thinking, embarrassing us like that in front of all those people?"

She smirked. "You told me you'd be in Portland. Or did I imagine that?" Sabrina shrugged away from his clutch.

He pulled out her chair and stood glaring at her. "I asked you a question Sabrina. What do you have to say for yourself after this disruption?" The other diners at the table sat with shocked expressions, waiting to see what would happen next. Adrian gave an apologetic nod to Ian who sat in silence and stared out across the crowd.

Sabrina realized Ian was at his limit and thought better of continuing the fight. She couldn't resist one last jab.

"Okay, Adrian. Go on back to your ex-wife if that's who you want in your life. You told me you wanted to escape from the boredom of that life."

Ian's face twisted in anger. "Enough, Sabrina. Remember, in future, you're not to ever invite me to go anywhere with you. You know how much I hate these scenes. Everyone around us is staring."

She kept an eye on Adrian's back, while he returned to his own table and stood behind his chair scanning the crowd. She smiled to herself when she saw the chair across from him was empty. Celeste must have left on her own as soon as she saw Adrian standing with Sabrina. She felt a warm glow as she knew her sudden appearance had spoiled Adrian's night.

Sabrina turned to Ian. She had to attempt to mend some relations with him. "Sorry. I didn't mean to involve you in all of this. Do you want to leave?"

Ian's face froze. "No. Although you've spoiled the evening for me. We'll leave when the group breaks up and not before." He nodded to the other guests. "Sorry about the disturbance. I hope you'll continue with your meal." He dropped his head and began to finish his dessert, refusing to look at Sabrina.

Chapter Twenty-Nine
Sabrina

Sabrina sat in silence beside Ian giving him a chance to regain equilibrium. He continued to talk golf with the men across the table and ignored her. She settled back subdued and watched while other groups as they packed up their belongings and headed back to their cars. Thank goodness they had donated the decorations and didn't need to worry about cleaning up. She finished her last glass of wine and gave him a quizzical look.

"What do you think, dear? Is it time?"

Ian stood up, he held his body stiff, a frown on his face. Without a word, he headed to where they had parked the Jaguar. She followed behind. As soon as they reached their old house, he got out of the car and stood by the driver's door, waiting for her to leave.

"Look, Ian. I had no idea that Adrian would be there. And especially with Celeste. How could I have known?"

Ian tensed his shoulders even more. "It doesn't matter anymore. Our marriage is over, and I was a sucker to go out with you tonight. I won't do it again. Call me only when we have investments to discuss."

She jumped out of his car and started towards her own, feeling her face red hot. "I've had all I can take tonight from the three of you. I need some time to myself. We can talk again when you've had time to reconsider."

On the drive back to her townhouse, Sabrina felt a new surge of anger towards Adrian. She pounded on the steering wheel with her fists. How could he do this to her? Had he been seeing Celeste on the side? Was that why he was so cool with her lately? Why he seemed to be avoiding her?

If he thought he could go back to Celeste as if nothing had ever happened, he could soon forget that. She'd call him tomorrow and demand some explanations. As she pulled into the safety of her own driveway, she felt relief at being alone and hurried into the house. With her anger still burning, she went straight to the bedroom. She lay on the bed and pounded her fists into the pillow. Celeste had won when she pulled that suicide stunt. Allowing Adrian to play saviour to a woman in distress suited him. She'd deal with him tomorrow. Right now, she needed sleep.

Her optimistic mood returned with the bright sun streaming through her window. Sabrina dressed in new ivory capris with a shiny gold and cream top and made up a breakfast tray for the back porch. While sitting in the sunshine, admiring the pink and red roses in full bloom, she plotted her next steps. Her mind was made up. She carried the tray back to the kitchen and picked up the phone. She perched on one of the kitchen bars stools as she dialed.

"Hello."

Surprised that Adrian had answered so quickly, Sabrina hesitated then plunged in. "I don't know what game it was you played last night but I expect an explanation."

The silence dragged. "Look, Sabrina, I had already asked Celeste to the dinner before you brought it up with me. It was as simple as that. I thought it would be easier to just say I wasn't going. I didn't think you'd go alone."

"Your lie isn't the point. When did you start back with Celeste and why didn't you tell me? Your efforts to avoid me is not a response. Did you forget we've been dating since the spring?"

A note of guilt crept into Adrian's voice. "We're not back together exactly. I've tried to make friends with her since the shock of Dennis's death hit me. I guess I realized we're all more vulnerable as we age."

So that was it. Fear of getting old had finally caught up with him. Well, she wasn't having any of his fears. "We're young if we choose to live our lives that way. One of the reasons I chose you was because of the obvious distance between you two. The spark had died who knows how long ago and you know it." She left some silence for him to think. "So. We've both enjoyed the summer. Where do we go from here?"

Another long silence. "I meant to tell you this in person, but you pushed the issue as usual. I need some time to see if there is anything left between Celeste and me. So far, she's resisting but I need to know if that's final. In the meantime, I don't want to keep seeing you. It wouldn't be fair to you."

Anger sharpened Sabrina's tone. "Oh, how noble you are. Wouldn't be fair to whom? You're leaving me hanging while you explore other opportunities. Well, Sabrina waits for no one. When Celeste dumps you for good, don't come crying back to me."

Slamming the phone down on the cradle, she paced back and forth across the kitchen floor. She'd been taken in by those foxy blue eyes of his. Adrian was just like most married men. They liked to stray for excitement and then went running back as soon as they were in danger of losing the homestead. What did this mean for her? She needed a plan.

Chapter Thirty

Celeste

Celeste stared in disbelief as Adrian and Sabrina snapped at each other in anger, while other guests hid behind the elaborate decorations, and listened mesmerized. What a mistake she'd made when she agreed to attend the dinner with Adrian. Sabrina raked over him like a jealous cat while Adrian, rather than a show of embarrassment, allowed his language to become more and more aggressive. He'd walked over to Sabrina and grabbed her by the arm and dragged her away from the table.

Meanwhile Celeste was left to stay cool and repair the damage. She checked out how their dinner partners were taking this. Most of them shifted their gaze away from hers. She felt the flood of humiliation with tears building up behind her eyes. She had to get out of here. She grabbed her clutch purse, pushed back her chair, and ran past all the other tables toward the clock tower. Adrian had picked her up, so she'd have to walk home but it would give her time to calm down. She slipped off her high-heeled sandals and carried them as her toes curled under in the soft grass of the boulevard.

With no one in sight, she let the tears come. It wasn't so much the shame for her but also Adrian's attitude when under stress.

She'd forgotten how he would always put himself first and ignore her feelings when he wanted something. He might have realized Sabrina would be at that dinner. It was, after all, her kind of thing. And then, just like in their past, when he'd been challenged by Sabrina, he'd gone straight to aggression rather than trying to soothe the situation with her in private.

She sighed. Now she had replayed his usual reaction to being challenged off her chest, she had to look at her own behaviour. Even though she'd confided to Marjorie her intention to keep Adrian as just a friend, she had to admit part of her still dreamed he'd want her back. Somehow, that was important to her. She still needed that reassurance. Perhaps this was the wakeup call for her. The next time he called, she'd tell him the rules of the game had changed. She began to enjoy the soft light of dusk over the greenery of the Commons as she continued down John Street closer and closer to home.

She breathed in the fresh night air and smiled when she stood on her own front stairs and turned her key in the lock. Once inside, Celeste went straight to the fridge and poured a glass of Chardonnay which she took to her favorite chair in the living room. She leaned as far back in the chair as it allowed and sighed. She could feel her jarred nerves begin to settle, as she inhaled the cool aroma of lemons and apples. At least his betrayal hadn't hit her deep in the chest like last time. What did she really want to do with the rest of her life? She'd discovered teaching nurses was important to her but preferred to have it under her own control which made contracts work for her. Good friends like Marjorie were so important to fill a huge gap in someone for her emotional needs.

Obviously, she needed to keep active through tennis and long walks. She sat up. Keeping in touch with Natalie had slipped lately. Although, she had her own life now in Ottawa and would probably marry someday, she was the only child Celeste would ever have.

The question she had been avoiding was men. But it always came back to men. Did she want a new man in her life, and if so, was she ready? How could she avoid falling into the same traps she did with Adrian? Celeste didn't have the answer to this and as she drained the last of the glass, decided it could wait until another day. Her eyes were heavy as she climbed the stairs and entered her bedroom, her sanctuary. She had a whole week ahead of her and would think about it tomorrow.

* * *

The next day, after a light dinner on her patio, Celeste drove to Marjorie's to pick her up. They were on their way to a jazz concert at one of the local wineries. Last year, she'd loved the vibrant notes of the clarinet and the love songs were superb. She was ready to face the pangs it brought right now.

"I'm glad you reminded me about this event earlier in the week or I'd have totally forgotten it was on." Marjorie smiled.

Celeste led the way back to the car. "I'm looking forward to it." The light breeze and lingering sunlight were exactly right for an outdoor concert.

Once they were both seated and headed down Lakeshore Road, Marjorie turned to look at her. "I wasn't sure whether or not to bring this up, but how did you enjoy that white dinner the other night with Adrian?"

Celeste grimaced. "Probably more than Sabrina did. Would you believe Adrian invited me there knowing Sabrina wanted to go as well? I bet he knew she might show up."

Marjorie's eyes narrowed. "Tell me more. Did she see you?"

"She not only saw us but came over to our table to confront Adrian. That caused quite a scene, I must say. I was stunned but also embarrassed for the other guests at our table."

"What did Adrian do?"

"Adrian was his usual self. Tried to skirt around the issue and played innocent. Then got angry with her and dragged her back to her own table. Sabrina had her eyes opened and I don't think she's likely to forgot how he reacted."

"But how did you feel? It must have been awful for you."

Celeste sighed. "Hurt, angry, confused. But not nearly as bad as the first time I heard about their affair. I must admit, I felt a little tinge of satisfaction when I saw how shocked and angry Sabrina was. Probably not my best moment."

Marjorie laughed. "You deserved your moment of jubilation over her. But, what about your feelings towards Adrian? Have they changed?"

"This friendship attempt was doomed from the start. I think it's time for me to give Adrian up for good. But we need to get to a place where we can run into each other in public without it being a big deal. That's what I'm working toward."

Marjorie nodded her head. "That sounds healthy to me."

They pulled into the parking lot. A huge crowd gathered at the entrance, so they had to wait for a turn to show their tickets and find a seat. Celeste sank back into her seat and drifted away with the mellow sound of the piano. That's why she loved jazz. She could lose herself in the music and leave with most of her issues resolved. She and Marjorie were both moving toward new chapters in their lives and it felt good. Adrian would have to find his own way.

On the drive home, Marjorie challenged her. "What do you think? Will we continue on as two mature women on our own with no men in our lives?"

Celeste sighed. "I can only speak for myself. Until I know what I'm looking for, I'm better alone. At times, I still feel vulnerable and not ready to take a chance. What about you?"

"Well, the initial pain has subsided over Dennis's death, but I have never imagined myself with anyone else. I guess I'd have to say I still feel married. It's like I'm waiting for him to return from a trip."

"But do you know what type of man you'd like if one came along a year from now?"

"I'd want him to be just like Dennis, which is probably not fair. I'm certainly not ready to date anyone."

"I know what you mean. But for me, I need to think about it and maybe try some casual dates to see if it's possible for me to find a totally different type of man. I'm not interested in marriage. I've already tried that twice."

"I know it doesn't sound romantic, but I think at our age companionship becomes more and more important to the relationship."

"Yes, you're right. But I still yearn for someone who lights a spark in me. I want to feel a yearning to have him around me. Maybe it's too much to expect."

"No. I'd like that too, but it doesn't seem to last. So, it's important to have someone who enjoys many of the same things you do. Sort of like a good friend."

As they pulled into Marjorie's driveway, they both laughed at the same time.

Celeste spoke first. It was so good to have a friend like Marjorie, someone with whom she could confide her inner most fears. "We're two senior women so why do we think we'll have the choice of anyone whom we meet? I must have regained some of my confidence."

Marjorie unbuckled her seatbelt. "Celeste, you're still beautiful and I see a great change in you over the past few months. You look and act alive again. I'm sure at the right time you'll find the right one."

After Marjorie went inside, Celeste sat quietly for several minutes. Marjorie was right. She was feeling stronger and more in control than she'd felt for the last few years of her marriage. One thing she knew was if she chose another relationship, she'd never let her partner take control over her life. It had been a big mistake both for her and for Adrian as well. By taking advantage of her, he also lost the respect for her which had attracted him in the first place.

Chapter Thirty-One

Celeste

The relationship between her and Ian had suited them both for many years. The romance had long disappeared, but they were good companions, and that was hard to find. They both liked their independence, but he seemed happier to maintain what was like a partnership. Sabrina needed something more. Until the affair, she hadn't realized he could be jealous. It was more likely he was embarrassed in front of his friends by her current behavior. She'd make an excuse to go to the club and soothe his hurt feelings. It wouldn't benefit her to make an enemy of her husband.

Always a good strategist, Sabrina waited a week then booked a lunch at the golf club with a woman she knew from the newcomer's group. They'd both arrived in town around the same time. Edith could be a bit boring, but she'd been available on short notice. The host at the club's dining room gave her a nervous smile when the two women arrived.

"Will you join Ian, or shall I set you up at a nice table for two near the window?"

"The latter sounds good. Give us the one looking over the water." Sabrina gave him a dazzling smile in return and followed him to the table. When they passed Ian's table, she lingered.

"You are here. I see old habits continue. Ian, you remember Edith from our social club days."

Ian frowned and then forced a smile. "Nice to see you again, Edith. I'm just finishing up lunch. The Cornish Game Hen was great. You should try it."

Edith shifted from one foot to the other. "Good to see you, too. Sabrina told me they serve great lunches here."

Ian dropped his head and sipped his coffee, dismissing them.

As they reached their own table and took their seats, Sabrina smiled at Edith. "Sorry, I didn't think he'd be here this late. He's usually on the course promptly at 12:30. Maybe he ran out of partners."

Edith looked puzzled. "What's going on between you two? I heard you've been living apart, but you always seemed like a close couple to me."

Sabrina sighed. "I guess it's my fault. The need for excitement seems to die for most of us, but that's not the case with me. I need to live my life right to the edge."

From the disapproving look on Edith's face, she could tell this lunch had been a mistake. Deciding to make the best of it, Sabrina chatted about people they both knew and then excused herself to use the washroom. On the way, she passed Ian's table once more. He was in the process of settling the bill.

"Since we're both still members, why don't we book a game together on Saturday? I haven't played for several months but I can still keep up to you."

A genuine smile came over Ian's face. She knew he loved a challenge. "I'd like that. It can be lonely here. Meet me for lunch at 11:30 and we can be on the greens by 12:30."

Inwardly, Sabrina groaned. Still stuck to his routine but at least he'd agreed. "That's wonderful. It'll give me a reason for going to the spa for a workout tomorrow. See you on Saturday then."

The remainder of the lunch with Edith was tedious but she'd accomplished her goal. Ian had allowed her back into his life, if only by an inch. One thing she'd learned about engineers was their stubborn personality and ability to focus in one direction could be a challenge. Well, she wouldn't be seeing Adrian this Saturday so she might as well be entertained, and Ian was a particularly good golfer.

*   *   *

On Saturday morning, grey clouds hung in the sky threatening rain. How could this happen to her plans? Sabrina pouted as she pulled on her khaki capris and tight knit top and laced her golf shoes. She was being silly. At least the two of them would have lunch and that was almost as good. Her mood lifted, she pulled her clubs from the closet, slung a small bag over her shoulder, grabbed a hat, and headed to the car. No umbrella for her.

When she'd maneuvered into the parking lot, she handed her car keys to the nearest caddie and instructed him to carry her clubs to the cart area. She went directly to the dining room and this time asked the host to take her to Ian's table. His inky black hair and stiff posture was visible to her from where she stood.

"Hello." She stood by the table until he gestured for her to sit. "I hope the weather doesn't spoil our game. I've been looking forward to it."

Ian nodded. "A little rain never used to stop us back in Britain. The weather report suggests we're not in for more than a shower." He turned back to the menu. "What are you having? The salmon filet with roasted vegetables looks good to me."

Taking her seat, Sabrina picked up the menu, and studied it closely. The club tended to cater to conservative diners. Where was the adventure in that?

Inwardly, she smiled. Ian acted like there'd never been a disagreement. "I'll have the honey garlic scallops with greens." She closed the menu and sat back.

After the waiter took their order and brought two glasses of white wine, Ian looked around the dining room. "Not as many members as there used to be. Especially, on a Saturday. Some people are just getting too old to play and others have moved on to other activities."

Sabrina was puzzled at his thoughts. "Does that mean you've having difficulty putting together foursomes or actually finding a partner to play with?"

"No. I'm just saying that the membership is down and that's not a good sign for the future of the club. We need to be attracting some new blood. The town has catered too much to old people like us. If they let me, I could teach the town how to attract a new group. Maybe I should be on the board."

"Aren't you still volunteering with that town committee?"

"No. I gave that up. They don't listen to us old people anyway. It's the consultants who count with that group."

Sabrina was surprised by the conversation. "You're not thinking of going back to work, are you?"

"Well, not full time. But some contract work might be something to do and get me recognized with the group. I seem to have lost my sailing partner and, thanks to you, my golf partner as well."

Sabrina scrunched up her nose. So that's what this was about. She chose to ignore his comments. Lunch had arrived, so she ate in silence enjoying the succulent seafood. "I'm looking forward to playing this afternoon. Did you order a cart?"

He stopped with a fork full of salmon halfway to his mouth. "Why don't we walk this time? It's only nine holes and I could use the exercise."

She squelched her annoyance. "Why not? We'll show those young people we can keep up to them." The walk would give them more time to talk. She didn't want to totally lose Ian. He was part of her history.

The game went well with Sabrina able to keep up with him until the last few holes. As usual, her swing deteriorated over time. When they returned to the club, Ian suggested a drink at the bar before they went their separate ways. It was deserted when they took their seats at a small table and ordered, scotch for him and a vodka martini for her. They chatted about the game, what had worked and areas where they could improve. She noticed that his jaw muscles were beginning to clench. That normally meant he was about to say something difficult.

"Sabrina are things between you and Adrian truly over? I mean is this just a break or is he gone for good?"

Her moth dropped open. "What do you mean?" She took another sip of the martini. "I told you we're not seeing each other right now. He wants some space."

She watched him suck in a deep breath. "I mean is it over for you or do you plan to win him back?"

Sabrina gestured to the bartender and ordered another round of drinks. After carefully taking a sip, she responded. "Dennis's death has changed Adrian. I think he can see himself as being next in line."

Ian took a gulp of scotch. "Dennis's death changed a lot of things. I miss him but didn't take his death personally. You haven't answered me. Is this temporary with Adrian?"

Forced to think about it, Sabrina replied, "I don't think things will ever go back to what they were with Adrian and me, if that's what you mean." Saying it out loud made her realize, Ian had guessed right. The relationship was over.

He sat silently sipping his drink. This was obviously something he'd gone over in his mind for some time. "What about us? Could we give it another try? I mean you move back home, and we become a couple again."

Shock hit Sabrina in the stomach with sharp pain like a broken piece of glass. She hadn't anticipated this outcome. What to say? She wasn't ready for resuming her marriage, but she didn't want to scare him off for good.

"I'm not ready to give up my own place just yet." She paused. How about we start a new relationship? We keep both houses for now but move back and forth."

Ian's eyes brightened. "It would be exclusive then. No dating other people. Back to just you and I." His silence felt heavy. "We could give it a try."

What did she have to lose? Considering what Adrian blurted out to her after the tragic dinner-in-white, she wouldn't be seeing him for a while. "Give me a little time to get used to the idea. How about I order us both dinner for Saturday at my townhouse? That can be a fresh start."

He smiled. "Good. It's a deal."

Chapter Thirty-Two

Sabrina

At first the new arrangement with Ian was exciting and fun. They'd have their dinner dates and occasional golf games, but then she returned to her own townhouse. After dinner at Ian's place a few weeks ago, she'd downed one too many martinis to attempt the drive home and she stayed over. Waking up in their old bedroom was strange. She'd felt Ian's hand rubbing her neck and shoulder and rolled over to face him.

"So where do we go from here, Ian? Are we now a couple like before?"

He pulled her up against his chest and nuzzled her ear. "Let's just enjoy this sleep-in for this morning. I've missed you."

She enjoyed the familiar warmth and responded by pushing him onto his back and massaging his chest and down to his thighs. Then she straddled him. Later, feeling the warm water of the shower caressing her skin, she wondered where this was headed. Could she really go back to being Ian's wife and, if so, why had she left?

Later, over croissants and coffee on the deck, Ian seemed preoccupied. He finally broke the silence. "Why don't you move back here? There's no need for us to maintain two houses."

Sabrina took a deep breath. She was feeling smothered. "Let's not rush this. I'm not ready to give up my own place just yet. How about my staying on weekends? Then I can go back to my place Monday to Friday to give us some space?"

Ian frowned. "Don't forget that we're not just dating. We were married for over thirty years." His face had that closed look that she knew meant there wasn't much bargaining room.

Maybe if she reversed the order, he'd be willing to try it. "What I'm saying is we need to take things gradually. I could move back to this home during the week and then go to my place on the weekends, if that suits you better."

He looked puzzled. "Would that include lunch and golf on Saturdays? Or does it mean I don't see you at all on weekends?"

She smiled in relief. "Golf and lunch would be great. I just need some time to myself."

Ian stood, picked up the dirty plates and headed into the kitchen. "That's settled then. I'll expect you back here on Monday. With lots of luggage, of course. I'm sure that your attraction to luxury goods hasn't changed."

She followed him to the kitchen and watched him fill the dishwasher. It still amazed her how self-sufficient he had become as a bachelor. He was more resourceful in a way than Adrian. She was free to go for now. Sabrina had planned an afternoon at a local opening for a new artist in town and wanted time to change her outfit.

Kissing Ian on the cheek, she opened the door. "I appreciate how understanding you've been. You can expect me here on Monday after lunch. I'll look forward to it."

*   *   *

The gallery had been packed and she'd enjoyed chatting with several women whom she'd not seen for the past few months. Their response was warm, and all hard feelings seemed to have disappeared. For a change, she made her own dinner and savoured the penne with shrimp, sprinkled with sundried tomatoes while sipping a glass of Chianti Classico. Back home, she realized her freedom had become important to her. She had doubts about moving back with Ian part-time, but she'd give it a try. She knew it was important to earn back Ian's trust.

While packing her suitcase on Monday afternoon, she kept hesitating. Did she really want to do this? Ambivalence washed through her. She'd lived through tougher moments. Slamming the lid down, Sabrina picked up the case and headed out to the car. Action worked best for her. She'd learn to deal with this new change.

Ian welcomed her at the front door as soon as she rang the bell. They both stood there awkwardly until he motioned for her to enter and took her suitcase to carry it upstairs.

"I've been looking forward to this week. It does get lonely sometimes, especially with Dennis gone and no sailing trips."

"Well, I can't fill in as a sailing partner. You know how bad I was as a crew member."

He smiled. "I just got back from my golf game. Found a new guy from Toronto who was looking for a partner. We're on again for later in the week."

Sabrina shrugged. "Sounds good."

He turned his attention back to her. "If you want to go shopping, I'll come along. Or Music Niagara has a jazz quartet at Riverbend if you want a drink."

He could be so thoughtful. She knew how Ian hated to shop with her. The women's shops were so small, he felt cramped. He'd usually tag along if she wanted company.

Sabrina went to the kitchen and filled two glasses with sparkling wine. "Let's sit in the garden for now. We can go out for a drink around four if you still feel like it. Maybe we can go shopping later in the week."

He followed her out to their deck. "I'd prefer to go over to the patio at Queen's Landing later while we still have some summer sun. We can have a light dinner there right by the water."

*   *   *

The week continued at first with their normal relationship—as though nothing had happened. Then Sabrina caught Ian checking the last numbers dialed on her cell phone once or twice. The next day, when she left her purse on the kitchen stool, she could tell he'd rifled through it. When she confronted him, he'd apologized but the look he gave her told her that his suspicions were still strong.

To make amends, he'd agreed to drive her to the Pen Centre in St. Catharines on Friday after lunch so she could go shopping.

"Are you sure you want to do this?" Sabrina asked. "I know how you hate malls."

Ian forced a smile. "I want to check out some of the new digital TVs. We need to think about replacing ours. The Bay has a good selection."

After they parked and entered the mall, Ian suggested that they meet in an hour outside The Bay's mall entrance. "We can find somewhere to go for coffee before we leave."

Sabrina noticed that he seemed more agitated than usual. Maybe he had realized she would be going back to her townhouse when they got back. She wandered through a couple of the women's fashion stores but didn't see anything glamorous or different. Although she hated the long drive back to Toronto, she'd probably have to go back to Holt's to get anything she really liked. Feeling bored, she was surprised to hear a familiar voice.

"Sabrina, is that really you? I heard you'd moved out here but found it hard to believe. You're such a city person."

With a quick glance, she immediately recognized, Jim Wood, one of their former neighbours from Toronto. He and his wife,

Eve, often went to dinner with them. That is until Ian had complained that Jim frequently flirted with her. "Jim, what brings you out here to Niagara? I thought you'd be playing golf on a Friday afternoon."

He pulled her into a hug. "It's great seeing you. Where's Ian?" He snickered. "He's usually following you around?"

She hugged him back. "Be careful, Jim. Ian's not far away and you know how jealous he can be. You didn't answer my question."

"I know we said that we'd never move out to the country, but here we are living in Grimsby near the escarpment." Their eyes held for a moment.

Sabrina's spirits picked up. "That is a surprise. How are you liking it?"

"We've adjusted. Trying to find good shops is a problem though. We don't want to always be going across the border."

As they walked down the mall, he kept his arm around her shoulders. Relaxed, she leaned against him. Out of the side of her head, Sabrina saw Ian approaching and started to move away.

His face was blotched red and his eyes like steel when he faced them. He grabbed Sabrina by the arm and jerked her away from Jim. "Can't I trust you alone at all? Even for an hour?"

Sabrina froze in shock. "Ian, get control of yourself. Don't you recognize our neighbour, Jim Wood. We were just catching up on how much our lives have changed since we left the city."

"I'm sure you were. He was always interested in you." Ian looked embarrassed, before he turned to Jim. "Sorry, about this, but we're on our way home." He shrugged. "It's a long story."

Ian placed his arm firmly around Sabrina's waist and directly her towards the door leading to the parking lot. "Let's go before this gets worse. People are already staring at us."

She bit the inside of her lip. Turmoil had caused acid to work its way up her stomach and her throat burned. How dare he treat her like a common slut? She took a deep breath and held it until they were back in the car and then turned to him.

"What were you thinking back there? How could you treat me like that? Jim must think you're crazy."

He watched her with a contrite expression. "I came around the corner and there the two of you stood, lost in each other like two lovers. What did you expect me to think?"

Sinking back against the seat, she closed her eyes for the remainder of the ride home. When the car stopped, she opened her own door, got out, and slammed it behind her. With her own key, she let herself in and headed straight up stairs to pack. She'd be going home early this time.

As she closed the suitcase, Sabrina heard Ian coming up the stairs and turned to face him.

He stood in the doorway of the bedroom. His voice was calm, and his reserved look had returned. "I guess I overacted back there. Won't you at least stay for dinner?"

She sighed. "For your information, I've never been attracted to Jim. It's been an interesting week, but this isn't going to work. You must realize it. I'm going back to the townhouse now and we'll talk later."

He moved out of the way to let her pass. "I'll give you the weekend. Then we need to decide. If we are officially separated for good, I need to know."

When she entered her townhouse this time, Sabrina knew this was her home now. She'd been away on an unpleasant vacation and now she was back. It was no use trying to live together. Ian had become more and more suspicious of her and couldn't trust her anymore. They wouldn't be reconciling.

By seven, she was hungry but didn't feel like cooking. When had she ever felt like cooking? A nice dinner at that new restaurant in town, Garrisons, would suit her fine. After renewing her makeup and changing into a new lime green pant suit, her spirits improved. The location was a short drive, and there was a parking spot right in front.

She gazed at the other diners as the host directed her to a small table near the window. Later, sipping her first glass of red wine, she was startled to see Adrian standing in line just inside the entrance. Should she say hello or pretend she didn't see him? She turned her head to look out the window as he walked right past her table.

The host seated him across from her and two booths down. He was looking in her direction, but without recognition. To ease her tension, she gave him a small wave. He raised his head from the menu and nodded at her without even a smile. But she couldn't let him get away with ignoring her. She rose from her seat and crossed the floor, to stand in front of him.

"Hello, there. We seem to have picked the same restaurant. Is anyone joining you?"

Adrian sat up very straight, his face grave. "No. I'm alone and want to stay that way tonight. Before I go back to Portland, I need some time by myself to think."

Sabrina felt her face turn hot. "There is no need to be unfriendly. I get the message, but we need to talk about what's next for both of us. We were a couple. So, you might as well own up to it."

After she returned to her table, she gulped her wine and ordered another glass. For the first time, it felt strange to dine alone. Where the couple at the next table whispering about her? That was one thing she hated about small towns. People kept bumping into friends and acquaintances. You couldn't avoid it. She finished her dinner and decided to go home for a brandy. Her earlier optimistic mood had been ruined by the nasty encounter with Adrian.

*   *   *

Several months passed while Sabrina fell back into her regular routine. She followed the art shows in the local area, especially when new, younger artists where featured. Ian had called a few times, but she had ignored the calls. What was there to say? Finally, she went to the golf club one morning just before noon to see if she could catch him. It was late fall but there were still many players on the course. He was at his usual lunch table, so she walked over.

His face registered surprise, but he smiled. "This is unexpected."

She sat across from him but waved away the menu. "I just thought it was time to catch up with each other. What have you been doing with your time?"

"I'm working with the town again. Not that useless committee I was on before but consulting a couple of days per week on the design for a new Wastewater Treatment Plant. My engineering skills have proven to be useful for something. Even if I'm only paid a stipend. How about you?"

"I've been meeting with an agent in Toronto to rent or buy a small condo in that complex we used to live in. When the lease runs out on my townhouse, I've decided to move back to Toronto."

Ian leaned towards her. "That's a big jump. I thought you loved this town."

Sabrina had thought about this for the past few weeks. Her bad memories about the loss of Adrian would always be linked to this town for her. Besides, the fun they'd had with their exclusive group of friends was gone forever. There was no one else here she cared about.

"I'm ready for something new. I plan to open my own gallery in Yorkville featuring new and emerging artists. Maybe even some of the artists I've experienced here in town. Investing in art has become extremely popular. I'll even invite you to the opening if you want."

His face turned serious. "I bet you'll do well. We made a great team for a good many years, and I'll miss your advice." He took her hand. "Of course, I'll come to your opening."

Her throat tightened. "Thank you. Your support and encouragement are important to me."

She rose, blinking back tears, and left the club. Back in the car, she breathed deeply and took a long drive along the Lakeshore Road, enjoying the fall colours and the fragrant breeze coming in the open window. Her future was settled. This gallery would work for her. She had to admit to herself, it wouldn't be easy. The art scene in Toronto was crowded and she had no idea where to start. It was a new challenge.

Chapter Thirty-Three

Adrian

After the unfortunate incident at the Dinner En Blanc, Adrian took steps to avoid running into Sabrina. Why had he ever gotten involved with her? When they were together as a group of friends, she seemed all fun and excitement. But when they became involved, her demands continued to grow. Her drinking had also put him off. His experience with this problem in staff at the hospital had soured him on drunks. Several colleagues who worked hard also drank too much every time there was a social event. When drunk, some of them were very unpleasant company.

The dinner had enlightened him in additional ways. He'd enjoyed Celeste's company and now that her depression had lifted. Her blue-violet eyes once again sparkling, and he could see that she was still an extremely attractive woman. She had made it clear, after the disastrous encounter with Sabrina, there would be no starting over for them. However, he hadn't given up on his new role as a friend. What could they do together? She wasn't a golfer, and he didn't play tennis. Maybe nothing in common had been part of the problem between them. They didn't really do anything as a couple except dinner. They both enjoyed the visual arts and entertaining. Could he work something out with that?

With Dennis gone, he had no real friends left in town. Ian, of course, was out of the question. Should he consider a move back to Toronto when his current contract wound up later this fall? Maybe not. When he and Celeste lived there, their lives had centered on the hospital and many of those people would now be retired and have moved on. Restless and dissatisfied, Adrian went out to his car, cranked down the top and headed for the Niagara River Parkway. The blanket of green grass on the riverbank and soft breeze playing in the leaves of the maples calmed his soul as he drove without any destination in mind.

By late afternoon, hunger drove him into town. From the parking lot of Casa Mia's on Portage Road, he pulled out his cell phone and pushed in Celeste's number. One last try was worth it.

"Hello."

He could hear the surprise and caution in her voice. "I'm just out for a drive on this wonderful Friday afternoon and couldn't help thinking of you. Right now, I'm parked at Casa Mia's and wondered about us having dinner here again. You always found it quite romantic. Remember our last Valentine Day dinner here together?"

"Adrian, what a surprise." Silence hung in the air. "I'm glad you found a way to amuse yourself. We're a long way from Valentine's Day."

"What about right now? I don't suppose you'd want to join me. I haven't gone in yet and would be happy to wait for you."

Her voice hardened. "No. I'm taking Marjorie out for dinner later tonight. Besides, I thought we'd had this discussion already. I hear you and Sabrina have split, but that doesn't mean that we have returned to being a couple."

Adrian sighed. "Can't we be friends? That's all I'm asking."

The silence dragged. "Look, Adrian. It's too early for me. With my own business underway, I'm feeling good about myself for the first time in years. I've worked too hard for my independence to give it up."

"I'm not suggesting that we get back together right now." Adrian's mood sank as he said these words out loud. "Can we keep in touch? Talk to each other when we need some support?" His hand gripped the phone, and he held his breath as he waited for her response.

"Not right now, I told you." He'd never heard her so angry. "You're not listening to me. No more dinners, lunches or social events for us." There was a long pause. "You can keep in touch by phone, if you really want to."

Adrian sucked in his breath. That would have to do for now. At least the communication lines were open. "Okay. Bye for now then and enjoy your dinner with Marjorie." He turned the phone off and entered the restaurant feeling defeated.

He casually flipped through the menu. Most of the main courses where pasta which didn't interest him. After ordering pork roast with mashed potatoes, he sat back to enjoy his scotch on the rocks. But he couldn't help himself. He still missed Celeste. They'd built up some great memories.

During their anniversary dinner, back in Toronto before they moved, they'd both been so excited. Both were long term residents of the city and this would be a new beginning. A move to this small, sophisticated town, less than two hours away would start their new life. With her eyes alight with emotion, Celeste's normal aloof manner had been replaced by sudden outbursts of enthusiasm.

"I can't believe all the space in the garden. We can entertain on that large patio. Hold barbecues with friends. It's all so new."

He'd smiled and held her hand. "We've got to make new friends first, but with more leisure time that should be easy."

She looked pensive. "That's what makes it so great. Since I was laid off by the hospital, most of my friends have avoided me. They make all sorts of excuses as to why we can't get together for lunch. The last time I was there to meet with HR, I saw Nancy coming towards me in the hall and she turned and quickly walked in the other direction."

Adrian winced. "I've been away for some time, so I forgot what that was like. That's why this consulting work is so important to me. Besides, I like that I've been able to work from my own space at least some of the time."

"Selling the house so soon was a help and at a good price. After buying the Niagara house, we'll still have some money for new furniture."

He'd thought their future together was secure. On the drive back to their current house, he was relieved they wouldn't be facing all this city traffic every day. When they'd hung up their coats, he poured two glasses of brandy and Celeste followed him out to cedar deck. Relaxing on the lawn chair, he reached over to grasp her fingers in his.

"Let's just celebrate tonight. We can think about all the work we need to do tomorrow."

She'd squeezed his fingers. "I'm glad we have each other. It makes the adventure even more satisfying."

He'd stared into the darkness, ready to move on to a new place.

His eyes stung as visions from the past engulfed him. He took another drink. Returning to Toronto didn't make sense for him. After paying his bill, he walked back to his car and drove carefully down the Parkway back into town.

* * *

Adrian closed the door to his condo and walked over to stare out the balcony. It was over then between them. Thirty-four years and four months washed away by his stupidity. Celeste had pushed him into freedom, a freedom he no longer wanted. He paced. What do I do now? The weekend had just started, and he had no plans. Moving onto the balcony, he stood at the railing and watched the people below. Couples holding hands as they strolled. Everything seemed grey and stale.

Tightness in his stomach, drifted upwards to his neck. He slammed the door behind him as he left the open air, crossed the floor, and grabbed a windbreaker. A walk outside would get rid of some of those knots.

Arms swinging at his sides, he kept up a brisk pace as the pathway meandered around the edge of the lake. Reaching the end, he stopped to rest on a wood bench. His shoulders slumped forward, his head in his hands, as he felt the sobs shudder through his chest. He'd forgotten how frightening it was to cry.

After a while, he was relieved to feel a quietness. His earlier decision was confirmed. He wouldn't leave this town. It felt like home now and there was no one in the city who would care if he returned. But he'd had it with living in hotel rooms. Consulting roles were for the young. From what was left from his share of the sale of their house in Toronto and the large payout from the hospital, he could invest in a small business locally.

His group at the Niagara Golf Club would have some ideas. He'd talk to them next week. His mind settled; Adrian strolled back towards home.

The following weekend, after he wound up the contract in Portland, he'd been invited to a meeting by the guys from the golf club. During the meeting, Karl did most of the talking for his colleagues. He found their proposal intriguing and it fit with his love of the wineries. The five partners were putting together financing to build and operate a wine processing facility for local growers with a storefront operation for the tourists. This group of small growers couldn't afford to process their own wine from their vineyards. Forced to sell their product at a much-reduced rate to larger local winery owners, they looked to these investors to offer an alternative. These men wanted him to take on the role of General Manager. This was a project with appeal because he could help small entrepreneurs and at the same time use his skills in operational management and marketing. His decision was quickly made. He'd stay right here in this unique town and make a new life. He knew he could do it.

Chapter Thirty-Four

Sabrina

Alone in the house now, Sabrina had lots of time to think about what happened to her. The affair had started as a mild flirtation with Adrian, blossomed into a level of satisfaction and excitement she couldn't have imagined. Did she and Ian ever have those feelings? She didn't think so. What was it about Adrian then? Her analytical side could see how his unavailability contributed. However, emotionally her whole being felt stimulated in his presence. He seemed to feel the same. Then why didn't the feeling last?

The easy way would be to blame Celeste for the break-up by offering a reopened door to him. She could see it was something else. Adrian went too willingly. He'd never really been in the relationship with her. It was just an easy conquest for him. Sabrina slammed her fist down on the kitchen counter and then licked her sore hand. She knew how to make him feel her pain. The one thing Adrian hated was a public scene. She'd make sure he got one.

A careful check of her wardrobe and she reappeared in tight white shorts with a matching white eyelet blouse which tied at her waist. In the mirror, she admired the silver highlights in her curly mop. It would do. She slammed and locked the front door with satisfaction and squared her shoulders. The drive to the golf club took about fifteen minutes with the traffic in town. Her plan was to arrive there just before the late lunch crowd showed up so Ian would already be out on the course. The lot in front of the golf club was packed but she made out Adrian's new red Audi convertible in the far corner. She was in luck.

Within a few minutes, she stood in the restaurant doorway and surveyed the room. Seated at a small table by himself, Adrian seemed immersed in the menu. Sabrina chuckled under her breath as she strode over and slide into the seat across from him.

Her voice sounded shrill enough for the next table to overhear. "Imagine finding you here, honey. I stopped in to have some of their great chowder before my game. I know you don't mind my joining you." She blinked her eyes at him.

Adrian pushed back in his chair. "Sabrina what do you think you're doing? I didn't invite you to sit." He paused and glanced over at the next table. "As a matter of fact, I was just going to leave for the course." He began to get up.

"Now Adrian. I can tell you haven't ordered your lunch yet." She lowered her voice, almost purring. "Do I make you uncomfortable or is it the others staring?"

A deep frown clouded his face. He glanced in both directions at other guests. "Okay. Sabrina. Let's have it. What do you want from me?"

"Why don't we just have a friendly lunch together?" She reached over to touch his hand, but he withdrew it. "Didn't you say, we'd be friends? That's your usual expression for former lovers."

His body went rigid. "Why are you doing this? And why bother now?"

Before she could respond, the waiter appeared at the table. She checked the specials. "I'll have your clam chowder with sourdough bread. Why about you, Adrian? Shall I order for you?"

Adrian forced a smile at the waiter. "Give me your smoked beef sandwich with lots of fries. I can use the energy boost."

"Maybe you need a partner? To play this afternoon, that is."

Annoyance caused him to grind his teeth. "No. I've a pre-scheduled game at one today. I'm playing with Jim."

"Oh. You've already found a new partner. I should have known."

The interruption as the waiter served their dishes was welcome for both. She watched his body relax. Sabrina could barely suppress a smile.

Her voice raised, she glanced at the table next to them. "I don't know why you're in such a snit. It's not like you and Celeste lunched here regularly like Ian and I did." She grinned in satisfaction as she watched Adrian cringe back into his chair. Now that she knew how badly he reacted to a public scene; this was going to be so easy.

He took a huge bite of his sandwich and chewed silently while he pretended to glance out a nearby window.

Sabrina fidgeted then concentrated on finishing her soup. It was time to go. He kept on ignoring her. He was good at that. However, she'd gotten what she wanted.

She savoured the last piece of bread, drained her glass and got up to leave. "Well, you'll soon be off for your game so I must run. We'll have to do this again." After picking up her purse, she turned and headed for the door.

With her luncheon success, Sabrina decided to give him a short break. The apprehension would be good for him. She waited until the next weekend before she decided to track him down at a local haunt. It took four swings past the Pillar and Post Inn before she was successful. His Audi was parked in front where he normally left it when they went to the Cannery Restaurant. Her car slid into a spot three over from his. She pulled down the visor mirror, checked her lipstick, smiled broadly, and opened the car door. The sky was beginning to get dark. As she climbed the stairs into the restaurant, another smile played across her lips. The host on the front counter was easy work.

"Do you have a reservation, madam?"

"Yes. I'm joining Adrian Gardner. He's expecting me."

While she followed the host to Adrian's table, Sabrina checked out the other diners. Without an audience, this wouldn't work. Good. The closest two were staring at her. She stood for a moment longer then sat across from him.

"Sorry I'm late, dear. Traffic was awful in the downtown."

Adrian's eyes widened as a frown crossed his face. "Sabrina what's this about?"

She pretended alarm. "Aren't you glad to see me?"

"Keep your voice down, will you. We don't want to disturb the other guests." He continued to eat his steak, not looking at her.

Sabrina sighed. "What are you worried about? The other guests have probably heard old married couples quarrel before." She signaled the waiter. "Bring me a menu and a large glass of merlot."

As he dropped his fork and sat back, Adrian replied. "What is it you want this time, Sabrina? Can't you find another way to amuse yourself? There are other men in town."

Her lips formed a pout. "There was a time when you welcomed this suntanned body next to yours. Why don't you reach your hand under the table and experiment?" She chuckled and took another sip of wine.

The steel in Adrian's eyes would have stopped anyone more timid than her. "Okay. I'm tired of these games. What do I have to do to get you to stop? Just tell me."

Sabrina leaned forward. "Well. A real date on Saturday night would be nice. You seem to prefer Casa Mia in the Falls. We've enjoyed ourselves there over dinner many times."

Adrian threw some bills on the table. "No way. Not with you anytime. And you can get the bill this time. I've business across town." He glared at her as he turned and left the table.

Her stomach clenched. This wasn't much fun anymore. He caught on too quickly and once he regained control, there was no moving Adrian. The tightness in her chest returned. How could he humiliate her by just walking away like that? She'd find a way to attack where he was most vulnerable?

On Sunday, she stopped by the golf club restaurant at noon, but he was surrounded by four other men. She'd forgotten how men stick together when threatened. The obstacle would be too great. On the way home, she passed the usual places the six of them gathered including Celeste's current house on Christopher Court. A jolt of anger spiked through her head. What was Adrian's Audi doing in the driveway? He hadn't mentioned Celeste since the incident at En Blanc. Back on adjoining Charlotte Street, she parked, her head rested on the steering wheel with her arms crossed. What did this mean? As her head cleared, she sat up, her mind clear. She had her answer. Celeste was his weakness. She could best get to him through Celeste. She smiled as she pulled back into the street and headed home.

Chapter Thirty-Five
Sabrina

The next morning, seated at her kitchen table, Sabrina sipped her second cup of coffee, deep in thought. She needed to be more strategic this time. No more time to run off with half a plan in mind. She'd seen Celeste around town at different restaurants during the lunch hour, but always with Marjorie. Marjorie could be a formidable opponent. She wanted to catch Celeste alone. Back at one of those coffee parties the women used to have, she remembered Celeste mentioned playing tennis. The only outdoor court in town was over in Memorial Park so Sabrina decided to check it out.

Sabrina felt a surge of excitement as she rushed upstairs to change into tight white shorts and a hot pink top. She relaxed against the leather seats of her leased BMW as she slowly maneuvered through steady morning traffic. Parked in front of the club house, she watched the action until she located Celeste seated at a picnic table with team members and sipping a glass of lemonade. The stunned look on Celeste's face, when she approached was worth every effort. The three women with her who had been chatting with enthusiasm froze. Sabrina took her time until she stood facing her rival.

"I planned a morning swim until I noticed you over here. It's time we had a talk, you and me. Don't you think?"

Celeste glared at Sabrina. "Why would I want to talk to you? I don't have anything to say to you."

Anger moved in waves over Sabrina. "That's what you might think. I'm sure you think you've clutched your husband back into your bosom. You don't think he can be trusted, do you?"

As she stood to face Sabrina, Celeste took a deep breath. "I don't know what you're trying to prove. If you and Adrian had a row, that's your business."

This was just what she wanted. Sabrina puffed out her chest and smirked. "Did you know he had another woman in his apartment last Friday night? I know he was with you at the Riverview Winery earlier that day." Although it was a lie, Sabrina would use what tools she could invent.

Celeste's face flushed bright red and her hands clenched. "Why should you care? He's obviously not seeing you anymore?"

Her determination surprised Sabrina. This wasn't the Celeste she'd known. Undecided about how to proceed, Sabrina watched one of her women friends with a determined expression on her face came over to stand beside Celeste. A team approach would shift the balance.

"I think you'd better go now."

The two of them made a formidable opponent. Sabrina choose to back away. Her plan hadn't worked. Celeste wouldn't run back to Adrian in distress like Sabrina had hoped. As she recognized she couldn't win this time, Sabrina glared at the women, turned her back and strolled back to her car. What was next for her?

*　*　*

Back at her home, Sabrina poured a large glass of Shiraz and retired to the back garden to lay on the lounge chair. As she relived this morning's encounter, she wondered what had gone so wrong.

Sabrina acknowledged to herself Celeste hadn't been hurt by the notion of Adrian cheating with someone new. She'd been shocked and embarrassed by Sabrina's confrontation in public in front of her friends. However, she didn't seem too bothered about who Adrian was now dating. Maybe their relationship was over for good. Today, she had faced a new Celeste. But, if Adrian hadn't reconciled with Celeste, it meant a worse situation for Sabrina. He was now more comfortable with going forward alone than being with her. Damn it. Like it or not, Sabrina would have to do the same.

She had to get out of the house and do something.... anything. Where had she left those flyers from yesterday's mail. When she moved back into the kitchen with her glass, Sabrina noticed a bunch of paper in the wastebasket. She flipped through them and picked out the one about a local art show. Stonechurch Winery was just down on Lakeshore Road and she could get another glass of wine at the same time. Her energy restored, she rushed upstairs, pulled on a coral sundress and strappy sandals before heading for the door. Before she left, Sabrina drained her glass.

A crowd milled around the entrance of the winery; friends who'd arrived together, acquaintances who recognized each other. She was the only woman alone. Rather than feeling sorry for herself, she checked out the few men who leaned against the bar. Too old and grey. No prospects for her. Seeking a distraction, she cruised the displays in the vestibule which were filled with paintings and ceramic vases, plates, and pots. Thirst soon drove her up to the bar where she experimented with a glass of their Cabernet Franc.

Back to the displays, she stopped at a wonderful oil painting of what appeared to be a street scene in Florence. The artist, a middle-aged man with curly brown hair, intriguing black eyes and muscular arms caught her attention. He smiled at her.

"You seem so interested in my work. I've got a show coming up in Toronto with some of my larger European pieces." He handed her a card. "Free wine and canapés for all who show up. Bring your friends."

Sabrina gave him a wide-mouth smile. "That's my kind of show. And I'm from Toronto. Is it in the Yorkville area?"

He shook his mop of hair. "No. That's for the artists who've made it. For emerging artists like me, we congregate in the new King Street West district. Studios mix well with the small designer shops and chic restaurants. It's now the in-place."

She removed a small calendar with attached pen from her handbag. "When is it then?"

"From Thursday to Saturday, two weeks from now."

"Mmm. Looks like just after thanksgiving on October 19th. I'll be there." Not wanting to seem too obvious, Sabrina gave a brief smile and moved on to the next display. It was worth the effort to show up just to see those mysterious eyes once more.

After she drained her glass, Sabrina glanced around the room but recognized no one and made her exit. As she drove back home, she felt an excitement which had been missing for her. A weekend in Toronto would revive her and it was just two weeks away. Back in her kitchen, she phoned and booked a two-night stay at the Marriott.

*   *   *

The two weeks dragged by as Sabrina checked out local arts exhibits and tried out a few new wineries. When she finally arrived in Toronto, the desk clerk at the Marriott, a young Asian woman, checked Sabrina in and handed her the door card, a small gift bag and mentioned the complimentary breakfast. She then signaled to a porter to take care of Sabrina's luggage. Wow. She hadn't had this much service in years. She'd have a good dinner here tonight, go over to the Eaton Centre tomorrow morning for some shopping and visit the gallery around four. She didn't want to appear overanxious to see the artist. The card in her purse carried his name *Emmanuel* in cool violet. She shrugged. With artists you could never tell. He might prefer men.

To Sabrina's surprise, the dining room was crowded in the morning, but the fresh coffee with a basket of croissants, crusty buns and a small pot of strawberry jam put her in a serene mood. A swim and sauna would get rid of the extra calories before lunch. She'd prefer to shop in Yorkville for higher end fashions, however, the walk would take too long.

After a careful check of the directory posted in the mall, she sighed. Probably the designer floor in The Bay was the best she could do. She made her way over there and watched the throngs of people on the escalators all going somewhere. The Fourth Floor teemed with busy women who checked out sales tags closely before taking items into the fitting rooms. A well-dressed clerk approached Sabrina and checked her out.

"I'd say about a size ten and something amber or peach. Have you looked at the Halston Collection? Good bargains in your style today." She led Sabrina over to a section of tailored dresses and suits.

She pretended to browse until the woman gave up and left. She didn't need more office clothes. Silk blouses and linen pants was more like it. By three, she felt fatigue and made her way back to the escalator. Four bags of items showed her restraint. She'd still have time for a short rest before her next adventure started.

The taxi driver checked the card and nodded his head. "Yeah. I got it."

Bumper to bumper cars the full way down King Street to the gallery caused Sabrina to recall one of the reasons she and Ian left Toronto. It was four thirty by the time she entered the shop and strode directly over to Emmanuel. "Hi. Do you remember me from the show in Niagara-on-the-Lake?"

He grasped and kissed her hand. "Mademoiselle. Of course. I never forget anyone who admires my work. Come with me. I'll show you even more." How she loved his European accent.

His section of the gallery was impressive. The white walls with track lighting on the ceiling showed off the paintings well. Although attracted to his paintings of Tuscany, she found herself drawn even more so of those done in Rome. After choosing one that showed a dark-haired mother and two sons in their enclosed garden, she handed over her Visa card and asked him to have it shipped. She wondered through the other sections while waiting for him to finish.

When she returned to his small desk in the corner, he was arguing with an older grey-haired man, arms swung over his head in gestures.

"Papa, why must you sell the shop? We're doing a good business here. Where will the artists go?"

"Emmanuel, I'm too old for this. It's time to retire. I told you. Why don't you buy the gallery and collect rent from the others?"

Emmanuel dropped his arms and groaned. "I talked to the bank, but they said no. Artists aren't good businesspeople. Too emotional, the man said."

Sabrina took a quick look around. "How much rent per artist?"

The older man stared at her. "From $1000 to $1400 per section payable each month. These are large rooms." He was probably assessing the cost of her wardrobe.

She remained calm while calculating in her head. "And do they pay? I don't take promises."

The old man checked her out more carefully before he responded. "I get signed contracts from each and make sure they pay. Otherwise, they go." He glared at his son. "That's good business."

"I might be interested, but I need more details. Can we arrange a meeting with your bookkeeper tomorrow afternoon? I need to review your accounts and take copies of income statements to my bank manager."

The old man took her hand in both of his. "Madame this might be possible. I have an office upstairs. Come back tomorrow at ten and Leo will be there. We don't need to rush. I'd like to retire before winter is all. It's much warmer in Italy." He smiled at Emmanuel and slowly climbed the stairs to the second floor.

Emmanuel's eyes danced. "What a find you've been. I'll say nothing to the others until we know. I've been worrying every day for months about this move. Believe me. We're all doing well in this location."

On the ride back to the hotel, Sabrina's stomach fluttered. Could this be her future? Her own business with space for new and emerging artists to build their careers. Why not? She'd planned to move back to Toronto anyway. There was nothing left for her in Niagara-on-the-Lake. She'd need to talk to Ian about the investment funds. Much of it was jointly owned and he might balk at cashing some of it out.

* * *

Back in her own bedroom, Sabrina worked out a plan. Ian was more approachable in person, so she'd have lunch at the golf club once more. If she arrived before he did around 11:15, she could catch him before he got seated. She selected a navy coat dress with white piping he liked and a pair of deep blue high heels. On the drive over, she rehearsed her business plan.

Her scan of the parking lot didn't pick up his car, so she waited in the entrance way of the restaurant for him to appear. After fifteen minutes, she had become impatient when the door opened, and she recognized his slim build in tan shorts and a buttoned-down shirt with his ebony black hair.

He stopped in the doorway and then walked over to her. "Sabrina, what brings you into town? I thought you were moving to Toronto." His tone was full of sarcasm.

She gritted her teeth and gave him a full smile. "Not yet, dear. I'm still setting up my new business." She watched his eyes narrow.

"That sounds intriguing. Tell me more." He signaled to the host who led them to a table. Seated, both checked the lunch menu, ordered, and waited for the waiter to leave.

Sabrina breathed deeply. She needed Ian's support on this. "I've stumbled on an art gallery for sale with a clientele of real paying artists."

Ian's eyes narrowed. "In Yorkville? The galleries are expensive in that part of town. Where do you plan to get the money?"

"That's just it. This gallery is on King Street West, a new area for studios and shops which is much more reasonable."

"It used to be only the new and struggling artists on the West side. Has it changed?"

"Yes. Definitely. I'd love to have you come with me to see it. It would have to be soon since the owner is older and wants to sell out right away."

Ian stiffened. "You have your own money. Why involve me?"

Sabrina knew she'd need to handle this with extreme caution. "We said the investment funds would be shared but we'd keep each other informed. Besides, I'd really value your advice on this deal, and I have the paperwork here."

Ian jerked his head around the room. "We're not discussing money here. You know better."

"Okay. Would you be willing to come over for dinner Saturday night and we can discuss it then?"

His face brightened. "You know my weaknesses. I hate eating alone. Yes, I'll be there around seven. After dinner we can spend some time going over the figures."

A trip to the local butcher for a sirloin roast and the open-air market for vegetables prepared Sabrina for the event. She knew Ian loved roast beef and it was one thing she could cook well. It seemed strange fussing over him after all the quarrels and separation. Dressed in a deep blue silk top over draped black pants, she was ready for the evening when the doorbell rang.

"Come on in. It's still warm enough for a drink on the deck. What will you have?"

His serious expression softened. "How about a good California chardonnay?

She poured two glasses in the kitchen before they moved to the garden.

"I've reviewed our portfolio over the past couple of days, and we can free up about $150,000. Do you think that's enough?"

"It will more than cover the down payment." She waved both hands in the air. "Let's not get into details just yet. After dinner, I'll go over the business plan with you in my office upstairs."

Sabrina felt a sense of elation rush over her. He was interested. In fact, he was eager. Just what she needed. She tipped back and drained the glass. "Come. Let's have our dinner while the roast is still warm."

Over dinner, they talked about Ian's golf partners and his volunteer work with the town. He was now recognized as an expert on sewage systems which was in greatly needed by the town due to the current building boom. She could tell he was proud of his accomplishments and was glad he'd found something for himself. Relieved, she realized the work had improved his mood.

Her patience was wearing thin when he dawdled over dessert and coffee. Clearing away the dishes, she motioned for him to follow her upstairs.

When both were seated in her desk, she went through the business plan with him in detail. As a former investment advisor, she knew what to look for to ensure a business was healthy.

He nodded and asked questions but seemed to agree with her. This business had value and could continue to be a going concern in that location.

He stood and paced the small office. "Okay, so what are you asking me. Are you seeking a business partner in this enterprise or just advice like you said?"

Sabrina breathed out. "I'd prefer a partner but if it doesn't appeal to you, then advice and discussion about what we should liquidate to buy it."

Ian scratched his head. Tension filled the silence. "As long as you understand, we're still separated, then I could be interested in this as a business venture. You'd be the upfront manager since I know nothing about art. I'd be the silent investor and would demand regular accounting."

Her face relaxed. "That's great, Ian. I appreciate your business knowledge and we can both benefit from this. I'll go ahead with the final arrangements next week."

As she later saw him out the door, Sabrina knew what had kept them together for so many years. It had never been romance. They were good partners and intellectually a great match. She'd enjoy this part of their relationship continuing through the business. Her confidence grew. It was a strong base to launch her new life back in Toronto.

Chapter Thirty-Six

Celeste

Celeste had firmly stood her ground with Sabrina, but she now felt the aftereffects. Her head ached and she just wanted to go home, crawl into bed and turn out all lights. But first, she joined the group at the table. It wouldn't look good to rush off.

"I'm sorry you had to hear our quarrel. Sabrina can be quite belligerent when she's crossed. Thanks for being there for me."

As usual, Janet took the lead. "Jim and I have been through our own bad times. We even separated for two years over an affair with his secretary. I didn't think I'd ever want him back, but then he changed. Wiser with age, I guess. For the past ten, we've never been happier."

Rachael next to her grimaced. "I can't believe how brazen that woman was. No sense of guilt, no understanding of your pain, just her own needs and wants."

Brenda dropped her head and rubbed her eyes. "I didn't tell you, but Claude and I have separated a few weeks ago. I've tried but I can't tolerate his drinking and arriving home late from the casino broke."

"I'm sorry to hear that, Brenda," said Janet. "Has this been going on for a long time?"

"Probably. When he was at the office every day, I didn't see it. He'd come home after too many; I thought it was from entertaining clients. Now that he's retired, it's different. And with the casino so close, he's gambling as well."

"I'm glad you shared with us," said Janet. "Let us know if you need anything."

Rachael put her arm around Celeste's shoulders. "Remember, we're here for you. Don't let that bully get you down. Maybe Adrian has had enough of her by now."

Celeste took a deep breath. "That's just it. I don't think I care. We go out for dinner about once a month, but I wouldn't want him to move back. I agreed with him to try friendship, but I don't love him anymore."

Rachael sighed in sympathy. "You're starting to find your new self, Celeste. Keep an open mind and experiment with what brings you satisfaction. That's what you pursue. We'll be here to back you up when you need it.

Chapter Thirty-Seven

Adrian

The cab dropped Adrian off at the Crowne Plaza late Monday night. Tomorrow would be a full day of meetings at the hospital, but his contract was nearing an end. Normally, he looked forward to winding up these projects, with most of the disruption for staff in the past. But tonight, as he sat at the bar with a last scotch, he dreaded the emptiness. No new contract was on the horizon. Maybe because he hadn't been searching as hard as needed. He ran his hand through his hair. He couldn't imagine what he do next if the investment group didn't work out?

He grinned. He'd handled Sabrina well in the end. Her demands and manipulation were more than he could tolerate. Did she think with his work in negotiations, he didn't recognize what she was trying to do with him? He shook his head, left the bar, and headed back to his room. He couldn't understand why he didn't see what she was really like sooner. Maybe he'd have been able to save the relationship with Celeste.

He entered the large room with the mahogany king-sized bed and walked to the window. From his dinners with Celeste, he knew she had moved on. It was time to give her up. Her new life provided what she needed, and she'd become wary of any renewed closeness between the two of them. On the weekends, he spent time at the golf club as before, but Ian no longer spoke to him. He had reason to hate Adrian with Sabrina now gone. Dennis, his closest friend, had died. Even though he still couldn't believe it at times. Klaus, Michael, and their three buddies seemed to like him. He wondered how far their dream of owning a winery would go. He'd seek them out again when he got back on the weekend. His entrepreneur genes tugged at him.

When Adrian entered the boardroom the next morning, he expected to see Jim and his group of new senior managers. His training program with them was complete except for the last piece on the culture of organizations. That one was never complete. To his surprise, the room was full of staff with a huge cake and pots of coffee placed in the middle of the table.

Jim stood at the front of the room. "Adrian, we want to express our appreciation for all the work you've done for this hospital." He placed a long package in Adrian's hand. "Since this is your last week with us, we're beginning the sendoff today."

A genuine sense of pride rushed over Adrian. He took his work seriously and knew he did it well. As he ripped open the gift, his face flushed. He held up the new golf putter for everyone to see. "This is great. I'll be taking a few weeks off when I get back so this will get good use."

An hour later, seated in his own small office, he looked up to see Jim enter. "I meant it, Adrian. You're incredibly good at what you do. I'm confident the hospital can move on toward a better future. If there's anything I can do for you, let me know. I'll have my secretary send a reference letter."

Adrian shook his hand. "Good. I like to hear those words. I've dedicated this last part of my career to saving hospitals. It's nice to hear I'm appreciated."

Before he knew it, the last round of meetings was over, and he was back on a plane to Toronto. His mood had improved, and he could look forward to going home. Maybe this would be his final job as a consultant. He called Michael to arrange a meeting tomorrow morning for a serious discussion about the investment in a new winery.

*   *   *

They'd agreed to meet at Klaus's home on Lakeshore Road. On his way there, his face smarted from the chilly wind, while he noticed the shrubs and trees along the roadside which had turned yellow and brown. Fall had arrived. Klaus lived outside town on the same property as his seventeen acres of vines. He followed Michael up the stained wooden steps, onto the wrap-around porch with two its wicker couches.

With the six of them seated around the oak dining room table, his wife Carole passed around large mugs of fresh coffee. Klaus, as usual, took the lead.

"Are you still in with us, Adrian?"

Adrian looked him straight in the eye. "You bet. I told you I'd be here today."

Klaus took a sip of coffee. "Well, you never know with these city people. Change their minds every few days." The group chuckled. He turned to Michael. "We know what's it's like to be left in the lurch."

Michael patted Klaus's arm. "We thought we had a deal several months ago. One of the big wineries, which shall remain nameless, strung us along with promises until we had our lawyer draw up a contract."

Klaus hit the table with his hand. "Sure, scared him off with the papers in front of him." He glanced around the table. "We got expensive buildings and equipment to construct and we're running out of time."

Adrian sat back, his mug in both hands, and waited.

Michael pulled out copies of the proposed contract from his bag and passed them around. "Adrian's not the type to put his money on the table until he sees the terms. We're giving you a week or two to review this and let us know."

Wow. Where they ready to accept him? "Is that all I have to do?"

"Well. Next meeting, we'll ask our lawyer, Wally, to join us. Then we need to see when you can commit and how much."

As he remained silent, Adrian rapidly went over the details on the papers to see if they had a viable business plan with a proposed budget.

"Any of the banks interested or are we in this alone?"

"The Credit Union." Klaus looked at the others and waited for some nods. "Out here we pretty much use the credit union."

Adrian needed more time to research how much would be needed and find out if these players had it.

"I'll take you up on the two-week review. In my experience, too much rush can result in a poorly thought out plan."

Klaus stood. "Okay then. I got others to talk to, so we'll meet here again in two weeks."

Michael pulled out his Blackberry and checked the date. "How about Wednesday, the week of thanksgiving? Does that work for the rest of you?"

Adrian already had figured out the players. Klaus was the lead, but Michael was the organizer and the catalyst behind the scenes. He liked him and trusted he'd made a solid plan.

During the drive home, facts and figures ran around in his head. He desperately wanted to do this deal, but his long-term caution said to wait until all the facts were on the table. No doubt, he'd be on his computer all day tomorrow. The most important aspect was to find out what people in town thought of the five of them. Where they solid citizens or fly-by night schemers? He knew how to find this out. He'd be playing a lot of golf over the next ten days.

251

*   *   *

His head reeled when he finally left the club house on Monday night around 10 p.m. From his foggy head, he knew, he'd consumed one too many scotches, so he maneuvered the car at low speed along Prideaux Street on his way back to the condo. All three of his golf partners agreed on one thing. Wineries were both very lucrative and a huge risk. Next, he needed to talk to the big player who dropped the group and find out why. Dinner with a couple of the board members from the club confirmed for him what he'd guessed. Klaus was known to grandstand so he should watch him. Michael retired from an investment business in Toronto and seemed to know what he was talking about.

He'd do some more online research tomorrow at home before he showed up at the Friday meeting with the large winery owners. Then it would be worthwhile to explore what pockets of capital he could free up. Satisfied, he crawled into bed and fell into a deep sleep.

The next day, he was so absorbed in the spreadsheets he pulled together, the light disappeared over the horizon before he shut down the computer and left to seek out some dinner. The Gordon House as usual teamed with locals when he strode to the reception kiosk and asked for a seat. He hadn't been here for a while since Sabrina wouldn't set her foot through this door. No atmosphere and too many calories for her.

He ordered a pint from one of the local micro-breweries with the special and sat back to people watch. Surprised, he overheard the three men at the next table talking about Klaus and his aspirations. Local gossip could prove useful to him.

"He was the one with big ideas even back in high school before he went away to college."

The second man, well-tanned and a little older, scratched the back of his head. "I'm not so sure he's on the wrong track this time. My neighbor, Joe, is a grower who sells to the new winery on Lakeshore Road. He knows the group."

"The thing is can they do it cheaper than the processor the other local growers use?"

"They're not the first growers trying to take on production for new wineries. But the older largest group, Wine Country, charges too much. That's why the owners are determined to find another way."

"But isn't it building the processor that's expensive?"

"I hear their plan is to build a huge processor to do their own and take in business for others. That might work."

The first man signaled to the waitress who brought them a bill. "I got to be on my way. Joyce worries if I'm home late after a long day in the fields." All three of them threw some cash into the middle of the table on top of their bill.

A smile crossed Adrian's face. His observation of people had benefited him more than he wanted to admit over his career. Usually, it was in the hospital's cafeteria where staff would let their real feelings show. This new information would be especially useful for his next owners meeting.

*   *   *

Friday morning, Adrian dressed carefully in a pale blue long-sleeved shirt, navy, and red stripped tie with grey summer wool pants. This would look respectful but not too Bay Street. He'd heard, the chair, Donald Longo, a shrewd businessman, expected some decorum from his members.

Adrian displayed all the confidence he didn't feel when the secretary ushered him into the boardroom. He noted there were only four men in the room, pouring their own coffee. He knew what Donald looked like from their website and strode over to him with extended hand.

Donald gave a firm handshake. "You must be Adrian Gardner. Glad we could get together." He gestured to the other three. "You can introduce yourselves."

Adrian made the rounds filing away the additional names for later reference. Part of his training as a consultant. His interest returned to their leader who gestured for them to sit.

"We hear you've been assessing the Klaus Richter group. Good move on your part to check with those who know what they're up to."

After a sip of strong coffee, Adrian joined them at the table. "I've heard mixed comments about Klaus, but Michael seems solid and their plan, on the surface, appears to have some merit."

Donald raised his eyes and sat back. "What do you hope to get from us? You know we made an assessment and walked."

Adrian gave a tight smile. "Just doing my due diligence, I guess." His manner changed, and his back turned to steel. "So, what turned you off? What am I missing here?"

"Klaus and I don't see eye to eye. Never did. I thought it might be different this time, but he's still all bluster. I don't know the rest of the group. It was enough to make me cautious and they never came back to the table."

Why was it always personalities which ruined deals? As he checked out the expressions on the faces of the remainder of the group, he could tell two of them didn't agree with Donald and the last one was a fence sitter. He wouldn't get much more here so might as well exit gracefully.

"Thanks for your time, gentlemen. I appreciate your candor." He stretched his face into a broad smile, shook hands all around and walked to the door to leave.

Donald's voice was strained. "My message to you is caution. It's the leader who usually screws up the deal."

Back in his car with the top down, Adrian drove back along the back roads while he enjoyed the breeze. Donald was right. From what he's heard, he recognized that it was both Klaus and

Donald who screwed up this deal from the beginning. The others just went along.

He spent the weekend checking all his investment accounts and scrapped together enough for a down payment. Early Monday morning, he phoned Michael to advise he was ready for a follow-up meeting with the group. It took a day before he got the call. The meeting was set for Wednesday morning and the lawyer would be there. He'd soon be a part owner in a new wine processor and tasting facility. A double scotch over ice on the balcony was all the celebration he wanted. He realized Celeste hadn't been on his mind even once over the past hectic week. Work was still his greatest escape.

Chapter Thirty-Eight

Celeste

Her meeting with Diane went well. Most of her program outlines were approved and she would start the real work next week. She knew the first day would be the hardest. Nurses tended to be skeptical and hard to win over. Well, she was up for it.

Walking into the empty classroom the next morning, Celeste felt bubbles of anxiety float in her stomach. She could have discussed her first class with her daughter Natalie. After all, she taught at university and would be challenged regularly by bright students who didn't hesitate to say what was on their own minds. With half an hour to prepare, Celeste knew she would be okay. Moving around the classroom, she set up flip charts beside each grouping of six with the last one firmly established beside her at the lectern. Next, she distributed a supply of paper and pens and organized her notes. She poured a large glass of water and drank most of it. Nothing like a little tension to make one thirsty. As she set the glass down, the first group of students entered the room.

A young woman of about thirty with short blond hair and deep blue eyes approached and stood directly in front of her. She seemed genuinely curious. "Teacher where would you like us to sit?"

Celeste caught her gaze. "Hi. I'm Celeste and I'll be teaching the workshop today. You'll be working in groups so you can choose any of the tables."

The woman smiled. "I'm Jeannie. Did you want us to sign in?" She scrunched up her nose. "Our nurse manager told us we had to come, so we need you to verify we attended."

Why did managers always do that to their nurses? That would only make Celeste's job more difficult. "I'll do my best to make it interesting for you. I expect I'll learn as much from you as you will from me, so we'll both benefit from it. Here's the sign-in list and you can pass it around."

Jeannie seemed satisfied and she and her followers took one of the tables.

The next group to appear was led by a tall middle-age woman with straight black hair, her face set in a dark frown. Celeste heard her mumble to the group. "I don't know why I have to be here. Just because I'm new to this hospital doesn't mean that I'm new to nursing." The other members of the group, who appeared much younger, nodded their heads.

Celeste pretended to study her notes while the remainder of the students arrived. She waited quietly until all had taken their seats. She started by introducing herself to the group and wrote her name and contact information on the flip chart. Although still nervous, she took a deep breath and addressed the class.

"While we have a range of different ages and levels of experience in the groups today, we're all working towards the same goals. Can anyone tell me what those goals are?" She stared at the blank expressions turned towards her. Panic was beginning to rise in her chest. Could she do this? She told herself to keep calm. Finally, she saw a hand rise.

"Jeannie, what do you think we're here for?"

Her face pink with embarrassment, she responded. "Well, we're here to take care of patients. We do our best to help them get better. Why else would we be here?"

Celeste turned and gave Jeannie a big smile. "That's a great answer. At this workshop, we're going to concentrate on what we can do to make sure we do them no harm."

The older woman, whom she'd learned was called Pauline, jumped to her feet. "Are you one of those officials who thinks doctors and nurses injure their patients through carelessness?" Her face was red, and her hands were clenched.

Taking in deep breaths, Celeste calmed herself. "No. I was a nurse for twenty-three years. Just in another city, which is why you don't know me. Our hospital, as well as many others had worked out new methods to streamline processes and lessen any potential for errors to keep patients safe. That's what we'll be talking about in this workshop. Only I want you to develop your own processes for your work area in this hospital."

Pauline was grinding her teeth. "Have you discussed this with our Union Steward? He'll have something to say about this."

It was the same old argument that Celeste had faced many times in the past. "Of course. We sat down with the President of the Union and the representatives and explained the full course to them. We have their endorsement."

She could see that people at the other tables were looking down avoiding eye contact with each other. "Those of you who want to learn should stay. Anyone who thinks this is a waste of time, is free to leave and I'll explain your absence to your nurse manager.

Jeannie, spoke up once more. "This sounds like it could be fun. Why don't you go ahead with the exercises?"

"Okay." Celeste relieved the tension by distributing documents to each table. Taking a quick glance, she noted that Pauline had gone back to her seat, mumbling to herself. "This is a real case study based on an incident which happened in a Toronto hospital a few years ago. I'd like each group to identify what processes went wrong and develop a better way to do carry out those activities. You have forty minutes and then each group will report back."

The noisy buzz in the room reassured her. They had accepted the task and seemed to be enjoying working together to find solutions. She knew she could get through this first class. Pauline would continue to be a problem, but she didn't have followers. By the end of the session, Celeste felt in control. The work was gratifying and her team building skills would make the workshop a success.

Chapter Thirty-Nine

Celeste

The next four weeks flew past for Celeste. After the final role play of this module, she set the markers back on the flip chart easel and turned to the room full of nurses. It was great to see smiling attentive faces and eyes alight with stimulation.

"This is your last session in the patient safety series. I'm pleased and proud of how you've progressed. Now I hope that you'll go back to your wards and practice what you've learned."

She noticed one woman in the middle row who was frowning as she raised her hand.

"What can we do if we try these processes and they don't work? Can we call you back for consultation?"

"We talked about how you are all part of teams. Try getting advice from your team members first. If that doesn't work, you can sign up for my next class on customer satisfaction and use it as an example."

The laughter she heard from the group reassured her. She didn't want them to become dependent on her. That wasn't what teaching was all about. She watched them file out of the room in groups. It was amazing to her how the experience from her former hospital job had allowed her self-confidence to soar. She'd managed to start up her own business and knew from the feedback it was successful. Celeste realized she had let herself become like a door mat while living with Adrian. Celeste knew that she couldn't blame it all on him. Her former self would have stood up to him long ago.

She'd had some satisfaction when he called her last week at home.

"I've been thinking that we gave up too easily, "he'd stated. "Couldn't we give it another try? We've both learned things."

At least he was consistent. He wanted her back. What would that mean for her? Did he expect the same old relationship they fell into over the past few years?

Celeste knew her voice had an edge. "Tell me what that means exactly. Would you go your way and I go mine? If so, it wouldn't work for me." Now with her eyes opened, she suspected Sabrina wasn't the first. He'd lacked the guilt which a first affair would have generated.

"Come on now, Celeste," he pleaded. "You know we had good times." There was a long pause. "We loved each other once."

That statement rang true for her. She had adored him. She'd loved his edgy behavior which attracted admirers and the sleek way he dressed when they'd go out. She missed his loving touch and flattering glances. But, when he embarked on his fling with Sabrina, things had changed. She'd never be able to forget the humiliation she'd experienced at the Diner En Blanc when Sabrina showed up. She knew then all her trust in him and much of her respect had vanished.

"Yes, we did love each other once. However, I've become an independent woman again just like I used to be and that's important to me." She couldn't afford to take a chance on losing her self-respect. "No. I'm not ready to try again. Not now and maybe never."

During the long silence. she swallowed hard and blinked back tears. Then she squared her shoulders. She'd made the right decision.

Adrian sighed. "Let's leave it at that for now. You're not ready and don't know when you will be." He sighed. "Can we be friends? Maybe go for lunch and talk occasionally? I miss you."

"Give me a few more weeks on my own. Then, if you still want to see me, give me a call and we can talk about lunch." She dropped the phone into the cradle. She was surprised to find she hoped he wouldn't call.

*   *   *

Driving back toward home, she detoured to pick Marjorie up for lunch. She'd already called as a reminder earlier to say she'd be there in half an hour. Marjorie was gradually coming back to life after the deep pit of depression she'd fallen into when Dennis died. Celeste had been very worried her friend wouldn't ever regain her stability, to be able to laugh and enjoy life again. Best to make sure she was up. She punched in Marjorie's number.

"What have you been up to this morning?"

Marjorie responded. "You'll be surprised. I met with the travel agent to finish booking our cruise, like I promised. I can't believe how much I'm looking forward to getting away. Maybe it will help."

"Great. The Mediterranean sounds wonderful, especially the southern part of Italy. And, of course, the south of France."

"I've taken the full month of October off from any charitable commitments. Even with Janice taking the lead role right now, it's still a strain since I'm still training her." She paused. "I'm not sure I'll ever want to go back to it."

"We'll talk about it over lunch. I'll pick you up at the same time as usual. Can you be ready? We're going to Zeke's this time so it's a little dressier."

"Sure. I'll put on the pale grey dress with a rose and silver scarf. It makes me feel good."

"I talked to Adrian last week. Since we're both still living in town I might as well get used to him being around."

"I'm glad to hear you've reached that stage. Good progress. Okay, I'm going to get dressed right now and wait in the living room. Bye."

She slowly set the phone down. Marjorie had sounded much better today. Still she wondered about her reluctance to return to the Heart and Stroke Foundation Board. The depression was still hanging on like a cloud. Last week when Celeste called on her, she opened the door wearing her pajamas, hair uncombed and no make-up on at three in the afternoon. Her speech had been so slow that Celeste wondered if she had taken an overdose of some drug. That had really shaken her up. Marjorie still had a long way to go but Celeste was committed to helping her get there.

*　　*　　*

This time Marjorie opened the door after the first ring and wore the dress she had described to Celeste. During the drive, she confided to Celeste she was now going for an hour walk every morning except Sunday. When they reached Zeke's, the young host took them to a nice table near the gas fireplace. Although it was only September, Celeste was feeling the chill. After a close look at Marjorie, she realized that her friend was making the effort just for her. Her face was drawn and pale, her normally wavy hair hung in limp strands, but at least she was well dressed, and her eyes had some sparkle.

"Really, I want to know. How are you getting along?"

"I don't sleep well. I wake up in the night and reach over for Dennis, but he isn't there." Her eyes were swimming. "I miss his quiet, steady presence and his ability to know how I felt before I did."

"I remember from my counselling, Amy said that when you lose someone, it can take up to a year to get used to the loss. You need to keep active. You're not thinking about leaving the Foundation?"

Her face clouded. "I have no enthusiasm for fundraising right now and feel I should ask them to replace me." She sighed. "Getting out helps. Thank you for taking me places. I wouldn't have the energy to do it on my own.

Celeste put her hand over Marjorie's "Don't rush into it. Give yourself time."

Marjorie looked up and attempted to smile. "Since you went back to hospital work, I've been thinking about myself. Before I got into fundraising, I always wanted to teach. The colleges are constantly looking for experienced teachers in the non-profit field. When I'm ready, I plan to talk to them to see if they'd consider me."

"That sounds like a good plan." She pulled a brochure out of her handbag. "In the meantime, I love this cruise ship we're going on. It seems to have everything. Lots of wonderful food and good entertainment. The webpage mentions international lecturers, Broadway shows and ballroom dancing every evening."

Marjorie chuckled. "We'll look funny being the only two women dancing together on the floor."

"The Silver Star line has thought of everything. They even provide escorts in the ballroom to dance with single women travelling alone." Celeste smiled. "Would you believe it? Apparently, they're normal single men who get part of their trip for free for their service."

Marjorie smiled back. "Well, I don't think I'm up for dancing, but I think you'd enjoy it. It's about time that you looked at other men and put Adrian in the background."

Driving home after dropping Marjorie off, Celeste thought back to her comment. Was this final between her and Adrian then? They'd shared so much. She didn't feel like going home and found herself taking the long scenic drive along the Niagara Parkway instead. Parking the car, she strolled along the public path until she arrived at the staircase leading down to the boat club at Smuggler's Cove.

Adrian hadn't really been a sailor, but she recalled the sunny fall day, the first year they'd moved to town, when he'd suggested a picnic and wouldn't say where they were going. They'd spread out their wool blanket on the ground right around here somewhere and shared roast chicken sandwiches on Panini. He'd pulled a cold bottle of Shiraz out of the car trunk with two glasses. She could still imagine him, after their lunch, perched at the top of the stairway with a broad smile on his face as they stared at the water.

"You've got to come and see this." He'd gestured to her. "The white sails against the deep blue water with the cumulus clouds overhead. What a perfect day."

They'd stood together looking out over the Niagara River and everything had seemed right. They'd chosen the right home in the right town and life was good."

Her mood felt sober driving back home. Adrian had been a big part of her adult life and like it or not, she couldn't ignore the fact. However, she couldn't take him back without the risk of jeopardizing what she had built up for herself. What were her other options? She didn't know.

That afternoon when she arrived home, the red light on the answering machine was flashing. Although she'd usually ignore it, she picked it up.

"Hi, Celeste. It's me again. Adrian. I know you said to wait, but I'm hoping you'll join me for dinner this Friday night. You can pick the restaurant." She waited to hear him continue. "Please, at least call me back."

Celeste sighed. His timing had always been good. She sat in the living room holding the phone in her lap. Over the past few months, as she had begun to feel better about herself, Celeste acknowledged that she didn't hate Adrian anymore. He'd remain her ex-husband and they were both getting older. She dialed.

He sounded expectant. "Hello."

"Hi, it's Celeste. I got your message and have had time to think about what you asked me. I drove around to one of our favorite places today—Smuggler's Cove. It's still beautiful there in the fall."

Adrian murmured. "I remember it well. So, any hope for dinner out?" He waited.

Gripping the phone, Celeste forced herself to respond. "Okay. I've agreed we can try this friend's thing. But, just to stay in touch since we're both living here in town. We can talk more over dinner on Friday. Let's try the new restaurant, the River House."

Adrian sounded excited. "Great. I'll pick up around seven then. You won't regret it."

After he hung up, Celeste sat back against the cushions. She felt a small twinge of regret but pushed it aside. Occasional dinners wouldn't make any difference. She shrugged. He was right. They could at least try something new and see if maybe they'd both feel about better about their marriage. It was in the past now anyway. He could no longer hurt her.

Chapter Forty

Celeste

Celeste felt a renewed sense of hope for Marjorie when she agreed to go with her to see The Light in the Piazza at the Shaw Festival. She was beginning to see slow progress in her friend. She seemed to have reached the stage where she could socialize in a crowd provided, she had a friend nearby. At the intermission, the tiny foyer was crowded so they were forced to stand squeezed around a small round table with two others. Celeste offered to pick up two glasses of white wine for them at the bar. When she turned away from the bartender, with both hands full, and started back towards the table, she sensed that someone was staring at her.

Dressed in a white Egyptian cotton shirt and baggy khaki pants, he reminded her of a guy she dated in college. His hazel eyes and grey rumpled head of hair and trimmed beard caused her to catch her breath. As he followed her back to their table, she noticed the bare feet in leather sandals. What fun. Perhaps this man was a rebel at heart. She set the two glasses on the table, then turned to gaze back at him but within minutes a middle-aged woman joined him and the two were soon engaged in conversation.

Celeste realized Marjorie wanted to discuss the play with her, so she pulled herself back to her friend.

"What did you think of Clara choosing a younger Italian man? It didn't seem realistic to me. Marjorie asked.

"Well, he was good looking. Personally, I loved the music. It's what attracted me to the play."

While waiting for Marjorie's response, Celeste looked over at the stranger, but the woman and he were both gone.

"Who was that man?" Marjorie had caught her glance. "He sure seemed to be interested in you."

Celeste's face felt hot. "I don't think I know him. Somehow he did seem familiar." She smiled. "I found him attractive. However, I hope that woman wasn't his wife. I know what that feels like."

Marjorie shook her head. "They didn't necessarily come together. Let's watch where they're sitting. It's a small theatre." She turned her head. "He's still there in the doorway looking this way."

What did this mean for her? Celeste was surprised she could even think about other men. She didn't want to open herself up to all that pain again. Celeste's hands gripped the glass tightly as she swallowed the last sip of wine. "Let's go in. I don't want to miss the ending."

They made their way through crowded aisles to their seats. For now, Celeste just wanted to enjoy being single again. All the same, she relaxed when she saw him, and his female companion settled into separate seats in different rows. Next time she'd work up the courage to speak to him. Unless he was a tourist, she might run into him somewhere in town. Or it could be some other good-looking man at another event. She was finally ready to reach out.

Later, on their way down the long flight of stairs to the exit, the stranger approached her. "I tried to catch you earlier, but I was interrupted by my colleague. I've seen you in the hospital cafeteria. Do you work there?"

Celeste smiled. "No wonder you looked familiar. I give a patient safety workshop to some of the nurses a couple of times per week."

"Great. I'm Dwight Sinclair, one of the new docs. Would you like to have coffee next time you're there?"

She hesitated. It would be opening new doors. "Okay. What about next Wednesday around ten? I'll meet you inside the main entrance."

"I'll see you then." He handed her a card with his phone number and asked for hers. "Just in case one of us has to cancel on short notice. It often happens to me." She was glad the hospital had printed up some for her.

Back in her car, Celeste turned to Marjorie to confide what she'd done. "Am I being stupid to open myself up again? Yes, he works at the hospital, but I don't know anything else about him. I wouldn't normally take the chance."

Marjorie nodded. "It's been months since the separation and it's only coffee. Give it a try."

"Just when I've decided I like being single, now this. I don't think I'm ready."

"The hospital cafeteria is pretty safe grounds, don't you think?"

"You're right. He is good looking and new in town. One of those nurses will soon snap him up, so I might as well take a chance."

*   *   *

When she realized, she had been staring at her computer screen for the last thirty minutes, Celeste decided to leave her lesson plan for now. Sometimes the words flowed smoothly and other times she was stuck. She realized from the sun it was almost time for lunch. She pulled on a pale blue skirt and soft pink flowered top before leaving to pick up Marjorie. With her friend teaching at the college four days a week, they both looked forward to an escape on their Friday afternoons off. Marjorie had reached another milestone. Their lunches were now down to once a week which was a good thing. Celeste had run out of new and interesting restaurants to explore.

As they drove along The Parkway towards Niagara Falls, on their way to the Victorian Restaurant, she felt a sense of relief. Marjorie was now so involved in her teaching; she rarely fell back into her dark moods.

"You know, I was so surprised when you first talked about teaching. You'd been into fundraising for so long, I couldn't imagine you doing anything else."

Marjorie said. "I surprised myself. When I kept delaying my return to the Heart and Stroke Foundation, I realized I needed a new outlet for my talents. I know the education and research the organization does is important. It was knowing the reality of how relentless heart disease can be that made me reluctant to return. I need to do something more active."

"Obviously, you did the right thing. You're brighter and more enthusiastic than I've seen you in years."

"Those young people are so eager to learn and so smart, I feel privileged to have anything to teach them. I look forward to my classroom every Monday. You must feel it, too."

"Hmm. I know what you mean. The nurses at the hospital are very bright and very committed, but they still want to learn. It helps that I have some real-life experiences to use as examples."

"We've lived through a lot, both in our early lives and since we retired. I'd never have thought I could make a life without Dennis and am relieved to say I'm getting there."

"The pain from the breakup with Adrian can still get me down, but I've grown so much since then. Maybe I needed a shock to push me out of my fog. I didn't dream I could have the life I have now."

Marjorie nodded. "Well, I was too comfortable with a lifestyle I'd lived most of my adult years. I enjoyed the excitement from those high-profile association events and had no reason to reassess what I really wanted to do when I grew up."

Both were laughing when they reached the front entrance of the restaurant. Celeste stopped to feel the sunlight on her face, then opened the door into the foyer and listened to the noisy chatter as they waited for a table.

Chapter Forty-One

Celeste

With these new nurses in her second class, Celeste couldn't contain her impatience, and gritted her teeth until the first coffee break. She could feel the tension in her neck and down her shoulders while she waited for them to quit their chatter and begin to leave the classroom. She couldn't believe how different they were from her first group. Younger and more into their own exclusive clusters. They didn't look to the facilitator for any expert advice.

After a quick look in her mirror, she refreshed her lipstick and hurried down the hall towards the front door. Her forced calm was shattered when Dwight wasn't there to greet her. She took several deep breaths, in an attempt not to panic and pulled out her cell phone to check for calls. Nothing. She groaned. This was like a first date in high school. About to return to her classroom, she spied a tall figure with grey hair headed towards her. I think that looks like him. She took a chance and walked to meet him.

Dwight's face brightened when he saw her. "I'm so sorry. I was with a patient and she seemed to want to talk on and on this morning. I worried you'd leave before I got here."

Celeste shook her head. "You did the right thing. It's one of our key points in the workshop. Focus on the patient and especially when they're older, don't rush them."

He smiled. "Great strategy, but some of them would keep you all day. Let's go to the smaller coffee nook. Otherwise, we'll both be interrupted by the nursing staff."

When they arrived, he took charge directing her to a table while he ordered coffee for both as she'd requested. Once seated at their secluded table in the back of the small space, he confided, "I've only been on staff for a month here. The Chief recruited me at a conference from St. Joseph's in Toronto."

"What do you think so far? My ex-husband and I moved here two years ago from Toronto. We both worked at UHN."

He took a sip of coffee and seemed preoccupied. "Yes, I enjoy the work very much. I'm still getting used to small town life. As you know, hospitals are fertile ground for staff rumours and general gossip."

Celeste sat back alert to a confession. "Hmm. When we first moved to Niagara, we expected that type of scrutiny. They'll move on after a time." She hesitated and then decided to be direct with him. "Do you have deep secrets to hide?"

He gave a deep laugh. "No. Not really. It's just I'm a new single man in town, I guess."

"Where you ever married?" Celeste continued to probe.

He sighed. "My wife, Donna, died of cancer almost ten years ago."

She dropped her head. "I'm sorry. I shouldn't have pried so much."

"It's okay. I can finally say I'm over it. I just wish I'd spent more time with her." The regret seemed genuine. "What about you? Anyone special?"

She bit her lip and hesitated. Since it was her who opened the topic, it was only fair for him to ask. "My ex-husband, Adrian, and I split up about six months ago."

He nodded. "That's not long. Are you still working things out?

"No." Once she'd blurted it out, Celeste realized it was true. "I know it's over for me. The issues went on for some time before the final blow. He had an affair." She was glad to see he didn't react.

"Adrian? I knew an Adrian Gardner when I was on a wait-times committee with executives from UHN."

"That would be him. He was a senior executive there for fifteen years before the down-sizing."

"I never ran into you though." He caught her eyes and held her gaze. "I would have remembered."

"Yes. But, as you know, the nurse managers and doctors didn't cross paths that frequently. Unless, of course, when you're on the same ward."

He chuckled. "Did I detect some criticism in your comment?"

She smiled and then glanced at her watch. "I'd better get back or I'll have some very irate nurses. They don't like instructors who waste their time."

He stood. "I've got another appointment soon, as well. I'd like us to get together again if you agree."

She nodded. Her curiosity aroused, she wanted to know more about him. It couldn't hurt.

The lines around his eyes showed when he frowned. "Okay. How about a drink after work one night for a start? When are you at the hospital next?"

Celeste smiled to herself. Maybe a bar was a good way to reduce the tension. "I'm here next Wednesday so let's make it around six before I leave for home. Any suggestions about a place?"

"We could go to Grant's Martini Bar. It's in that mall along with the Best Buy store. Do you know it? I don't know all that many places yet."

"Sounds good. I'll meet you at the bar for one drink since I'm driving." One drink with a near stranger, she could endure. This might be the last time. They said goodbye and both rushed off.

Celeste found her Wednesday afternoon class dragged as she thought ahead to her date that evening. I guess you could call it a date. After she located the bar and parked in the lot, she strolled towards it checking both shoulders to see if she saw anyone she knew. Settled on a comfortable leather bar stool, Celeste felt the thrill of being single again and enjoyed it. When Dwight arrived, she turned and waited for him to join her.

"How was your day? I see you're on time."

The corners of his eyes crinkled. "You sound just like Donna." He sighed. "Sorry. Now you know why I miss her, even after all this time." He sat still. "That wasn't a good way for me to start. I'm just not good at this dating game."

"That's okay. I'm also learning as I go along."

The small bar and café had a subdued elegance with its dark oak tables and matching chairs, low lighting from the brass wall lamps. He ordered a rum and coke while she choose a vodka martini. They drifted into a comfortable chatter.

Celeste talked about her team of nurses at her former hospital. "The old guard still called the new recruits *the kids*. I remember how I hated the expression when I graduated. I made sure to call them all by their names."

Dwight mentioned the rivalry between the group of surgeons in St. Catharines. "I'm still the new guy. Not to be trusted in the operating room on my own. I've showed them some new procedures. I know I'm good at this. They grudgingly had to admit it."

Celeste remembered the physicians at UHN were also incredibly competitive. "I know what you mean. It's great for me to feel confident in my work again."

He turned serious. "I do remember Adrian. Very bright guy and serious about his work. Everyone said he had a roving eye with the nurses. There was lots of gossip about him back then."

Celeste gulped. "Obviously, some of them were true. I didn't know. Maybe I was willfully blind, but his recent affair came as a shock."

He continued. "The woman you saw me with at the theatre, Blanche, was my live-in partner for five years, until recently. She wanted something more permanent and I couldn't give it to her. After we moved from Toronto, she confronted me about my lack of commitment. I just couldn't reassure her, so she got her own place. So, we keep in touch. Go out together when we need a date and that's it."

For Celeste, this was a warning light. Still in love with his deceased wife and afraid of commitment. She considered this new information carefully. Neither of them was ready to seek a long-term partner right now, so why not keep each other company. He seemed fun to be with and she could use another friend.

"I've enjoyed tonight. Why don't we get together again sometime? I'd love to show you what we've got in Niagara-on-the-Lake."

An intriguing smile floated over his mouth. "I hear there's a wonderful Heritage Trail out that way. Why don't we make it a Sunday and go for a long hike? I love to walk, and I don't do golf. We can set up a date over coffee the next time you're at the hospital. Call me. You have my phone number."

It was good news for Celeste that he wasn't another golfer. A few casual dates would be fun, and she was in good shape thanks to her tennis games. Her focus right now was on her new contracts. And besides, Marjorie still needed her, and it was a friendship she valued. New beginnings weren't easy but the opportunity to grow was worth it. She'd call him and set something up.

She wondered what Natalie would say about her plunge into a new life. Next time they talked, she'd bring it up and listen for her reaction. Her daughter was becoming a strong sounding board for her. Their relationship had deepened since the break-up.

On the way back home, she crossed the bridge over Lock Three. A chill crawled down the back of her spine as she gazed at the cold water. She never wanted to be that vulnerable again. When she closed her eyes, she could still feel the darkness in her mind, the day her car left the road bank and plunged into the canal. She shook her head to clear it. It seemed so long ago.

Right now, she loved her teaching job. Dwight was a nice diversion, but he might not last. In the meantime, thoughts of Adrian were slipping farther and farther away.

*   *   *

Celeste smiled at Julie, one of the nurses who had voluntarily stayed after class to talk to her alone.

"What can I help you with? Did I go over that material too quickly for you?"

Julie smiled and pushed back her long hair. "No, it was just the right pace." She looked down and Celeste noticed her hands were shaking. "It's something else. Did you ever wonder if you made the right choice? Choosing to be a nurse, that is. Sometimes I feel like an alien—like I'll never learn this stuff."

"Let's go over and sit at one of the tables. I'd feel better if I could see your face."

Julie followed her to the student's area and they both sat. Celeste turned to her and said. "It's more common than you might think. There's a big jump from the classroom and all those texts to dealing with some extremely sick patients. And you're right. It's not a career for everyone."

Julie sighed and dropped her shoulders. "When a patient tells me all about her symptoms, I'm supposed to know what to do. Instead it feels like an overload of words and I can't sort them out."

Celeste asked. "When did you graduate?"

Julie responded. "One year ago, I got my piece of paper and I was supposed to be a fully qualified nurse."

"You're right to question yourself if you don't feel the confidence you expected. It might help to get more involved in the role plays we use and contribute some real live situations." She looked at Julie to see if she was responding but her head was still down. "However, if you're sure you've tried everything and it's not getting better, it would be a good idea to ask for a session with your Nurse Manager to discuss this. She'll have your records and can tell if you're making progress."

Julie smiled. "I think that's a good idea as a last resort. Otherwise, I've been thinking about resigning but hate to give up two years of college."

Celeste shook her head. "What you learned is never wasted. You'll use it again sometime or somewhere in your career, but you need to clarify this issue, or you'll be very unhappy in your current job."

Julie stood and extended her hand to Celeste. "Thank you for giving me the time and for helping me to make a decision."

Celeste gave her hand a gentle squeeze. "I hope to see you next week and you can tell me how it went with your manager."

After Julie left the room, Celeste felt a warm glow creep up her neck. It felt so good to be needed by someone again. She moved back to her desk and picked up the phone to call Dwight. A few rings later, it went to voicemail. "Hello, this is Dwight Sinclair. Please leave a message and I'll call you back."

Celeste scrunched up her face in frustration. You could never get anyone on the phone anymore.

"Hi. This is Celeste calling to see if you're free for that hike you mentioned this Sunday. I'll manage about 10 km and then we can find a deli somewhere close by. Let me know if it's a go. You have my number."

She hoped that wasn't too direct for him. Then they had to get used to each other. This time she wouldn't be so eager to please.

The women at the tennis club had taught her to ask for what she wanted and expect it to be delivered.

*   *   *

Dwight had called back to say he was eager to try out a new trail. Hiking was something he'd done regularly on the trials north of Toronto. When she woke on Sunday, the sky had a moody grey tinge and puffy clouds edged in smoky tones. Oh no, it might rain and spoil their day. Celeste had a bowl of hot cereal, a fruit cup and coffee. When the phone rang at seven, she hoped it wouldn't be a cancellation.

"Hi, it's me. It looks like a perfect day for hiking. I hate toiling along in the heat. A good misty day gives me extra energy."

Celeste's mood clearer. "You must be a morning person. Cheerful and ready to go."

Dwight chuckled. "What about you? You sound a little pensive."

She sighed. "Pensive is me in the morning. My body wants to take its time to come to life. I'll be fine when we get there. Are you picking me up?"

"That I am, and I'll be there in half an hour. Just need to pack the car. I'm bringing lunch for two and some water."

"Are you that hungry or is some for me?"

He laughed. "Of course, some is for you. Today is my treat and I'll expect the same from you next time. If we don't make it a competition. I've never been a great cook."

"Okay. I better finish getting dressed and try to find my hiking boots. I've haven't used them since the last time I was up north at a cottage."

As Celeste rummaged through the basement storage area, she felt a surge of energy flow through her limbs. It was a long time since she'd done anything so adventurous. She'd last hiked with some of the nurses in Toronto on the Bruce Trail in Tobermory, but that was ten years ago and all women. She wondered if she'd be able to keep up with Dwight. He was tall and therefore probably walked faster than the norm. Once she dusted off the boots, they didn't look too bad. She had to admit they hadn't had a lot of wear.

She had them laced up and her knapsack packed when she heard the doorbell. When she pulled it open, she stopped in amazement? Dwight stood there in faded blue jeans, old navy t-shirt with a red and black checkered jacket over his shoulders. She should have remembered men either went with the latest gear from Eddie Bower or the dressed down outfits which suggested the Salvation Army.

"Ready to go? I like to be comfortable on weekends. Sort of being out of uniform which makes me happy" Dwight said. "You look great in that blue jacket."

Celeste picked up her stuff and headed out the door, locking it behind her. "I'm looking forward to a good long hike. It's something I haven't done in years. What about you?"

Dwight opened the car door for her and went around to his own. "I need to get out in the outdoors on weekends as often as I can. It clears the head and opens the chest."

Celeste found herself enjoying this new person with new ideas and new perspective. If this were a date, it wasn't as bad as she'd expected. Sharing an activity broke the ice and they both soaked up the lush greenery on both sides of the road during the drive to Laura Secord Trail. Once parked, they got their gear and picked up a map of the trail.

Dwight studied it closely. "I'm suggesting we take the portion up to Fireman's Park which is about 8 km. Do you think you can manage that far?"

Celeste squared her shoulders. "Of course. I've hiked farther than that before." She wasn't about to refuse a challenge. When she turned back to Dwight, his eyes twinkled.

"Okay. Let's get going then. If I walk too fast, let me know."

She was glad to see the first part was down a dirt road wide enough for them to stroll side by side. She watched the strong muscles in his legs as he seemed to move without effort. Her tennis had helped due to the need to run so at the beginning she felt no pain. Before long, the road narrowed which caused them to go single file. For the next half hour, he strode just in front of her and she could follow his back. Then Dwight began to disappear down the trail and she had to work hard to keep up. Her breath came in gasps as they began to climb. She'd lost sight of Dwight at least fifteen minutes and kept moving in hopes he'd be around the next corner.

Finally, she could see a small group of hikers sitting in a small meadow. There was Dwight with his back leaned against his knap sack. He waved her over.

"Sorry I lost you for the last half hour. Are you okay?"

She dropped to the ground with a sigh. Yes, of course. I'm tired and thirsty, that's all." Celeste pulled her water bottle out of her bag and drank for several minutes.

He laid out a green garbage bag and covered it with sandwiches, fresh strawberries, cheese, and snack bars.

"Help yourself."

Celeste grabbed a sandwich and took a large bite. "This is delicious. Exercise always makes me hungry." She watched as he sampled the sandwich and nodded.

"I confess, I bought them at the local deli this morning, but they're good."

Celeste chuckled. "You're such a fraud."

He laughed. "Don't say that until you've tried the strawberries."

The half hour break went fast, and they were soon trudging down the trail once more. This time, he hung back, and she could keep him in sight. They had both slowed down when the park came into sight. Dwight headed straight for a picnic table and she followed. As usual, the first thing out of the bag was their water bottles. They drank in silence.

Celeste touched his hand. "Thank you for a wonderful day. I've haven't been hiking since I worked as a nurse back in Toronto. It was great."

His broad smile crinkled his eyes. "I'm so glad you enjoyed it. It helps me decompress from the tension at work. Not every patient has good results."

Her mood turned sober. "I know what you mean. That's why I teach what I do."

Dwight said. "Well, I guess it's time to go. I could use a warm shower." He picked up his bag and headed towards the car. "You ready?"

Reluctantly, Celeste packed up and followed him. "I hate to leave but you're right. A long hot bath would feel good when I get home."

Before he started the car, he put one hand on her knee. "I hope we can do this again some weekend. I have to be on call next week but another time."

Celeste smiled. "Sure. I'd love that. We can try bicycling on the Niagara Parkway trail sometime too." She sat back in her seat and enjoyed the short ride back to her house but didn't invite him in. It was enough. She wanted to be alone for a while to take in all these new feelings. They said goodbye at her door, and he backed out the driveway. She knew she'd be seeing more of him.

Chapter Forty-Two

Celeste

The next Thursday when back in her classroom at the hospital, Celeste found her concentration wandered. Two students had to ask their questions twice before she pulled her mind back to reality and responded. She bit her lower lip in frustration. What was the matter with her? Just because Dwight was in the building didn't mean she'd hear from him. He'd said this was a busy week. Should she call him to meet for coffee or would it be too forward? Like many men, he seemed to be sensitive of his own space. When the class was over and the last student had left, she picked up the phone. She'd probably get his voicemail anyway.

His now familiar voice responded. "You've reached Dr. Sinclair. Leave a message."

Celeste sighed. So impersonal. But then, it was probably mainly his colleagues who called this number. "It's me, Celeste. I was hoping you'd have time this afternoon for a quick coffee break. Call me back when you can."

She opened her laptop and found the file with her next lesson plan. She might as well spend an hour here revising this plan instead of doing it when she got home, she had finished the last class for the day anyway. Half an hour later, she'd almost completed it when her cell phone rang.

"Hello"

"I got your message but couldn't break away until now. Do you still have time to share a break with me?"

It was Dwight but she detected a subdued tone to his voice. Something had happened. "Sure. I was just getting ready to leave but I can stay for another twenty minutes. I'll meet you at the small café in a few minutes."

"Good" He hung up the phone.

Celeste felt a tinge of worry as she packed up the rest of her things and hurried over to the place they usually met. As she approached, she stood back for a few minutes and watched Dwight before he looked up. He had leaned both elbows on the table and rested his head in both hands. That didn't look good.

When she got closer, he heard her shoes on the ceramic floors and sat back. He attempted a smile. "I'm glad you called. I needed someone to talk to."

That didn't sound like him. "What's up? Has something happened?" When he didn't respond she stopped. "Let me pick up the coffees. I'll be right back."

She returned with full hands and he took one cup from her before she pulled up a chair. "Now, Dwight, talk to me. You're scaring me."

He wiped one hand over his forehead. "I don't know why this has hit me so hard. I've had many other operations that went bad over the years. But this was a child, and I was so sure I could save him."

"She placed one hand over his. "Tell me what happened." In health care staff got used to these events. They were never easy, but they were bound to occur. Often only another staff member could understand the impact.

"I was the lead surgeon for removing an abdominal tumour in a ten-year-old boy. Ken Arnold was supervising as usual and it seemed to be going well. Then there was a sudden gush of blood. I tried to get it stopped but eventually he pushed me aside and took over. But it was too late."

Celeste held her breath. She knew losing a child was awfully hard to take. "Did you follow all the procedures? Did any of the team see what happened to cause the bleed?"

He shook his head. "I did everything according to the book. It seemed like a normal abdominal surgery. There was no mistake. But Ken never liked me, and he's determined to put the blame on me."

She nodded. "He sees you as the big city physician who knows everything. Or do you think he's directing the blame away from himself?"

"No. At the point it happened, he was observing and not involved in the operation."

"What did the nurses say when he accused you?"

"Most of them are junior and are afraid of his status so they said nothing."

"They'll be asked to write out their own version of what they saw. Something might come of that." Celeste cringed at the look of pain and defeat on his face. "Dwight, you need to go home and rest. There'll be investigations and you'll have a chance to tell your version of the event."

"I'm on call for the rest of this shift so I might as well stay here. Can you stay with me a little longer? It feels good to have somewhere to unload my fears."

"Of course. I have nothing on this evening but let's go to one of the small meeting rooms, so we aren't being overheard."

"You're right. We can go to my office. It's quiet there and no one will disturb us."

She followed him to the elevator, and both got in and stared at the row of buttons while people jostled around them. After they entered his office, he closed the door and locked it.

He walked over to his sofa and slumped into it while he reached out a hand to ask her to join him. They sat staring at each other. His face was still distorted with strain.

"I know they say physicians need to be young to operate but my hands are steady, and my mind is clear."

"Dwight, why are you blaming yourself? Is it because of something Ken said, or do you doubt your own skills?"

He sat still deep in his own thoughts. "I followed all the procedures correctly and made no mistakes. I can tell them that with no qualms." He twisted to look directly at her and picked up one of her hands. "I guess I'm worried about what happens next. I love my work, but I know there is a time to let others take over the fine hand work of surgery. Maybe that's what's hit me more than anything. Do I have to give up operating?"

Celeste squeezed his hand. "It's a good sign when you can question yourself. What I believe is as health professionals, we need to watch carefully for any mistakes and question our abilities regularly, so we'll know when it's time. If you're doing that, it will keep your patients safe."

He hung onto her hand tightly for several minutes. "Thanks for listening to me. I miss my old team in Toronto and haven't had time to develop a new one here. I'm not ready to give up my practice. However, there are signs I need to be watchful."

He stood and helped her to her feet. "I've got to stay to the end of the shift, but you should go home and have your dinner. You've helped so much."

On the drive back home, Celeste, concentrated on the road. These few hours with Dwight made her realize there was something missing in her life. Relationships were about sharing, and it went both ways. She'd always remember what Dwight had shared with her today. Whether or not their feelings for each other would deepen in future, she could appreciate him as a deeply sensitive person who was open to sharing with a friend or partner. This new journey with him would lead to new experiences if she just let it happen. She relaxed knowing she was ready to open that door.

About the Author

A graduate of the University of Toronto Master of Health Administration, Karen had a nineteen-year career with the Ontario Ministry of Health as a senior manager. This included leading two Ministry joint teams with the Ontario Medical Association and the Ontario Hospital Association. Prior to that, she was part of the Ministry negotiations team and worked on policy for physician services. She gained hands-on experience in operational management as senior manager of the Assistive Devices Program from 2001–2005, working with a broad range of community stakeholders, health professionals, and a staff of 50.

Karen next assumed the role of executive director of Bellwood's Centres for Community Living for seven years, working with a professional board and providing accessible housing and support services for people with disabilities. Following her retirement in 2009, Karen began writing fiction novels. A member of the Canadian Authors Association since 2009, Karen was president of the Niagara branch between 2011 and 2017. She chaired the CAA Branch Support & Development Committee from 2013 to 2016 and the Program Committee from 2017 to May 2020. From 2016 to 2020, she was also one of two Regional Directors for Ontario on the board.

In March 2018, Karen released her first self-published novel, *Differences Between Us,* is a psychological suspense that is available on Amazon.com and Kobo.com. A short story, *Canal of Destiny*, was published on the *Quick Brown Fox* blog in 2010. She is in the process of submitting her second and third novels to agents and editors.

For www.Amazon.com use https://amzn.to/2LSVDnx or
For www.kobo.com use https://bit.ly/2L9PSk4

Acknowledgements

Special thanks for my friends at the Fiction Guild Writers Group in Oakville, Ontario who helped me during the early days of my writing career in 2001 to 2008 through many hours of feedback and critique: especially Sheila Gale, Barbara Fraser Winter (Wood), Donna Kirk, Kimberley Scutt and Liz Hegge Bryant.

I cannot forget all the support and encouragement I received from fellow members of the Niagara Branch of the Canadian Authors Association Fiction Writers Group through later stages of development of this novel. You are too numerous to mention each one by name but all of you encouraged me to continue with my writing and in shaping the final version of this book.

Thanks to my husband, Ken Gansel who was supportive about my potential career as a writer right from the beginning. Ken continues to offer great advice about the design and structure of the book and has learned to leave me alone at the computer in my home office when I'm engrossed in writing.

Thank you to my professional mentor, Brian Henry of Quick Brown Fox online newsletter who taught me how to develop a great story that informs and entertains readers. He also edited a portion of my first book *Differences Between Us,* also published on Amazon.com, a psychological suspense about a young mixed-race couple who overcome both diversity issues and a crime ridden city after a major storm. If you like this book, you might want to check it out as well.

www.ingramcontent.com/pod-product-compliance
Lightning Source LLC
Chambersburg PA
CBHW051528260626
47170CB00003B/840